Vanishing Act

Patricia Ferguson

Vanishing Act is the final volume of a trilogy. It can be read on its own, but some of the characters appear in the earlier books. If you want to know their more youthful stories, the books are in this order:

The Midwife's Daughter

Set in 1900, this is the story of Violet Dimond, the local "handywoman", devout, principled, called in by the poorer inhabitants of her home town of Silkhampton, in Cornwall, to look after women in childbirth. Though trained only by her own mother she is an expert, with a lifetime of experience and traditional skills. Her career is derailed by the passage in 1906 of the Midwife's Act. She can't write well or quickly enough to pass the new professional exams, and is soon barred from practice. Her life is further complicated by her adoption of a foundling Black baby, then in the care of her twin sister Beatrix, who runs a local orphanage. The baby resembles Violet's own long-dead little daughter, and because she is piously convinced of God's hand in her decision, she names the baby Grace.

Grace Dimond is a clever pretty child, painfully aware from a very young age that she is different. Her teenage years are particularly difficult, and a love affair goes very wrong, though as the disaster of the First World War comes to an end she eventually makes a happy, if brief, marriage to another outsider, the injured soldier Joe Gilder.

The book ends with the birth of Grace's son Barty, and with the first local Armistice ceremony in 1921, and the unveiling of the town's war memorial statue.

Main Characters:
Violet Dimond, pious "handywoman". Known locally as The Holy Terror.
Bea Givens, Violet's twin sister, entrepreneur, currently in charge at Rosevear House, a nearby children's home.
Grace Dimond, Violet's adopted daughter
Lily Houghton, Grace's best friend
Tommy Dando, Grace's admirer
Joe Gilder, a soldier

Doctors and midwives
Dr Summers, elderly GP, friend and supporter of Violet Dimond
Dr Philip Heyward, his new young partner
Miss Goodrich, professional midwife
Miss Dorothy (Dolly) Wainwright, her junior
Miss Marion Nesbit, successor to Miss Goodrich

Extras
Rosie, a young visitor to the town, whose baby Violet delivers
The Redwoods, wealthy aristocrats, who own the nearby stately home, Wooton Hall
Mrs Thornby, a wealthy middle-class lady engaged in charitable works.
Norah Thornby, her daughter
Guy Thornby, her son
Alice Pyncheon, local gentry, kin to the Redwoods, and also, by marriage, to Mrs Thornby
Frederick Pyncheon, her younger brother, photographer and early cineaste
Mrs Ticknell, shop-keeper, and Grace's employer

The date is now 1932. After her mother's death, impoverished Norah Thornby decides to take in a lodger, the apparently respectable midwife Lettie Quick, who has come to Silkhampton partly to set up a highly discreet clinic for married women (talk of contraception is still largely taboo), and partly for reasons of her own, some very personal, some entirely illegal, if lucrative: she is involved in a regular conspiracy to conceal illegitimate or otherwise inconvenient pregnancies.

Her latest client is the beautiful film star Rae Grainger, now in hiding at Rosevear House, no longer an orphanage but still the home of Bea Givens, employed there as housekeeper.

Slowly Norah and Lettie become friends, and put themselves and Rae in more and more danger as they at last discover who was responsible for the violent untimely death of local midwife Dolly Wainwright.

Main Characters
Dr Marie Stopes, pioneer of contraception, and author of the global best-seller "Married Love" was a real person, and I have not been very kind to her. Though perhaps like most pioneers she was by all accounts pretty hard to live with.

Lettie Quick, trained by Dr Stopes, professional activist and midwife
Norah Thornby, her landlady
Rae Grainger, silent-film actress and would-be screen writer
Joe Gilder, the baker
Barty Gilder, aged 13, his son
Frederick Pyncheon, blinded in the War
Alice Pyncheon, his elder sister and carer
Dr Philip Heyward, local GP
Marion Nesbit, midwife attached to his practice

Extras
Dorothy (Dolly) Wainwright, the other practice midwife
Minnie, once a child at the old orphanage, now employed by Mrs Givens as a maid
Dr Pascoe, partner to Dr Heyward
Mrs Lily Bettins, nee Houghton, once Grace Dimond's friend. Now works at Joe Gilder's bakery
Mr Pender, of Bagnold and Pender, estate agent and auctioneer: Norah's boss
Miss Pilbeam, his office manager

Vanishing Act

PART ONE

April 1945

It was a very ordinary room, bare, clean, painted institutionally in various shades of green. The window was high, she couldn't see out of it. She sat at the table, and waited. It was quite noisy, footsteps going past in the corridor, voices. She told herself: keep quiet as far as you can. Don't volunteer anything.

The door opened, and Davey came back in again, this time with a young woman in a bulky uniform Norah could not recognise, and another officer, not much older than he was himself, but clearly senior, authoritative, tall in a dark blue suit. The stranger's face was very pale; he didn't look quite well, Norah thought. She got up, and shook the hand he held out. Cold and damp.

"Mrs Gilder?" he said. "I'm Detective Inspector Thouless. Sit down please." His eyes were very dark in his white face. He was from a higher social class than Davey, she thought. Though not much. Lower lower middle, as against upper working.

Without looking at her he indicated the woman in uniform: "This is WPC Hendricks, who is joining us while I talk to you." It took Norah a second to work out *WPC*. She could not look quite look him in the eye, she found, nor manage more than a quick glance at the woman. Heavy dark blue jacket, that fitted nowhere. The merest impression of the face, round and pale as she stood to one side behind the men.

"And Sergeant Davey here will be taking notes. Well now. Let's get on with things, shall we?"

Norah waited, her hands folded. Keep quiet, as far as you can, she reminded herself.

"Now then. You have claimed that you were nowhere near Rosevear House on the night in question, that is, 17th March, 1932. Is that right?"

"Yes it is. I never went there at night."

She caught the fractional change in his eyes as she began speaking, and saw that her own social class had surprised him. So Davey hadn't mentioned it, either because he hadn't thought it was important, in which case he was a bit stupid, or for reasons of his own he had purposely let Inspector Thouless be disconcerted. Which was also good, thought Norah.

"You were alone at home all night, is that right?"

He had quite a nasty hair style, Norah noted. So much brilliantine, holding the comb-marks in stiff clarity. Her step-son Barty had had a brief Brylcreem-phase, at sixteen. It had been something a relief to her at the time, she remembered, as it had completely put a stop to any secret desire on her part to caress his pretty curls in passing. "Anyone else there, Mrs Gilder?"

"No," she said. "I lived alone, at the time."

"A witness has come forward. Places you there that night. At Rosevear. And in the morning afterwards."

Not a question, thought Norah. Keep quiet.

"Well? What d'you think of that, Mrs Gilder?"

"Your witness is mistaken."

Thouless leant back in his chair, folding his arms. "Seemed quite clear about it."

"But mistaken, nevertheless," said Norah.

"How well did you know Dr Heyward?"

"Hardly at all."

"You didn't consult him?"

"No. He wasn't my doctor."

"And you didn't meet him socially? Parties and so on?"

"No."

"Never went out with him, took rides with him anywhere?"

"No."

"You never got into his car at all?"

"No."

"Well, that's very interesting, Mrs Gilder. Thankyou very much. Now – I want you to look at this, and tell me if you've ever seen it before. WPC Hendricks?"

He turned, and the woman in the ill-fitting jacket gave him an envelope, with official-looking writing and stamps on it. The sight of it made Norah's insides heave with fear. He took his time opening it, and taking out something small, wrapped in paper. Slowly he unwrapped it, took out the something, and held it in his palm for a moment, so that she could not see it. Then stretched his arm out on the table between them, and opened his hand.

Cheap theatre, thought Norah, as dismissively as she could.

"Whose is that, Mrs Gilder? Is it yours?"

"I - I don't - "

"You recognise it?"

Norah tried to think. In his palm lay what looked very much like one of a pair of small silver brooches that had belonged to her mother. They were shaped like clusters of leaves, one fanning left, one right. Sometimes Mamma had worn them close together, sometimes separately, one on each lapel. They were the only thing of Mamma's that she had kept. But they were both at home, in the jewellery box. Weren't they? Oh, Lettie. Did you take it?

Thouless turned his hand, and let the brooch fall onto the tabletop. It was an odd colour, she thought, something bad had happened to it.

"May I hold it?"

"Be my guest."

She was certain as soon as she picked it up, even though it was so mysteriously altered. Apart from the discolouration one tip was bent, she saw, and several of the tiny garnets were missing.

"Can you read the engraving on the back? No? Well, you practically need a microscope, it's GMT, that's Gwendolen May Thornby. Your mother's name. And we know who did the engraving, here in Silkhampton, because the jeweller looked up the old books. Very obliging. 1896, it was."

"It was my mother's, yes." An anniversary present, she thought, from Papa. In their days of plenty.

"Left it to someone else, did she?"

"No."

"You sold it on?"

"No."

"So it belongs to you, then."

"I didn't ever think of it as mine, exactly - "

"But you wore it."

"No." Should I have said Yes?

"What, never? You just kept it, did you?"

"Yes."

"Where? Where did you keep it, Mrs Gilder?"

"At home. In a jewellery box." With the other one, she thought. Have they already found that? Proceed, she told herself, as if they have.

"When did you last see it?"

"I couldn't say, because I never wore it, I didn't know it had gone."

"You hadn't noticed it was missing?"

"No,"said Norah.

"So, you didn't ever wear it, and go for a ride in Dr Heyward's car with him?"

"No. Never," said Norah, but the hideous possibilities were instantly clear to her, she heard the edge of panic in her voice. Lettie, no, you couldn't have been so careless, you never got into his car, did you? Don't let it be true, she thought wildly, but he said:

"So you can't account for this pretty little brooch, as belonged to your mother, being found under the passenger seat in Dr Heyward's car? Eh? The car at the bottom of Rosevear Lake? With Dr Heyward's dead body in it, let's not forget."

"No,""said Norah steadily, "I can't account for it."

"Been down there thirteen years, Mrs Gilder. That's a long time. Your mother's nice brooch, as you never wore, in the car, with Dr Heyward."

Norah had often dreamed of the gallant little car over the years, watched it rolling forward so blithely into the shallows, until at last it had reached the hidden edge, and tipped over and disappeared, as she had thought, for ever, in a rush of boiling bubbles. Two hundred feet down, she had thought. Safe.

"I don't know anything about it," she said.

Thouless leant forward, spoke softly. "I think you do," he said.

She looked down. She was in his hands, a man who could tell her outright that she was a liar.

"What have we got? Let's see." He pretended to count on his fingers. "One, we got a witness puts you at Rosevear that night. Two, we got your little brooch in the car. And three. He didn't drive it into the water himself. Not with the back of his head bashed in. So, you know what I think?"

"No," she said, as coldly as she could.

"Someone killed him. And got him into his car, and ran it into the lake. And maybe that was you."

"No.'

"Not on your own. Someone helped you. Or you helped him. Was that the way it was?"

"No."

"Perhaps you didn't mean to kill him, it was an accident. Was it an accident, Mrs Gilder? You can tell me."

"I know nothing about it. I wasn't there."

"Long time, though, thirteen years," said Thouless. "You must've thought you'd got away with it."

"I didn't do anything."

" 'Course the funny thing is, you nearly did. You'd a got clean away with it, but for Mr Hitler. And his merry men. Which is quite ironic, don't you think?"

"I don't know what you mean," she said.

"I expect you'd stopped worrying about it. Had you, Mrs Gilder? Forgotten all about it?"

Her own tone was serious. "How could I forget, when I know nothing about it?"

She sounded, she thought, not only steady but convincing; she saw from his eyes that part of him thought so too. And that really was quite ironic, she thought. Because of course the real truth was that she had forgotten nothing, and knew all there was to know.

EARLIER

It was a late marriage. Still Norah's small circle of family and friends raised its collective eyebrows in polite distaste, as Miss Thornby was connected, if distantly, to some of the county's most distinguished families, whereas Joe Gilder was about as far from being a gentleman as it was possible to be, and not even a known local quantity, but a Yorkshireman. With an accent.

"But darling isn't he, isn't he actually, you know – the *baker*?" That was Norah's cousin Alice, in tones so tremulous that Norah had laughed out loud.

"He is Joe," she had answered, smiling, and perhaps something in her tone had made itself felt even to Alice; certainly the words had given Norah herself a conscious inner thrill of physical happiness.

In the style of the times Miss Thornby had been brought up in careful ignorance of the most basic facts of life, and taught also to maintain a certain willed incuriosity about them.

Over the years though she had been forced to acquire a little information. A brief stint as a VAD in the Great War had made it impossible for her to remain completely in the dark about male anatomy and the nature of masculine sexual arousal. But no book or film or conversation had ever hinted to her that there might be any matching female preliminaries, so the sexual act itself remained largely unimaginable to her. Miss Thornby had preferred not to imagine it. She knew it must hurt.

But she was not quite contented on the spinster's shelf. Sometimes in the cinema, when the hero at long last passionately kissed the heroine, Norah in her cheap seat towards the back of the stalls would feel her own insides meltingly turn over with delight, and on the way home would think of the kiss again and again, and in bed at night re-play the scene in her head, and often felt an echo of that delicious excitement.

As far as she allowed herself to think of it at all, Norah vaguely considered this as enjoying romance, which was the mainstay too of most of the library books she read, and of course entirely permissible. Certainly it never occurred to her to connect romance with any of the lower body parts she herself had no names for, other than the collective *private*.

But one day at the Auction Rooms, shortly after her thirty-seventh birthday, when she was helping to organise one of the Art sales, the curiously rococo frame of a small faded watercolour of gambolling lambs had come apart in her hands as she examined it. She had pulled away the remaining tacks, and to her horror had found beneath the lambs a black and white mid-Victorian print of three smiling moustachioed men in armchairs in a grandly baroque apartment, each with an almost naked but corseted woman, also smiling broadly, on his lap. The plump black-stockinged legs of each woman were spread apart to show the beginning of the root she sat astride.

It was by a long way the most disgusting artefact Norah had ever seen. After a second or so of baffled shock she had quickly slapped the gambolling lambs back on top, gathered the wrecked frame together as well as she could, wrapped the picture up in the newspaper it had come in, and stuffed it back in its box, her heart pounding.

Then thought again. She had looked around, making sure there was no one else about. She could hear her boss, Mr Pender, moving slowly about in the office downstairs. The urge to take another look at the disgraceful picture was overpowering. Had she really seen what she thought she had seen? Trembling, she had unwrapped and uncovered it again, and it was exactly as she had thought, unspeakably vile, the women smirking up at her, the men grinning.

One of the women sat with her back to the man, she saw. The other two facing him, their heads turned to smile out at her.

The words her mother or any other respectable person would have used about the picture, disgusting, obscene, appalling, came into her mind too, and stayed there repeating themselves over and over, but at the same time, especially when she looked at the smiling woman in the foreground, who sat with her back to the man, seeming so very pleased with herself and the large thing stuck inside her, Norah felt a shifting flutter within, very like the excitement she felt at the cinema when the romantic hero kissed the heroine, but then, further down, she also felt a direct crude throbbing in her private parts, a thump of awareness, as matter-of-fact, as mechanical, as a light switch being flicked from off to on. It made her breathless.

Shakily Norah put the picture down on her desk. Oh, she thought. Is that...?

Since she had no vocabulary to describe female sexual arousal the thought had to end there, and almost dazed with confusion she had wrapped the picture up again and hidden it right at the back of a box file about local sewage systems. All that night it had stayed there, prompting sleepless scenarios in which someone innocently looking for information about septic tanks in the Silkhampton area came upon her hidden disgracefulness, and everyone found out.

It was hours before Norah remembered that no one knew the print existed but herself and whoever had hidden it, presumably a long time ago. And he was almost certainly dead anyhow; the rococo frame had come from a house-clearance. Should she hand it over to Mr Pender? But then he would know she had seen it. And she would know he had seen it too. Impossible prospect. She must destroy it.

The next day she had fitted the lambs back into place, neatly mended the frame, and officially added it to Lot 37 with several other pictures suitable for nurseries. She had also rolled up the black and white print, and with pounding heart covertly slipped it into her handbag.

Were you still a thief, if you were stealing something that was in itself a crime, and simply to get rid of it? Of course not, she told herself, but she felt criminal all the same.

Though strangely she cheered up as soon as she was safely home. This was in the days of her maidenly solitude, and she took the picture out of her handbag straight away, in the hall, unrolled it and held it up to the light to take another look at it. How disgusting it was, what a good thing it would be to put it on the fire!

But perhaps not straight away. There was no particular hurry, she told herself, now it was safely out of any public domain. After some thought she hid it in the suitcase under her bed, inside an old copy of *The Film Lovers' Weekly*.

As she did so she was aware and at the same time not fully aware that she intended to keep the picture and from time to time visit it. Over the next few months she told herself many times that she could not imagine why she had not yet got round to throwing the nasty thing away; but then, she did not try to. Instead she grew to recognise that matter-of-fact throb of localised awareness, to wait for it, though she was not sure why, as it did not strike her as particularly pleasurable. Except that she was obscurely disappointed when from time to time it did not happen.

Then she would worry that the picture no longer worked because she had grown used to its depravity, and like any addict needed stronger further doses. Since there was no hope of any such thing and she was ashamed already, these were unhappy moments.

It never once occurred to her to touch herself while she looked at the picture; the early training of her caste and time ensured that her private parts remained private even to herself. She had no idea what she was doing and still no language for it; but then its mystery went some way toward safely making it more like something that wasn't really happening at all.

It would be strange one day to look back on such virginal obscurities. To remember the stunning moment on that summer evening walk together when Joe Gilder had first taken her hand, his touch as instantly, overwhelmingly effective as once the black and white picture had been! She had snatched her hand away, hot with shame, and nearly put an end to everything before it had begun.

Norah's pursuit of Joe Gilder began with a dress; she would never, she thought afterwards, have had the courage to try at all, without the extra help of that blue silk wonder.

Her friend and one-time lodger, Lettie Quick, had sent it to her, with not so much a friendly note as a set of instructions.

Dear Norah,
the address is on the other side if you dont like it. They got
lots of other good stuff your size, you want to go there sometime.
Can you thro out that brown tweed thing its godawful its to
old for you and Pete's sake get your hair done, tell them
shoulder length bob. Yould look great

Lx

The address was that of a London dress-agency, though the blue silk had looked and smelt perfectly new. All the same Norah had felt a certain distaste. Holding it up she had noted its modest curving neckline and plain panelled skirt; certainly a nice enough day-dress, but what was Lettie playing at, sending her someone else's cast-offs? Though there were a surprising number of beautifully-finished curving seams inside the bodice, she saw. And the skirt was lined with tussore.

Putting it on at last she had looked in the mirror in her bedroom and seen a curvaceous but elegant stranger staring back. The skirt swung gracefully with her every movement, while the closely-fitted bodice pulled her waist in but at the same time did something almost miraculous to her bosom, warmly smoothed and upheld it in some way, not emphasizing it, but not trying to hide it either.

Norah had been embarrassed by her breasts ever since the first shock of their arrival, which in retrospect had seemed practically overnight. They were essentially comical, she soon came to understand, a big coarse joke for all to see, as well as yet another way in which there was far too much of her. She was too tall, too strapping, with a great big bottom to match the bust and hands like a navvie's. Such a thumper of a girl, as Mamma had once said. Mamma who had been so dainty.

Can you thro out that brown thing, its godawful.

So rude, thought Norah lightly, her eyes still meeting those of the stranger in the mirror. She had relied on her everyday costume of decent hard-wearing tweed so long that she had more or less stopped seeing it, just kept it clean and well-pressed. It's comfortable, Lettie, she thought. And respectable, and easy, I'm fond of it, what was *godawful* about a well-made calf-length skirt and matching long jacket? The linings were stout, the seams nicely finished; there was every chance, Norah had often thought - gratefully, as there was so little money when poor Mamma's annuity died with her - that the loosely-tailored jackets and plain roomy blouses would last not just for years but forever.

But perhaps I shouldn't want such things to last forever, thought Norah, as she tried to see the blue silk dress from the back. Perhaps I fancy a change.

Pete's sake get your hair done

Norah's hair was fine and pale, and since girlhood she had worn it in a neat bun at the nape of her neck, or in two plaits pinned into flat coils about her ears. Either style looked perfectly at home with the brown tweed costume. But the blue dress was somehow different, made earphones look wrong, almost bizarre, like a poke bonnet worn with a swimsuit. She pulled the hairgrips out and shook her hair free, held it looped at her shoulders, trying to see what a bob might look like.

Yould look great

For a week or so she did nothing, though she tried the dress on every night at bedtime. By day in the office she thought of it sometimes, hanging in her wardrobe, a private source of strength, and finally took herself by surprise late one afternoon by turning into the hairdresser's salon on her way home after work, and simply making an appointment. She need not actually go, she reassured herself, several times, as the day neared. She could always ring up and cancel.

But she had dreamed the night before that the drowned car was found.

Really, what was getting a haircut, compared to facing a possible murder charge, Norah asked herself next day, with a sort of grim excitement, that held her up all the way to the perfumed shop and into the terror of the hairdresser's chair, where she had sat in apparent calm, watching the weight of thirty years fall away in the mirror.

"Lovely natural wave, Miss," said the hairdresser, when she had finished. Norah leant forward. Her hair was still pale, neither blonde nor brown, but now it stood up differently around her head, looking softer, thicker. When she turned her head, her hair swung, this way, that way. If she bent forward it hid her face, in soft warm curtains.

Norah fell in love with her hair. At night when she took off her blouse she would sit in front of the dressing-table mirror for minutes at a time, turning her head to feel the lovely tickle of her hair on her shoulders as it swung back into place.

Consulted in the mirror, the dress said *Yes.*

In London, calling by appointment at the dress agency herself, she had in confidence been told that her blue silk had once belonged to a certain quite well-known though of course as far as Norah was concerned completely anonymous stage actress (married *ever* so well, said the owner of the agency, with a little sigh). Luckily for Norah it seemed that the quite well-known stage actress also had a disinclination to wear anything more than twice, and a generous but still finite budget.

"So distinguished," said the woman at the agency, as Norah slipped on the actress's dashing and barely-worn light summer coat in fine black and white houndstooth.

"Was there a hat?"

The agency woman shook her head. "Don't go in for 'em. Says she's too tall."

"Oh does she," said Norah with interest, looking back at her own reflection. Like the blue dress the coat seemed to speak for her, its message warm and lively, and robustly in her favour. Look at me, said the coat, though not stridently. Look at me, and *be cheered.*

That first visit though she could not afford the coat. She bought a dark blue chenille cardigan, and a beautiful silk blouse with a cigarette burn on one lapel, which she planned to disguise with embroidery, at a cost of more than a fortnight's salary.

I really must do something about that, thought Norah in the train on the way home. She caught her own eyes in the dark reflection of the train window, remembering that she had recently acted with fine despatch in a crisis.

I shall do so again.

Four weeks later, after a great deal of thought and some careful correspondence, she had knocked on her employer's office door at the estate agency where she worked, and walked in.

"Miss Thornby – what is it?" Pettish; Mr Pender seemed displeased, though it was just after tea-time, when he was usually inclined to be jovial. For a second Norah considered delay. But that would be cowardice, she decided.

"May I sit down, please, Mr Pender?"

"Certainly." If you must, implied his tone. He did not move aside the papers on his desk. Keep this brief, said the set of his shoulders.

Norah tried to look blank. "I'll come straight to the point, if I may," she said. "I've been offered a position by another estate agent."

Mr Pender seemed unable to take this in. "I beg your pardon? What d'you mean, offered you a position - what are you talking about, Miss Thornby?"

"They are offering me a job, Mr Pender."

"But you are not seeking employment. You already have a position."

Norah, who had spent much of the last decade appearing to agree with everything Mr Pender said, now squeezed her hands together hard in her lap, and was silent.

"This is most irregular!" said Mr Pender, taking his glasses off. "What other agency - d'you mean Berry and Toms - d'you mean James Berry, over in Exeter?"

"I'd rather not say, at present," said Norah.

"And when did you apply for this position, may I ask?"

You may not, thought Norah. Aloud she said: "It's a generous offer; I'm inclined to accept it."

"But you - Miss Thornby. I must tell you that I regard this as an outrage. I am most displeased."

Say nothing, Norah told herself. She kept her eyes lowered.

"I thought you were suited here," said Mr Pender, changing tack. "You certainly seemed so all those years ago when I first offered you employment."

Here it comes, thought Norah.

"May I remind you that few then would have taken you on at all, completely unqualified as you were; I did so as a kindness, and out of respect for your late father."

Norah looked up, her heart beating fast with excitement, for so far, she thought, he had not landed a single unforeseen blow.

"Certainly I am grateful for the experience of working here," she said. "As you say, I have done so for many years, and I've learned a great deal; I am now a most valuable employee, especially in the auction house, as Mr - as another company has understood."

"Ah, now we come to it!" said Mr Pender. "You want more money."

Well of course I do, you mean old besom, thought Norah zestfully. She sat back in the chair for the first time. Let him see that she was not afraid.

Because, strangely, she was not.

"I should prefer to remain here," she said, in perfect truth. "But not on the same terms. Quite apart from the auction sales, I'm essentially managing the entire office - "

" - with additional emolument!" Mr Pender put in.

She had foreseen this too; *small additional emolument* was one of Mr Pender's stock phrases, and in the outer office the younger clerks sometimes vied with one another to insert it into daily conversation. Norah managed not to smile.

"I will of course be happy to stay on for a while," she said, after a pause, "to help my replacement settle in." Let him imagine the full horror of the replacement, who might know something about pictures, but nothing at all about Mr Pender's morning cup of coffee, or precisely how thick he liked the butter on his afternoon scone; who might not be persuaded to care much, either.

Mr Pender leant back in his chair, and drew a deep contemptuous breath in through his nose. "Well, Miss Thornby, let us hear it. What exactly are you asking for?"

Go above reasonable, Lettie had advised her. Don't tell him what you really want. Go higher. Let him think he's beaten you down.

Norah watched Mr Pender across the desk. He looks so tired, poor old thing, she thought, as she so often had. It was true that he had employed her when no one else would, and for her dead father's sake; but true also that he had browbeaten and cheated her for years.

And I have let him do it, Norah reminded herself. No: I have *helped* him do it.

Now pay me properly, old man.

So she went higher; and when a few minutes later she left his office, instead of going back to her desk she hurried outside, and walked quite fast along the High Street for a few minutes, until she could be sure that she wasn't going to burst out laughing. In the chemist's window she caught sight of herself, her own face alight with triumph.

A pale face still, she thought. Colourless, like her hair. She went inside, and presently began a pleasant but brief and on the whole unrequited love affair with make-up.

Norah's mother had belonged to that Edwardian generation most disapproving of cosmetics, employing the relatively few items then available in secrecy, if at all, for only trollops openly painted their faces. So uncapping her very own new Max Factor gave Norah an almost giddying thrill. How delicious it smelt! For the rest of her life Norah would love the look of a good lipstick too, the small heft of gold that slipped into the silken inner pocket of a handbag, its opening click, the smooth glide of the outer casing, the neat tab within to raise or lower the glorious waxen scarlet.

A little colour in lip and cheek, a natural wave, more money to buy a dashing coat of black and white houndstooth. A blue dress that said *Look*.

Strange to think how much these small changes had meant to her at the time. How they had made it possible to pretend to herself that shyness had no part in her, that she had as much right as any other decent-looking woman to go up to Joe Gilder should she happen to come across him in the market, say, and ask him in a friendly way how he was, and generally remind him that she was there. And decent-looking.

Strange also to remember the time just after their marriage, when she had walked about, gone shopping or to choir practice or to the library just as usual, but all the time wild inside with new knowledge. She had felt as if her whole skin might be glowing, as if it must be impossible for other people not to notice how different she was. Was it like this for everyone? Did every married couple share this delicious lightness, this unspeakable, unspoken happiness?

Every couple she knew made her wonder, even elderly ones she had known all her life. The headmaster of the council school, Mr Vowles, and Agnes: oh yes, they had, surely, and perhaps still did! The vicar, and Mary: yes, probably. The Canfords: oh, absolutely! Sometimes this new secret game made Norah smile to herself in the street.

But some had surely never unlocked the shared vital secret. Not Mamma and Papa. No. Beautiful Mamma in her filmy-throated lace gown, coolly pouring tea. She made him feel coarse, thought Norah, seeing her father's broad hairy hand take the cup. Poor daddy. And for the first time in her life Norah had known the deeply consoling luxury of feeling sorry for her mother.

One Sunday afternoon, about a year after their marriage, on a sudden impulse she had hopped out of bed and rummaged in the suitcase beneath it and taken out the old black and white picture of men and women coupling. Looking at it gave her a reminiscent flicker of sensation.

"I forgot", she said lightly, "a picture frame fell apart at work the other day - look what was hidden behind it."

Idly Joe had taken it from her. "Bloody hellfire!" He had sat up and burst out laughing. "What did old Pender say?"

"I didn't show him. I just – well, hid it, really. What's so funny?" she asked, though she was smiling too.

"Their moustaches," said Joe weakly. "And look at the curtains, they've got *bobbles* on - " He could hardly speak. "Dear God." He wiped his eyes. "Ain't seen anything like that for years. Not since France." That sobered him.

"So – you've seen pictures like this before, then?"

"Course I have. In the army. Not antiques, though - proper photographs."

"Like this?"

"No, just - women on their own. You know, girls."

"I wouldn't want a photograph," said Norah slowly, as she got back into bed beside him. "That would mean people being paid. You know, poor people, desperate people."

"But this is alright, is it?"

"Well - I see what you mean about the decor. The bobbles. And the moustaches. But I do rather like the way everyone looks so happy."

Joe gave the picture another long look. "Anything else you like?" he said. "In particular?"

There was a pause, and then she had leant across, and pointed.

Seven years, a little more than seven, for they had celebrated the anniversary. If the baby had lived, he would have been six. It was a late marriage, and a happy one, but then it ended.

Barty arrives on a twenty-four-hour leave.

The war has added another layer of emotional difficulty in dealing with him. He was too old for mothering when she married his father, a silent watchful fourteen-year-old, prone to disappearing on his bicycle or into his books. If she came into a room he quietly left it, not straight away, but soon. He was carefully polite. He was out a lot.

It was painful; she had known him all his life, had longed to hold the fat little rosy-cheeked baby, pet the motherless toddler; had occasionally dared to smile at the small boy helping out behind the counter in the bakery. She had thought, before her marriage, that he might one day want to talk to her about his long-dead mother, Grace, whom she had known and loved as a child. For a year Grace and Norah had been at the same local school, Norah aged ten, the adopted foundling Grace just turned five, and so spectacular a creature, almost fabulous to the other children: a pretty little girl who sounded just like them and yet looked so very different, a foreign exotic brown colour all over.

We might have been real friends later on, Norah sometimes told herself. If only I had not been so shy. If only I had not let shyness rule me. All those years we sang together as girls in the church choir. All those times I might have tried to approach her. How chilly and aloof I must have seemed!

Grace had wanted to be a writer, Joe had once said. She had wanted to write something she wouldn't be ashamed to show to Katherine Mansfield. Norah had pretended not to be baffled by this. It turned out that Katherine Mansfield had been a famous short-story writer, who had also died young, though not nearly as young as poor Grace, who had only managed to finish three stories herself.

"I gave them to Barty, when I thought he was old enough. But perhaps I was wrong. He's never said a word about them." You could ask him, Norah had thought, but did not say. That was the end of the only time Joe had spoken of his first wife. And Barty has never mentioned his mother at all.

Barty is nearly twenty-two now, and has grown a little Ronald Coleman moustache. He lights a cigarette, and Norah notices the new scar on his light-brown hand, it still looks sore, two inches of burn.

He has been shot down twice, to her knowledge. Once he crash-landed in Kent, in a cornfield. Once he had to bail out into the Channel, aimed his burning aeroplane into the sea, leapt out of it into the falling air and the cold rough seas far below.

How do you *chat* to him, knowing that? How can he walk about being normal, queueing for a bus, being overcharged for a cup of tea at the railway station?

An angler in a rowing boat hauled him out of the sea; if he hadn't been close enough Barty would have died of cold. Suppose the man had decided not to bother with fishing that morning?

How can Barty sleep at night? Does he? As well as escaping death he is trying to kill people. He is out there killing the country's enemies. Slaying them, like Achilles. Can you say to him, *scrambled egg alright? Would you like a scone?*

Norah was almost feverish with shyness the last time Barty was on leave, blushed all the time like the desperate girl she once had been.

Today all that seems to matter less.

She has been busy trying not to understand that Joe is dying. He's had bronchitis many times before. The whiff of gas he took in on the Western Front left its mark on his lungs, tickled further ever since with flour dust and tobacco smoke, he's officially Chronic Bronchitic. This time though it's not just the usual acute-on-chronic. There's something else behind the expected X ray opacities, a new growth, the doctor suspects. Norah has chosen to ask no further questions.

But Joe can't finish the small bowl of his favourite soup. He doesn't want to read. He's too tired to listen to the radio. The beautiful bones of his face stand out in hollows and shadows, his skin is waxen, the cough hurls him sideways in the bed.

On the other hand he's recovered so many times before. Norah tells herself that all she needs to do is keep going, keep him clean and warm and comfortable, tempt him to eat, try another steam inhalation, acquire a urine bottle for him because getting out of bed and across the landing is so exhausting, first at night, then by day, then at all. All this has become normal, become the path ahead, and she is still trying all the time not to notice how steeply it's leading downhill, and where to.

Still quite poorly, she wrote in her last letter to Barty. *Sends his love.* But then something stopped her, something that felt external, a command, and she took the letter out of the envelope again, and pencilled in a post script.

Come as soon as you can.

Writing to Barty had quickly become one of her allotted domestic tasks. At first it was a lot like the Sunday evening letters she had been required to write to her parents from boarding school, a list of her small dull doings to which only her father made occasional perfunctory reply.

She had been surprised and pleased when Barty wrote back, and beginning *Dear Dad and Norah,* from what seemed to be a training camp of some kind – whether he was doing the training or being trained was not clear, but somewhere cold and rainy, where he had gone for walks, he said, and seen a barn owl in the daytime, in silent flight right over his head.

Since then she has written to him weekly, as entertainingly as she can, about domestic mishaps, cheerful queues, successful gardening, a decent film he might try to catch himself, signing for Joe, *with love from Dad and Norah.* Sometimes she'd done re-writes, getting the story just right, picturing Barty smiling to himself as he reads about the stray cow that wandered into St George's and relieved herself all over the Jacobean memorial brass, or about the six nervous little Brownies playing hand-bells at the Christmas concert, slowly and precariously wobbling through *Jingle Bells* while the entire audience held its breath in agonised suspense, willing them on, desperate not to laugh.

She left out worries. She made no mention of the terrifying frequency of local air-raids. No, of course Silkhampton itself wasn't a target, said the ARP men, though of course you had to bear RAF Silkhampton in mind, but odds were the bombers were just off-loading, getting shot of anything they'd got left over before the long trip home, bad luck on Cornwall but there it was. Porthkerris harbour was badly damaged, and two cottages on the cliff above was flattened, though luckily no one had been at home at the time. Something massive fell in the very grounds of Rosevear House; the blast killed a dozen sheep and left a deep crater, which quickly filled with water.

Norah told Barty only about the ducks that shortly flew in and made themselves at home there. Often enough Barty has answered, short letters that of course hide almost everything about his life, and what it has become, though now and then he too writes something in perhaps his real voice. Though when that happens she knows that he is really writing to Joe.

When she comes in with the tea this particular afternoon Barty is half-sitting half-lying on the bed beside Joe, who looks better than he has for weeks, his eyes alight again, his face all smoothed out with happiness.

Still it is clear that he can hardly speak for breathlessness.

"Look!" is all he can manage, lifting his shaking hand to the bedside table, where there is something spilling out of tissue paper.

"Are those grapes?" They are blue-black, heavy with bloom, fragrant.

"Hothouse," says Barty, and smiles his mother's beautiful smile. He has already outlived her, Norah remembers.

"Got himself a posh.... lady friend," Joe manages.

Norah pours tea, careful to only half-fill Joe's cup. If they were alone she would use the spouted cup, but Joe would not want his son to see this.

Dearly she would love to know if Barty's lady friend, posh or otherwise, is nice and kind and loving and funny. Is Norah his mother enough to ask for more about her?

No, she decides. Of course not. She might embarrass him. "Sugar?" she says.

"What else...you bin up to....my lad?"

Barty shrugs. "Training, mostly. Two please. Thanks."

Training again, thinks Norah. Barty seems to do or get a lot of training. Perhaps it's true. Perhaps it's just the kindest thing to tell your sick old father.

"Had a bit of a Do the other night," says Barty. "Coming back from - " he pretends an elaborate look all round the room, checking for listening Nazis, lowers his voice - "from Norway."

"What were you doing there?" asks Norah, instantly remembering that this is a silly question. He shoots her a smile, and her heart gives a little thud of pleasure, because it seems a tolerant affectionate smile, and he has never looked at her like that before.

"Not much," he tells her. "Got a bit lively, met a Dornier, gave it a bit of a hammering. But we were in trouble as well, some of the rudder got shot off, thought we'd have to bail out there and then, so I get the escape hatch open - " here Barty raises both hands above his head, wrestles with imaginary catches, "and the other chaps open the cabin door all ready - "

Other chaps, thinks Norah. Navigator. Wireless operator. Other young men like Barty. Even younger, perhaps.

"We're corkscrewing, can't fly straight, everything's shaking about. But we're still in the air, so we keep going, towards base."

Scotland, thinks Norah. She knows that much. East coast, presumably. How far is that?

"Straight into a thunderstorm, then night comes on, it's like, it's - "

He trails off, as well he might, thinks Norah, who is sitting with hands tightly clasped. How could sitting in the open cockpit of damaged aeroplane bucking through a thunderstorm in the dark over the North Sea be like anything else at all?

" - it's quite tricky," says Barty at last. "Can't see much. I tell the chaps, be ready to bail, soon as we're sure we're over land. All this time the Wireless Op's trying to mend the set - got bust in the fight – takes him two hours, but then he's done it, contacts Base, asks for our position. They get back to us in a little while, and it's a bit of a facer, because we're right out over the Irish sea. We're on our way to the Isle of Man!" He grins.

"I've heard it's... very nice there," says Joe deadpan, after a pause.

"That's what the navigator said."

"I don't understand," says Norah.

Joe explains: "Flew right across ...the country. And over the sea again....out the other side."

"The blackout," says Barty. "Missed the whole country. Had to turn round and fly all the way back again."

"Oh, Barty!"

"So that took another hour, and by then I'm thinking, we've got so far, maybe we can try for a landing after all, so I ask the crew, and they're game."

Game!

"So we go ahead, the tail's kicking around, it's like landing a crab, we're all over the place. And there's a bit of a crowd on the ground by then. See the berk who overshot England. See what sort of mess I make of landing -" He laughs. "But it was just a few bumps. Got a round of applause. " He finishes his tea.

Norah meets Joe's eyes, and they exchange complicated messages, mainly *talk about this later.*

"Never thought England could look so black," says Barty.

It is by far the most Norah has ever heard him say. She thinks about the story while she washes up the tea things and starts on the potatoes for dinner.

Got a bit lively. Met a Dornier, gave it a bit of a hammering.

So laconic, almost a drawl, the RAF argot as defining as uniform. But he chose his story well, she thinks. It's full of crazy danger, of course. But it's essentially cheerful, reassuring. Not just, *damaged aeroplanes can still fly*, not just *I can fly damaged aeroplanes*, but also *a chap can sit in a damaged aeroplane and get on with repairing his wireless set.* And *Base always at the ready. It's not just me, dad. I'm not on my own.*

Presently Barty comes down. Joe has gone to sleep, he says. He lights a cigarette, and she sees the new burn on his hand.

"Not too good, is he," he says.

"No. I'm sorry - I thought I should let you know."

"'Course. Got any whisky?" he asks suddenly. This cordial stranger who looks like her step-son.

Startled, she has to think about it.

"I'm not sure. In the drawing room. Possibly." He follows her up the stairs and into the room that still always brings her mother forcibly to her mind, they spent so long in there, years of evenings spent on embroidery. She opens the corner cupboard, which makes exactly the same high-pitched squeak it made in the days of Mamma, and there is the slightly dusty bottle from several Christmases ago, with barely a toffee-coloured inch and a half left in it.

"Top notch," says Barty. He takes two glasses from the other cupboard and carefully divides the drink between them.

"Are *you* alright?" he asks, passing her one.

"Me?"

"Can't be easy."

For a second she again imagines his flight from occupied Norway, the overwhelming racket of vibrating half-wrecked machinery, things streaming and shuddering in the darkness, and the freezing barrage of the air. *Bit of a Do.*

"It's nothing," she says.

"Yes it is," says Barty. "I'm glad he's got you. Looking after him." She flushes, but the pleasure is mixed with something lowering. It isn't so much that he has forgiven her, for marrying Joe and inserting herself into his life, she will work out later: it's that he has grown out of caring. He can be friendly to her, even appreciative, now that she no longer matters at all, except that she makes his father a decent nurse.

Now Barty touches his glass to hers, and they drink.

"He's very brave," she tells him. "Never complains."

"Is he - " He breaks off, tries again: "Will he get better? D'you think?"

The sip of whisky burns her throat, she's never liked it. But it strengthens her.

"There's a growth, in his lungs," she says, and looks away when his eyes at once fill with tears. She hears him take a breath.

"How long has he got?"

She shakes her head.

Barty sinks into the armchair Mamma covered in tapestry stitch, and covers his eyes with his burnt hand.

Norah sits down in the other armchair, and waits for him to get back in control. She herself is dry-eyed, strangely calm. She notices how the embroidered chair-covers have sagged with the years, that the colours Mamma chose so carefully have mottled together into several slightly different shades of grey and beige.

Barty looks up at last, passes the back of his hand over his eyes.

"Here's to him, then," he says finally, holding out his whisky.

"Joe," she says, and they touch glasses again, and drink.

The telegram came less than a fortnight later. It was addressed to Joe, of course. She opened it and read it, folded it quickly back into its envelope and put it in her apron pocket, went on energetically mopping the kitchen floor.

Posted missing.

Joe need not know, that was her first thought. Not yet. While there was possibility, while there was hope, why trouble him? The news would get out eventually, she thought. The telegram boy had given her such a keen look: Barty was almost public property now, so many knew what he was doing. But no matter what was murmured in the shops or pubs Joe would not hear it, Norah told herself. She would make sure of that. The telegram promised a letter to follow. She would wait at least until that came.

Several days afterwards Joe for the first time fell briefly into a state of strange confusion. "Where am I?" he asked Norah, as she washed his face and hands that morning.

"You're at home, darling."

"Am I hit?"

She had not understood, not then.

"Is it bad? Where am I?"

It was so dark, he said. He couldn't move. He was so cold.

Nothing she said or did could comfort him. The strange fit only ended when he fell into what looked like natural sleep, except that she couldn't rouse him.

"I'm afraid the growth in his lungs may be affecting his brain," the doctor said later, which she could make no sense of at all, but carefully asked no questions about. By then Joe had woken up as if nothing had happened, except that he was weaker, had trouble sitting up. She had slid her strong right arm around him and drawn him upward, feeling almost consciously that she could impart strength to him by force of will, that she could give it to him by wanting to.

She had to be really careful though, Joe's skin was suddenly so fragile, and sometimes lately it hurt him to move, his poor back had grown so thin, she thought, the bones so present. The district nurse came every morning, to help her move him, to turn him gently onto the clean undersheet.

Sometimes in dreams he shouted. "Christ – take cover, take cover!"

"He was injured in the War. The last one, I mean – he was in a shell-hole for hours," she told the doctor next morning. "More than a day, until they could get to him. He's always had nightmares."

Joe was back in the trenches daily now.

"Wake up, darling, you're here, you're safe – " As if Death had gone back to its earlier plan, she thought once. Had kept the shell-hole waiting for him, all this time.

"Perhaps a soothing draught," said the doctor. The prescription was for a dark syrupy drink that smelt pleasantly like cough mixture.

"Just up the dose as needed, Mrs Gilder. It's very calming."

"Have you heard from the lad?" Sometimes Joe seemed completely himself. "Bin a while, ain't it?"

Norah was ready. "I think he may have been posted abroad," she said smoothly. "Just something he let slip."

"Where abroad, did he say?"

"Well, he's not meant to, is he! But I think it might be India," she said, because that sounded safe enough. Adding, as if the thought had only just occurred to her: "Of course the post takes simply ages from there."

Nine days went by, ten nights, and the following letter promised in the telegram at last arrived.

I regret to inform you that a report has been received from the War Office to the effect that

It was a form letter. She somehow hadn't expected that. There was a gap for Barty's number and rank. Then one for his name, in that order, confirming that he had been *posted as "missing"*. The letter added nothing, in fact, except those inverted commas. *"Missing"*, as if it was a new word, or slang. Or ironic.

If he has been captured by the enemy it is probable that unofficial news will reach you first. In that case I am to ask you to forward any postcard or letter received at once to this Office, and it will be returned to you as soon as possible.

I am, Sir or Madam, Your Obediant Servant – here a further gap had been filled in with an indecipherable squiggle of signature, by the *Officer in charge of Records.* Officer Squiggle had crossed out *Or Madam* with a single stroke of his pen; had of course sent his official form letter only to Joe.

She kept the letter hidden, with the telegram. It was easy enough to keep the secret. Joe's visitors now were fewer, were frightened, each staying only a few minutes; it was simple enough to warn them what might and might not be said.

More days went by, more nights. Once as she eased him back onto the freshly plumped-up pillows he smiled at her, and raised a hand to touch her cheek, in a familiar caress.

"Thanks, Gracie," he said.

In the kitchen her tears seemed to scald her eyes.

He began to be unconscious for longer than he was awake. She sat or lay beside him, turning him every two hours to stop him getting bed sores, giving him sips of broth, soothing his poor dry tongue with drops of glycerine. A neighbour dropped off shopping, Norah's cousin Alice took on the laundry, the doctor came daily, the district nurse twice, three times. The world outside fell away, largely stopped altogether.

"Is Barty coming? Where's my boy? Is he alright?"

"He's abroad, darling, I'm sorry, I know he'd come if he could."

Lying to the dying. It made Norah's heart pound in her chest.

One afternoon, drowsing in the big chair beside the bed, she awoke to him saying something, asking her for something.

"What is it, Joe? What do you want, my darling?"

He hesitated, looked at her almost shyly. "Will you sing for me, sweetheart? Like you used to?"

Norah felt her mouth drop open in surprise. She had never sung to Joe in her life, what a crazy idea, of course he was lost in some dream, she thought; then she remembered Grace Dimond's beautiful soprano.

For several years she and Norah had both sung in the church choir, Norah of course in her own unresplendent contralto. Once, just before the end of the Great War, they had stayed behind after normal Friday evening practice, to have another go at the quartet from Stainer's *Crucifixion,* "God So Loved the World." Easter, it must have been 1918, thought Norah: herself and Grace, and Mr Thatcher the choirmaster singing bass, and Ted Cernow, back from France with his golden tenor intact, for all he'd lost his right hand.

God so loved the world, that he gave his only begotten son, that whoso believeth, believeth in him, should not perish, should not perish, but have everlasting life!

Just the four of them gathered in the lamplight by the altar singing into in the dark empty church. Norah had always rather despised Stainer's *Crucifixion,* as trite and sentimental. That night, their four matched voices sang the simple harmonies with such perfection that her own voice began to tremble a little with emotion, gaining a rich vibrato that had blended exactly with Grace Dimond's. Afterwards they had all smiled tentatively at one another, almost embarrassed, aware that they had made something beautiful, they'd all heard it.

Now Norah breathed slowly in and out, remembering all this, and after a little while she could look at him again, and Joe was still waiting, still hopeful.

"Go on, love," he whispered.

She smiled at him, wondering how he could see her, even in this twilight, and still mistake her for his first wife Grace Dimond, who had died at nineteen. And who had above all been so unmistakeably different from everyone else, her skin a warm dark caramel brown.

"One a the old songs? Please, Gracie."

Where did he think he was? At least he was happy, not in the shell hole; thought he was home, and somewhere safe. Would the sound of her wrong voice break the spell, hoist him back to this desperate present? But she would not deny him anything, not now.

She wouldn't do anything cheerful, that would be wrong, and she couldn't manage it anyway. Something sad. Everyone liked a sad song somehow. Norah made her choice, closed her eyes, thought out the first note, and began, breathless but clear enough:

My young love said to me, My mother won't mind,
And my father won't slight you for your lack of kind.
And she stepped away from me and this she did say:
It will not be long love, til our wedding day.

"Grand," he whispered, closing his eyes. He lay smiling slightly. Perhaps she had hit on the right song. Or a right song anyway. The tremor in her voice reminded her of that special evening so long before, in the dark of St George's, when she and Grace had sung together, and made a perfect sound.

She stepped away from me and moved through the fair
And fondly I watched her move here and move there
And then she turned homeward with one star awake
Like the swan in the evening moves over the lake.

She kept running out of air, taking more and more breaths all over the place, not just as the end of a line. Mr Thatcher would have frowned, she thought.

The people were saying, no two ever wed
But one had a sorrow that never was said.
I smiled as she passed with her goods and her gear
And that was the last that I saw of my dear.

She closed her own eyes then, thinking of Barty and the young woman who had given him hothouse grapes for his father. So hard to keep going, she was snatching in big breaths halfway through some of the words now, almost panting as she sang.

Last night she came to me, my lost love came in

So softly she came and her feet made no din
She laid her hand on me, and this she did say:
It will not be long, love, till our wedding day.

Norah's voice broke at last, made a rattle of sobs in her throat. But Joe didn't wake, nor did he fully rouse again. He breathed more and more slowly, sometimes seeming to stop altogether, then starting up again. He breathed like that all night, without struggle, until dawn the next day, when he stopped.

There was another air raid during the funeral; the congregation had to decamp to the cellars of the George and Dragon, which Norah herself had helped set up as a shelter the year before, there were chairs and tables, and corners discreetly curtained off, and oil lamps. She remembered the bustle, the pretending, the determined brightness.

She had the house to herself again, as in the days just after her mother's death. But she had been younger then, still full of hopes and possibilities as well as fears.

Now she didn't feel anything very much most of the time, except that it had occurred to her that living like this, being this most recent wretched emptied version of Norah Gilder, was not actually necessary. Norah Gilder herself was not necessary at all. That was something to hold onto.

Her cousin Alice kept popping by, often with a small gift, a double-yolked egg, a bunch of chrysanthemums from her garden. Sometimes Norah, sitting in the basement kitchen, spotted her feet on the pavement before she reached the front steps, and moved into the shadows beside the cooker until Alice gave up knocking and went away again.

Once she saw a pair of familiar brogues, a man's, very well polished, pass by the railings. It could only be her old employer Mr Pender, she realised, and then came the knock at the door. What could he want? Norah didn't care. But the habit of years pushed her up the stairs to let him in.

"Mrs Gilder. How are you?" He took off the ancient Homburg as he followed her into Mamma's chilly drawing room, and presently at her invitation sat down, his hat on his lap.

"What can I do for you, Mr Pender?"

Mr Pender embarked on a long speech. It had many subordinate clauses, and Norah soon stopped fully attending, though when he fell quiet she was able, with the ease of long practice, to replay his last few sentences in her head.

"You mean you want me to come back?"

Mr Pender looked a little scandalised at this crude summary.

"A great deal of work is in prospect, Mrs Gilder."

"But why Rosevear House?"

"It is large and commodious. Its isolation I dare say makes it seem at least relatively safe. As of course you know, the house has been uninhabited for several years, and a certain amount of repair work has been required, though the roof is sound. The ah hospital itself is being equipped with items from several other such places – so many have been obliged to close, due to ah damage of various kinds, and medical and nursing staff have already been appointed. Progress has been remarkably fast. But for the accounts – for general administration - the board turned to me for advice, and I, Mrs Gilder, thought at once of you."

"Thank you, Mr Pender."

"The place is familiar to you, which I feel would a considerable advantage. The position would be part-time. But fully paid." Perhaps he had not intended the last words as a sneer, Norah told herself afterwards. They had certainly sounded like one though.

"Perhaps I could think about it," she said, to get rid of him.

"Certainly," he said, and began to get up. He knew what she really meant, she thought. "I should be most grateful if you let me know as soon as possible, Mrs Gilder."

"Of course, Mr Pender."

In the hall he spoke again: "I should only wish to add, on a personal note, that when my own dear mother died, I myself found a certain consolation in the daily routine of regular office work." He bowed as he put his hat on, and creaked away.

She stood for a moment leaning her back against the door, trying to imagine going back to Rosevear House, where so many things had happened, things she had once put a great deal of energy into not thinking about.

The drowned car was coming to mind less and less often, she realised. Once it had made her catch her breath almost daily, prompted by nothing at all; the surging bubbles had entered her dreams. No longer, now Joe was dead, and Barty was "missing."

Barty flying through a storm with the emergency hatch open. Barty dropping helplessly into icy seawater, the fisherman in just the right place. Barty using up his luck.

Another air raid killed three people, one of them a six-week-old baby. It also tore up the water main, and sliced off the back wall of her cousin Alice's house.

"Just like a doll's house!" said Alice, and could not be prevented from nipping upstairs and looking out from her own bedroom, now entirely open to view, especially since the blast had stripped all the leaves from the cherry trees in the garden, as if winter had come overnight.

Though it turned out that everything in the room only looked intact from a distance. Every surface was thick with dust and broken bricks, and the dressing table mirrors had burst apart into lethal splinters, some of which had studded themselves right into the wallpaper, little pink flowers all run through with glass, said Alice.

"Most extraordinary!" she said, drinking the tea someone had brought her. She was leaning against her front-garden gate, where everything looked completely normal. "As for the study," she went on cheerfully, "I couldn't even get the door open! Heaven knows what Freddie's going to say!"

"Alice," said Norah gently. "What are you talking about?"

Alice's usual expression of lively girlishness stayed intact while her eyes changed. Norah felt a little spasm of fear at the sight.

"Oh, how silly of me," said Alice at last.

"Perhaps you'd better come and sit down," said Norah.

For Alice's brother Freddie had died just before the War began.

"Poor darling, of course he should never have troubled himself with such things at all. But he could do almost anything by touch, you see. Well – you know, you heard him play the piano so beautifully – and of course he'd done it many many times before, so in fact the gun must have been loaded all the time – all those years, so it could have gone off at any time, when you think about it! So really one might almost say we were lucky, don't you think, that it took so long!"

It had been hard to know how to answer this. The verdict of accidental death had surely been a kindly one, Norah thought. No matter what Alice said, how likely was it that a blind man should take it upon himself to clean his old service revolver?

It had been an exploding shell in the last days of the Great War that had first damaged the retinas of Freddie's eyes. Despite a series of operations he had eventually gone completely blind. He had never married, and presently he was rarely seen anywhere without his sister on his arm, guiding, warning, describing.

"I am Freddie's eyes!" Alice used to say, proudly. She had taken her duties seriously, become expert.

Once Joe and Norah had stood beside them at an Empire Day parade, and caught some of Alice's by then almost unconscious muttered commentary:

Now it's the Scouts, the boy carrying the flag has orange hair, like marmalade, the flag's too heavy for him, he's drooping, quite pale, they're walking three abreast, not quite in step, one of them's just done a little hop to get back in time

It was not simply an account of what Freddie was missing, Norah had realised at the time, it was about detail, preferably scabrous.

Mrs Hopkins is wearing something silvery-grey and tight, she looks like a sea-lion, she once heard Alice murmur at a party.

A little of Alice went a long way, Joe had said once. "She's like his jailor."

Norah had been surprised, and indignant. "How can you say that? I think it's more the other way about. And she adores Freddie, she always has. Despite everything – he's often really unkind to her, a real brute. And all the time he completely relies on her - I don't know what he'd do without her."

"What would she do without him?" said Joe.

The War had answered that one, thought Norah.

They left the borrowed hand-cart ready in the front garden, guarded by an anxious woman in ARP overalls, and ventured inside with their suitcases.

"Documents, Alice," said Norah. "Your passport – title deeds – birth certificate. Where are they?"

"I must fetch some things from upstairs first," said Alice.

The wooden stairs looked normal at the bottom, apart from dusty, but grew steadily more speckled and gritty, the higher you went. In the shocking open daylight of Alice's bedroom every step crunched underfoot. A single brick lay exactly in the centre of the pillows on the bed, Norah saw. With the back of her sleeve Alice swept the rubble and broken glass from a small wooden stool and stood on it to reach up to the several round and octagonal boxes stacked apparently untouched on top of the wardrobe.

"Alice? What are you doing?"

"I can't leave Mother's hats," said Alice.

Alice had always been fond of Barty, Norah remembered, as they manouevred the laden cart across the Square. As a schoolboy he had occasionally earned a few shillings helping her get the barn ready, when she and Freddie wanted to show one of their old silent films there.

They had bought the tithe barn before the Great War, and turned it into the county's very first cinema, the wildly successful Silkhampton Picture Palace, packed every night, while Freddie played the piano, a brilliant one-man orchestra. But then had come the plush warmth of the purpose-built Rialto a few streets away, and the Talkies, and precipitate decline, until the Palace was opened up only for Alice's occasional soirees, one of Freddie's extensive collection of British two-reelers served with sherry.

"I remember his mother used to come twice a week in the old days," said Alice over supper that first evening. "Grace Dimond, I mean. She absolutely adored Charlie Chaplin, had her own favourite seat. I told him which one it was, Barty, I mean. Found him sitting in it more than once, poor little beast."

She picked up the photograph Norah had had framed. It was the most recent one she had of Barty, with an earlier more luxuriant version of the moustache.

"Such a dear pretty little thing. And so handy with a broom," said Alice, as if she were seeing quite a different picture.

The hatboxes took up a great deal of space in the spare room; there was only just room to walk past them to reach the bed.

"Let's put them up in the attic," said Norah. "It's perfectly dry."

"Oh, far too much trouble," said Alice. "I shan't be here for long, after all."

Next day, resolutely cheerful, she went back to work at the clothing depot.

"Best to keep busy!" She was running several first aid courses, and never missed a Sewing Night, so she was out a great deal.

Which was a relief, thought Norah.

One night she dreamed that she was walking down the carriage drive at Rosevear, the lake sparkling to one side. As she drew nearer she saw Joe's van parked by the front doors, and she ran towards the lake, knowing that he would only be there a little while, and saw someone standing on the little wrought iron bridge at the far end of the water. Was it Joe? He seemed to be looking straight at her, but he made no sign.

In the morning she remembered that she had not yet said an official No to Mr Pender. It was his fault she had dreamt of Rosevear, she thought.

Dear Mr Pender, thank you so much for putting my name forward to the Rosevear Hospital board, but after consideration I

She stopped, put the pen down. She had not done any considering, she thought. Not really.

Barty had at one time cycled there twice a week, she remembered, delivering bread to his grandmother Bea Givens, who had been housekeeper there.

It was a nice day, she saw, looking out of the basement windows. Some connection of thought she could not afterwards trace then led her to Joe again, and she wept for few minutes; she had quickly learnt that there was nothing she could do about these sudden storms, except wait for them to pass.

When this one was over she got up, washed her face, and went out to find her own bicycle. It had been a present from Joe after the baby, and it had taken her months to learn to ride it, she had never felt fully confident. Had she in fact ever ridden it without him cycling along beside her, shouting encouragement and reminders?

It was locked in the garden shed, which was full of Joe, she had to keep her eyes down as she went inside, trying not to look around too much.

Outside she leant her bicycle against the wall and looked at it. It was a pretty shade of blue, and had a basket at the front. Joe had always looked after it for her, he had done mysterious things to its brakes and chain. Gingerly she squeezed its dusty front tyre, tried the back one. Both felt almost solid to the touch, and that was good, wasn't it?

"Don't go too slow," said Joe in her head. She wheeled it out into the road. There was far less traffic now, of course.

Could she ride six whole miles to Rosevear? It would take hours, she would fall off and break something, or get a puncture and have to abandon the bicycle in a hedge and walk all the way back. She wanted see the Lake again, and the wrought iron bridge where Joe had stood in her dream. She had an odd moment of a kind of double awareness, of knowing that she had now decided to cycle all the way to Rosevear, but at the same time had sensibly decided not to, as if there were two of her.

But going back to her empty kitchen suddenly seemed unendurable. She hesitated for a moment more, trying to remember how you got on a bicycle, famously supposed to be one of the things you never forgot. You simply had to be firm with it, she thought. You had to use speed to make it balance itself and carry you. And never trust it too far.

Out of the Square, through the familiar network of streets and the straggle of bungalows, out into the countryside, past the fields, more fields, woods, and the long stretch of moorland. Presently the weather changed, it grew cloudy and grey. Sometimes she had to get off and push the bicycle uphill, then brake carefully all the way down again on the other side. After about an hour she realised that she must have missed the turning to Porthkerris, that she had somehow cycled past it. How had that happened? She got off in the middle of the road – it was half an hour since the last lorry had passed her – and turned round. Perhaps she should just go home now, she thought. It was lonely on her own, and several times she had barked her shins getting on or off, and the saddle was sticking into her more and more painfully, she had to keep standing up in the pedals to vary the pressure.

She went past a lane to her left, and for the first time understood that there was no signpost where one had always stood before. She went and had a closer look; yes, there was the deep hole where someone had wrenched out the concrete. No wonder she had ridden past the turn to Porthkerris; she had been looking out for the signpost, and it had been taken away, like all the rest, to confuse invading soldiery.

I'd forgotten about that, she thought. I'll just have to keep going until I recognise something. She tried to picture the turning to Porthkerris. Wasn't there a hollow oak tree on the other side of the road? Or was that somewhere else, quite a different crossroads?

Turn you round and you're lost, said Joe, from the past. They had cycled out the other way, towards Wootton and the cliffs. They had taken a picnic, and it had rained, and she had helplessly cycled through a puddle on the way home and drenched herself, he had brought her a cup of tea to drink in the bath.

She had to get off the bike for a while.

Then she set off again, and went past several possible turnings until at last she saw what looked like the right hollow oak in the right place. Another deep hole, where the signpost had been. If you cared about things, she thought, you would mind, about the lost signposts. It wasn't just the lost utility. They had meant something, they had stood for order, for the idea that impersonal helpfulness was a good thing. They stood for civilisation itself. All gone now.

She turned towards the sea, and Rosevear. The lanes now ran between by deep high hedges. Grass grew in the middle, there were occasional potholes to look out for. But the road was easy enough, thought Norah. Even with the wrong turning the journey had not taken that long.

As she took the final turning towards Rosevear she was able at last to look properly at what she was doing, and why. In some deep hidden way she had been contemplating this ever since Mr Pender's visit, she thought. Once she had stood at the bottom of the cliffs at Godrevy, and looked up, trying to imagine standing on the edge, taking that last step out into the air. It was possible; the bad part would not last long. But you would strike the rocks below so violently. Anyone who found you might suffer.

She herself had once been that Anyone, she had gone walking along that stretch of beach one sunny morning and come across death smashed open on the rocks, and it had taken her months to stop seeing that poor broken body every time she closed her eyes. Whereas Rosevear lake would simply receive you, take you in and keep you hidden, especially if you had a few stones in your pockets. The bubbles would rise for a little while, and then stop. She had seen them do it.

I am here to see if I can, thought Norah clearly, and her heart beat fast with a new sort of excitement. To work out exactly where. And if, and when.

Of course the lake was supposed to be haunted. Many claimed to know someone who had seen the ghost of a girl standing in the shallows, in the long white nightgown she had been wearing in life when she drowned herself. There were other local legends: of people who on certain nights rose singing from the water and walked around it holding spectral hands; of lights that moved in the darkness; that even by day the lake itself would somehow pull you in if you stayed beside it too long. And dear old Janet, Mamma's own parlourmaid, used to swear she had once heard a church bell tolling there, where no church was. How thrilling that once had seemed!

But believing in ghosts, even pretending to, was just another way to hide or deflect the fear of death, there was a feeble kind of hopefulness in it. She had no time for that sort of thing now.

She leant the bicycle against a tree just inside the front gateposts, took her handbag out of the front basket and walked down the carriage drive, as she had in her dream. Her bottom still hurt from being pinched against the saddle, and the drive was much more rutted that she remembered, and straight away to one side she noticed the sort of rope fencing the Silkhampton ARP used after a raid, to screen off danger. She made her way towards it across the lumpy moorland grass. The crater was enormous, and still looked new, though the bottom was full of stagnant water. She had told Barty about the ducks seen floating there, she remembered. She had tried to make this vileness cosy.

She went back to the drive and walked on. It was past five in the afternoon, a grey day now. One end of the lake began to appear round the side of the house. She would go straight there, she thought, make her way through the ruined kitchen garden and out onto the path to the nearer bank. She would be able to see the iron bridge from there. She was thinking so intently about the dream of Joe standing there that it was some time before she noticed that the house was no longer empty, that the tall windows on the ground floor were alive with movement, there was a car parked behind the laurel bushes outside the kitchen. As she went nearer she could actually hear voices, and hammering from somewhere, and catch a whiff of something cooking, potatoes on the boil.

Closer still she saw someone in nurse's uniform come right up to the window, give her an incurious glance, and begin drawing down blackout blinds. Music was playing from somewhere, a tinny orchestral whine from a radio.

"Hallo, are you lost?"

Norah turned, saw someone she knew slightly, a smallish woman in a grey coat, with short greying hair.

The woman came closer, her tone less friendly: "You're not a patient – what are you doing here?"

Norah had no idea what to say. She was still floundering when the woman's face suddenly relaxed.

"Did you – are you Mrs Gilder?"

At this, by some odd untraceable flow of ideas, Norah remembered that the woman in grey was a nurse from Silkhampton, and even managed her name.

"Sister Nesbit – hallo, I'm... sorry I didn't let you know I was coming." Norah was rather impressed with herself, coming up so quickly with something that sounded so normal.

"Come to see how we're doing?"

"I - "

"Quite well, actually," said Sister Nesbit, with a cool smile. "None of us have slept for days. But we're open. And running. First baby born last night!"

"Goodness," said Norah.

"I'd show you round," said Sister Nesbit, "except I can't. Short-staffed. Dr Broughton might be able to see you, for a minute or two. If you like. Maybe a cup of tea somewhere, if you're lucky. Come on in."

Unable to see any way not to, Norah followed Sister Nesbit up the familiar side path to the kitchen door. "Twelve patients at present," Nesbit was saying. "But essentially a cottage hospital for the wider public, fully-equipped operating theatre, minor ops mainly of course - " The smell in the corridor was almost overwhelming, more steamy potatoes, gravy, fresh paint, putty, and a deep base note of disinfectant. It was noisy, too, several voices raised in the front room, backed by more tinny music, and louder hammering noises coming from the floor above.

"Still working on the nursery," said Nesbit, stopping outside a door, knocking on it, and swinging it open.

"Sorry, this is Mrs Gilder. For the accounts."

"Oh, I - " said Norah, but meekly passed her into the room, where a woman in paint-spattered brown overalls was sitting at a large desk talking rapidly into a telephone. Norah turned in time to see Nesbit closing the door behind her. The woman in overalls gestured to her rather imperiously, sit down, and went on talking:

"I do see your point, Mr Harper, absolutely I do, but the question is one of priority. There are new born babies here. By tomorrow we will have three. This is not about luke-warm bath water."

She went on looking hard at Norah while a voice quavered at the other end of the line. She was about Norah's own age, pale-faced, crop-haired, with a high gleaming bridge to her nose and intelligent dark eyes. Norah looked away. Like the rest of the room the desk was empty, apart from a clean new blotting pad and a small very colourful framed picture on a stand, a reproduction of the Nativity, with angels and shepherds and, central in His mother's deep blue arms, the tiny shimmering golden baby Jesus.

The woman in overalls made a snorting noise of contempt. "Well, I'll talk to her myself if you like. Happy to, believe me."

...

"I'm sure you can."

...

"No, early as you like."

...

"Seven's fine. We're a hospital, Mr Harper, we're always open, that's rather my point. Good day to you."

She banged the phone down. "Right. Who are you again?"

"I'm Norah Gilder. Mr Pender - "

"Oh him," said the woman. "Very picturesque, but not in 1940, we haven't got time. You here about the accounting job?"

"I had no idea you were open yet," said Norah. "I haven't really thought about it."

"What is there to think about? We need someone who can do sums, basically. And type. That's about it. You like my picture?" She nodded at the small golden Nativity.

"It's lovely," said Norah, in surprise.

"Notice anything odd about it?"

"Well, no, I don't think so."

The woman sat back in her chair, and smirked. "I was present at a virgin birth myself once."

"I beg your pardon?"

"Absolutely true. Virgo intacta. Girl of fifteen. Fully intact hymen, in labour."

"Well - "

"Not the Holy Spirit though. Just messing about with a man in a taxi, poor kid. Hadn't actually done it at all - so unfair." She stood up, and something fell out of the pocket of her overall onto the desk. It was a screwdriver, Norah saw. The woman picked it up. "Well, nice to meet you and all that, but I've got to get back to work now. Can you see yourself out?"

"I – of course," said Norah.

The woman seemed to remember something. She came round the desk, tucked the screwdriver into the top pocket of her overall, as if it were a pen, and held out a hand. " I'm Edina Broughton, by the way."

Norah shook it. "You're the Matron?"

"Doctor in charge."

"Oh...sorry."

"No need," said Dr Broughton. "Happens all the time. Start on Monday? There's probably a cup of tea in the library, if you want it. But you must excuse me. Goodbye."

And Norah was suddenly in the corridor outside the office, watching Dr Broughton stride away, and then she was alone. She stood still for a moment. Though she had been to Rosevear many times before, the house had always been nearly or entirely empty, a dark echoing place of locked doors and cobwebs. Now it felt full. First baby born already, Nesbit had

44

said. Three by tomorrow. She could hear music, and a tap running, and hammering and sawing noises from upstairs, and when someone opened a door further up the corridor there was a sudden murmur of voices. Someone was clattering in the kitchen at the other end of the corridor, and there was a growing and poignant smell of frying onions.

Norah went back the way she had come, past the kitchen, out into the gathering dusk. Her stomach had growled at the onions, made her remember that she hadn't eaten all day. But food had been playing tricks on her for a long time now, turning into something inedible as soon as she picked up her knife and fork. She wasn't really hungry, she decided. Just as well, as there was still so long to wait.

She walked past the front of the house. Not a chink of light escaped, despite the size of the windows. The blinds alone must have cost a fortune, she thought. Who was paying for all this, the War Office? She made her way to the old kitchen garden, and felt lost for a moment, it looked so different. The great straggling banks of bramble had all gone. Revealed beneath them, some of the large rectangular beds had already been dug and planted, and someone had taken pruning shears to the espaliered plum trees. The cinder path crunched cleanly beneath her feet. The gate had been mended.

She walked far enough round to see the wrought iron bridge at the far end of the lake, set there by some eighteenth-century enthusiast to make the lake look even longer. It was unchanged, slightly more rusty perhaps, already barely visible in the failing light. No one was standing on it. She waited a few minutes just in case, then turned and walked back to the bank nearest the house, dipped her hand in the water.
Cold, but not too cold. She would have to be careful about shoes, she thought. The ones she had on would slip off, perhaps betray her, when what she wanted most was to disappear. She must remember to wear the lace-ups.

On impulse she spread her handkerchief on a fallen tree and sat down. The lake was a steely grey, darkening as the light faded. Soon the house fifty yards to her left was the merest silhouette, a dark line of roof just visible through the trees. Withered leaves whispered a little overhead, and she could hear a faint trickle of water, a streamlet joining the lake. The air was very still. Some stars began to show.

Dare you, thought Norah at the lake, but she knew there was nothing to be defiant at. The truth was this constant roiling weight of grief, this nothingness.

For a while she wept again, so that she did not at first notice the change in the water in front of her. It was black now, and softly gleaming, almost as still as glass, and presently mist began to form. It was very faint at first, a haze, gathering here and there into delicate twisting eddies, milky in the moonlight, slowly forming a soft low cloud over the whole lake. The far side disappeared. For a while she sat, rocking a little, just looking.

After a long time an owl hooted, far away, and she noticed that she was shivering with cold. When she stood up her feet were numb. Stiffly she bent, retrieved her handkerchief and her handbag. It was time to go home.

The thought that came to her most vividly as she made her halting way back through the kitchen garden in the dark and past the blinded house was the idea that the lake had always done this. It was not ghostly people who rose singing from the lake on certain nights, it was the living water itself. Every time the season and the weather was just so, mist arose from the water, and spectacularly hung there, milky in the moonlight, it had happened over and over again for millions of years, it had happened before there was a house, before there was a village, before there were people at all, unpredictable, fleeting, a grand event of stillness and water. This time she had been there to see it.

Think about that later, she told herself.

Her bicycle was still propped against the tree near the gatepost. She wiped the wet saddle with her handkerchief. There was just enough moonlight, she thought, to get through the lanes, but not to see all the ruts and potholes. She could easily get lost too, in the strangeness of the fields at night. No signposts either.

"Just in case," said Joe in her head, and she propped the bicycle against the tree again and with some difficulty in the darkness undid the stiff leather buckle on the small saddlebag, and found the torch inside, with the bicycle repair kit, and the spare inner tube. Was the battery still working? She clicked it on, and there was the bold golden beam, greening the hedges as it touched them.

Don't waste it, she thought in Joe's voice, and she turned it off and wedged it with her bag into the basket in front of her, easily reachable, and set off into the lane. She had not noticed the incline on the way down to Rosevear; now it was hard going, a long steady climb that at least warmed her up, soon she had to stand in the pedals, her heart thumping with effort. Looking back on that night she would remember that as she finally reached the relief of level ground she had seemed to hear the roar of the sea.

Then directly overhead the whole sky seemed to convulse and solidify, to hurtle over her all close fiery weight and roaring thunder. She shouted something wordless, half-fell from the bicycle, shaken at once out of her private dreaming self. For a second that felt like a long time she straightened up, made sense of things, thought clearly *aeroplane, crashing*. Then she kicked herself free of the bicycle, bent and plucked the torch from the basket, and ran. The first impact came as she was hauling herself over the five-bar gate, a violent rushing, a groaning grind, another long splintering crash.

Norah went on running. The field sloped slightly downhill, she ran faster than she had ever run before, faster than she would ever run again. She met the long curving gouge the aeroplane's belly had left in the earth, and raced along it past various scattered flaring scraps to the great sounding wreck itself, big as a house, standing high in a hot stink of burnt fuel, its nose skywards, looking impossible, a monster rearing up alive.

What to do, what to do?

She dithered for a second. The cockpit was too high to see into. Everything was out of reach. Everything stank of fuel, something fell off with a shivering crash as she stood there, the torch in her hand. She switched it on, saw in its frail light that the body of the plane seemed fairly securely wedged on the other side, against the stump of an oak tree. Perhaps she could get onto what was left of the nearest wing, it was maybe just low enough. For a flashing moment she saw herself hopelessly clumsy on the leather gym horse at school PE, then she put the torch in her pocket, and awkwardly set first one knee on the wing, then the other, hauling herself forwards onto it, metal groaning beneath her, the whole thing shifting horribly with her weight. She inched forward, found the torch, lit up the cockpit, and there was the pilot, sitting ahead of her like someone in the next row in the theatre, it was a shock to see him somehow, she gave a little gasp.

He was just sitting there, not moving. Blunt leather head, goggles. Was he dead? She smacked her palm on the outer casing of the cockpit.

"Hey – you, are you alright?"

He seemed not to hear her, went on gazing ahead, not moving.

The plane was a bomber, she thought. Maybe armed. Maybe not. There might be other men alive in there, navigator, wireless operator. Inside.

Wireless Operator trying to mend the set, said Barty in her head. She banged on the side of the plane, shouted again, "Hallo, hallo!"

How did the cockpit open? She inched forward on the ticking wing, there were other sounds as she moved, a groaning, a soft pattering; there was a deep heavy smell of oil. Aiming the torch, she found a sort of knob or grip on the cockpit perspex, and pushed at it hard. It shifted slightly, then suddenly gave, opened, fell right off sideways, dropped away, and there was the pilot unsealed, she could smell him, used air, sour sweat, scorching Bakelite, petrol. She could right reach in, and grasp his shoulder.

"Hey!"

He turned then, and seemed to look at her. Goggles half-covered his face. With what felt at the time like irritation she reached out and swiped at them, he winced as they fell off, coiling about his neck. His face was wet, blackened with filth. He screwed his eyes up in her torchlight. He looked like a child.

"Listen to me. Wake up now. Wake up!"

Was he injured? Was he only appearing to sit there dazed? Only appearing to sit, oh dear God! For a second she could not bring herself to look further.

"Come *on*!" she cried. Still he made no move, while the aeroplane went on shifting, groaning, muttering to itself, saying *petrol*, saying *smouldering*, saying *bomb*.

Strapped in, said something in Norah's head. He's strapped in. Norah reached forward further into the cockpit, and shone the light at his chest. Harness. Meeting in the middle. A thing like a buckle. She thrust at it with the fingers of her other hand, and it suddenly gave, sliding apart with a smooth metallic click.

The sound at last seemed to rouse him. He shifted, began struggling in his seat.

"Yes," she shouted at him, "Yes, quick, get out, get out!"

She hauled on his arm, and gasping he rose, the whole man, he unfolded higher and higher, leaning against her shoulder.

"Quickly!" He turned and got himself up onto the seat, kneeling first one knee on it, now the other, like a very old man, now he could half-lean half-fall out onto the wing as she side-stepped quickly along it to get out of his way. On the ground himself he cried out in pain, one leg giving way, but she wouldn't let him fall, she held tightly onto him.

"Run, run, come on!"

She had her arm round his waist now, his other arm heavy across her shoulders, she hung onto his wrist, hauling him forwards.

"Quick!"

Uphill now, the ground uneven. He was staggering wildly, the heavy flying boots kept tripping him, once he fell forward onto his hands and knees, pulling her over, but she yanked them both up again.

"Not yet, keep going!" and they toiled upwards, towards the safety of the field wall, but before they reached it there came the enormous explosion, the ground burst open in a great breath of heat and knocked them both over. Norah's spine seemed to flick and slither inside her, dissolving away in animal terror, but quickly she found that she could turn, and shift herself somehow, she could cover the boy with her arm, then with her shoulder, she could partly shield him with her own body. Clods of earth rained down on them, a thudding of stones, bits of aeroplane, metal, burning stuff, setting little fires here and there on the grass beside them, one hit his shoulder and she reached over and flattened it at once with her hand.

It was only afterwards that she wondered at how quickly help arrived. Where had the truck come from, and these soldiers? It was an entirely unfamiliar face bending towards her, London accent far from local.

"You alright, lady?"

Though he was close his voice was oddly muffled. She lay still, she felt relaxed and cosy, lying there on the grass. The air was full of smoke and movement.

She remembered something: "Were there others?" she asked, and thought how odd her own voice sounded too, it felt internal, as if she were talking with her fingers in her ears.

The soldier looked over at where the aeroplane had been, and shook his head. He was RAF, she saw.

"Where have you come from?" she asked him, but he made no reply, except to tap the side of his nose with his forefinger: don't ask.

Now there were several of him, with a stretcher, they were setting it down beside her pilot, who lay prone beside her as if he were asleep. Gently they pulled him away and turned him over onto his back, and she heard the sighing groan he gave. His eyes opened. He turned his head, and saw her.

"Hallo," she said. She couldn't help smiling, and after a few seconds he managed a near-smile back, keeping his eyes intently fixed on hers while the soldiers turned him partly onto his side, pushed the stretcher beneath him, laid him back upon it, briskly covered him with a blanket. He was shivering violently.

"You're going to be fine," she said. His lips moved, as if he were trying to speak. She leant closer, and he worked a hand free, reached out, and touched her arm.

"*Danke*," he said.

At the hospital the pilot was wheeled away, in a sudden eager excited knot of nurses, two ARP wardens and a policeman, and then Norah was alone in the waiting room. She went to sit down in one of the armchairs by what remained of the fire, then realised what a state she was in, covered in mud, or was it oil, her good skirt was actually torn at the front, ripped right open showing tattered oily petticoat underneath, her stockings were the merest strings, they were joke stockings with dirty scratched legs showing through, smeared with blood, and her shoes were an absolute ruin, the left one completely missing its heel. And all her teeth ached, and her left hand hurt; then she noticed with surprise that she was trembling all over, as if she were very cold.

Am I cold? It seemed impossible to tell. Slowly she made her way over to the table in the middle of the room, and sat down in one of the plain wooden chairs, though even there she was still a little worried about staining the seat.

Presently a nurse came in, and said something in a friendly tone, and Norah tried to explain about the chair and how shockingly dirty she was, but her voice was shaking too much, she could hear herself that the words came out garbled. The nurse went on cosily chatting, something about bicycles; she seemed to think that Norah had simply fallen off hers on the way home. As she talked the nurse tucked a big blanket round Norah's shoulders, which Norah thought very kind, and then produced a cup of hot sugared tea.

Norah hesitated, for a second afraid that she would somehow say *Danke* by mistake.

"Thank you," she said, and was relieved, but the nurse was looking concerned, she took Norah's left hand and turned it over, and they were both surprised by the tense blister of burn all across the palm.

"Oh dear, now how did that happen?" said the nurse, but Norah had no idea. She drank the tea and began to feel more herself, began to wonder what time it was, and then she remembered the bicycle, and the bicycle basket, everything abandoned in the lane several miles away.

There was a knock at the door, which opened.

"I come in?"

It was the RAF man who had tapped his nose at the crash site. He was quite young, she saw now, with a confident stride and a lively freckled face. The nurse sat up straighter.

"Alright?" He came forward, made a little sound of longing: "Was that tea?"

"Maybe," said the nurse.

"You know I'm gasping here," he said to her, and presently she went off with a swish of her skirts. The RAF man sat down at the table beside Norah, and tilted his head at the door the nurse had just gone through. "You said anything to her? About the plane?"

"No, not really - "

"Might be best if you kept quiet about that," he said.

"What? Why - d'you mean, because he was German? You think I should be ashamed of helping him, because he was German, is that it?"

"Keep your hair on," he said. "You want to go around saying you saved a Nazi bomber, you go ahead. But leave me and the lads out of it. We weren't there. Savvy?"

"But that's - well, if you weren't there, how did I get here, then? How did the pilot get here?"

"We was out on manoeuvres," he said promptly, "just passing, see the plane come down, enemy aircraft, do a recce, take him in, get to town, there you are, knocked off your bike, oh dear cycling in the blackout, happens all the time. We pick you up too."

"Oh," said Norah.

"Simpler, see," he said. "Anyway, mind telling me, what was you doing out there? Middle a nowhere?"

She looked at his uniform, trying to judge his authority-level.

"That time of night," he added. Whatever his stripes, his confidence was unnerving.

"If you must know," she said, "I was visiting the hospital."

"What hospital? This is the hospital."

"The new hospital," said Norah. "At Rosevear House," she added, as he looked blank.

"What - out there? Near Porthkerris, is it?"

"That is the nearest place, I suppose."

"You hear a siren?"

Before Norah could answer the nurse came in with his tea. He smiled at her and there was a moment's full silence before she said briskly that Well now, Mrs Gilder, we really should see about that hand, was she up to walking, or did she need a chair?

But later, after a difficult ten minutes for Norah, he appeared again, as the nurse was tying up the bandage.

"Sorry," he said to the nurse, and to Norah, "You show me? This hospital a yourn. This it?" he held out the map, folded in the right place, and turned the lamp onto it.

"I need my spectacles, I'm afraid," said Norah apologetically.

"They in here?" In his other hand, he held up her handbag. "Picked it up. Along of your bike," he said.

"Thank you so much!'

"Least we could do," said the RAF man, glancing warmly over at the nurse. "Got your specs in there then?"

She had. She fumbled them out – the bandage was going to be a nuisance, she thought – put them on, and took the map in her uninjured hand. There was Silkhampton, where she had lived nearly all her life. Trace the railway line westward, towards the coast as far as Porthkerris, the fishing village so besieged by artists every summer; then back along the lanes, to the lake:

"Yes," she said, "here."

"Marked Rosevear House."

"Yes."

"Been there long?"

"Not as a hospital."

"How d'you mean?"

"I told you, it's only just opened. This week, I think."

"What, women there now? Having babies and so on?"

"Yes."

"Right." He seemed - no, what did he seem? Norah could not tell. Perplexed, perhaps. A distant bell rang, and the nurse disappeared to answer it. He got up too.

"Well, I'll be off then. Me and the lads."

"Back to where you aren't."

He shot her a look, grinned. "That's us. Not there."

"Thank you for bringing my things, my bag and so on."

"Pleasure." He stopped at the door. "I saw what you done," he said. "Got to hand it to you. Jerry or not – you was top rate."

"Oh," said Norah. Instantly she was almost overcome. "How very kind of you to say so!" Her voice shook with emotion: so it was true, then, real, she had done something remarkable, saved a life! "Thank you," she added, recovering herself, "but really, I didn't think about it, I just ran. Not brave, just idiotic."

"Both,' he said.

"Of course I thought he was one of ours," said Norah. "It was all so quick, you see, and he was flying so low. It was so dark." She heard herself sounding as if she were trying to convince him, and shut up.

"Would you still a done it, then? If you'd known?"

Norah felt herself blush. "I don't know," she said.

He looked at her as if he knew she was lying. "Well," he said. "Here's to you anyway." He gave her a formal salute, and to her own embarrassed surprise her eyes at once filled. Then he was gone.

Ten minutes later Norah was slowly wheeling her bicycle home in the darkness, limping awkwardly in her ruined shoes.

"Fine, far as I know," the nurse had said dismissively, when asked about the pilot. Maybe he was still here. "Or they've taken him away already. Why?"

Because I saved him. Because he is mine. "Just wondered," said Norah meekly.

It was strange to think that she would never see him again, never so much as know his name. Nor he hers. But he will remember me, she thought, for always, as I'll remember him. His eyes on hers, his hand touching her arm. His grey dirty face.

"*Danke.*"

And I was top rate.

Had she still done something tremendous, she asked herself, if she'd done it for the wrong person?

She tried to imagine herself spotting the obvious swastika on the tail and holding back, standing there with her arms folded, watching the enemy burn alive from a safe distance.

Then had a sudden moment of uncertainty.

She stopped dead in the street, thinking back. Again she saw the plane shudder overhead, so close she felt she could almost have jumped up and touched it. She had grabbed the torch and raced along the gouged fiery path and come up behind the wreck, there had been no fin to show her its swastika, no, that was completely gone, shattered away; but absolutely plainly, no getting away from it, she had seen the black cross on the aeroplane's battered side. She could see herself seeing it.

How can I have seen it and not seen it at the same time? Black cross, white background. I saw it and ran straight past it, took no notice. As if it meant nothing.

Of course I thought he was one of ours, I told the RAF man, and it had felt peculiar at the time. Was that because I already knew I was lying, in some unconscious way? On the other hand, I know I didn't think *Oh, a German, but I'll try to help him anyway*. There wasn't time, for one thing. I really didn't think anything at all.

It came to her that if she had acted without thought she had not acted without feeling. Standing in the middle of the empty street she closed her eyes, and felt her way back in time again, and saw that as well as a rational humane impulse to help someone in danger there had been something else, something incoherent, more personal, a kind of magic. Primitive stuff.

I saw and didn't see the black cross. Identity was beside the point, because all men now were Barty. I was trying to do magic. I pulled him out of his harness and his daze, I ran him to safety, I saved him. I saved him, Joe.

Oh Joe.

Norah usually thought of herself as a sensible everyday robust sort of person, and so could not allow herself for long to stand *snivelling in the street*, as she soon pointed out to herself, as unkindly as possible. Stop that at once, and go home!

Drying her eyes briskly with the back of her uninjured hand she heaved the bicycle up again, onto the cobbles of the market square, and bumped it slowly across that large handsome space, past the war memorial's stone soldier, who still was and was not her long-dead brother Guy. Everything was in blackout darkness now, of course, all the buildings on all four sides unlit, as if every tall private house, every shop and pub, stood empty, abandoned.

Perhaps it was actually rather fitting, she thought, that the only people who had witnessed her being top rate weren't ever going to tell anyone about it. She dragged the bicycle inside the railings round her own front door, and felt in her handbag for the key.

It was fitting, and right. Because after all, Norah reminded herself, if ever a woman deserved to keep quiet about saving someone's life, that woman is me.

Making her way shakily down to the kitchen she was surprised to find that it was only eleven o'clock. The hectic lorry ride back to Silkhampton had been so much faster than cycling would have been, she thought, and she had surely spent no more than an hour at the hospital.

But it feels as if I've been away for days on end.

On the kitchen table was a note in Alice's huge scrawl: *Pie from Mrs Hennessy, bartered for eggs!*

It was in the meat safe, a nice-looking plate pie, onion and potato, with cheese in it, judging by the golden smell, and missing Alice's frugal dinner, just one thin slice. Norah got herself a plate, and carefully herself another slice just like it, but found that she had immediately eaten it with her fingers. She cut another, and quickly ate that too. Then another bigger one. There was hardly any pie left now, just a fairly small bit that was hardly worth keeping, she thought, so she ate that too, put the dirty plate in the sink with the clean one and went upstairs.

Drawing a bath would be noisy, the boiler roared in use, and the hot water pipes shunted and rattled and then as they cooled knocked at intervals for at least half an hour, but needs must, thought Norah as she turned the taps on. Sorry, Alice, please don't wake.

Slowly, with some difficulty, she pulled off her clothes one-handed, the ruined skirt, the torn blouse. Even her underwear was muddy, and there was earth in her hair, she could feel it gritting beneath her fingertips, but that would have to wait until morning. The steamy, dripping peace when she turned the taps off was wonderful.

The water pained as she climbed in, she seemed to have scrapes and bruises everywhere. She propped her bandaged hand on the bath tray and lay back as far as she could without getting her hair wet. Would she ever be able to sleep again, she wondered. Even in the lovely hot water she was aware of her own thrumming excitement, her mind racing all over the place. The instant she closed her eyes the wing creaked beneath her weight, saying petrol, saying *smouldering*, saying *bomb*.

She sat up again, splashing water onto the floor. Think about something else, she told herself. The hospital at Rosevear, three newborn babies. The lake. The mist rising.

It occurred to her that the only thing she had knowingly taken with her on her extraordinary adventure, on this unforgettable night of nights, was her handbag: doorkeys, spectacles, one almost-finished lipstick, a small comb with several teeth missing, half-a-crown, and three old bus tickets.

Once she started giggling it was very hard to stop.

Waking the next morning, almost too stiff to get out of bed, Norah was all the same aware of a certain change within herself. She had done something large, she thought. She had once more acted with dispatch in a crisis. It was impossible not to feel pleased with herself. The secrecy of the act was in itself a good thing too, no one was going to exclaim at her or ask silly questions. Or write embarrassing headlines.

The important thing, she told herself, as she inched her way over to the window to pull aside the blackout, was not to indulge in any nonsense. The important thing was to know that nothing she had done could have any effect on what had happened to Barty.

She must face the fact that he was "*missing*" until he was found, which might never happen. The angler had been there last year, but if he had decided not to bother with fishing and stayed in bed, Barty would have been "*missing*" then. Perhaps forever. One must always bear in mind that there might never be proof of his death. No trace might ever be found. And nothing she could do would ever make any difference.

"At all," Norah said aloud to herself.

The trouble was that some part of her would already have none of this, it was suffused with magical hope. The thought kept singing in her head: chance had saved the German pilot. His plane had missed the field wall, been braked by the oak tree, come down on the one night she had gone to Rosevear, when delayed by the beautiful mist – by *weather* - she was cycling by at exactly the right moment, and there had just been time enough to get him out safely. A chain of unlikely chances, and there he was alive at the end of it.

Unlikely things still happened. Help could arrive just when it was needed. "Missing" might still mean missing. Missing might still mean alive.

Stop that, Norah told herself sternly, as she hobbled downstairs to put the kettle on.

Stop that, you are being ridiculous.

But as if in defiance of logic and rational thought, the postcard came the following week. It was much bent and stained, and addressed to Mr and Mrs Gilder, a single thickly-pencilled line.

Am safe, prisoner of war in Germany, don't worry. I'll send address soon. Love to you both, Barty

The date was months ago, a world ago, when Joe was alive. Using her magnifying glass under a strong light Norah could just read the stamped word *Dusseldorf,* along with a few other bits of words and numbers that hadn't printed clearly enough.

For several days, before duty compelled her, and she sent it off as demanded to Officer Squiggle at the War Office, she kept the postcard tucked inside her bodice, next to her heart.

Love to you both.

It was a small thing, perhaps, but it was more than enough for Norah.

PART TWO

April 1945

LATER

The new day, a Saturday, dawned cold but still and very bright. Presently Dr Edina Broughton, in her cosy tartan wool dressing gown and carrying a rolled-up towel, opened the kitchen door at Rosevear House and stepped out into the brilliance.

To the far side of the house the edge of the lake shimmered in the sunshine. She set off on the weedy gravel of the old carriage drive, through the kitchen garden, and down to her favourite bank behind a few scrubby hawthorn trees. Some creamy waterlilies lay fresh upon the water. To one side a moorhen picked its way through the reeds.

She hung towel and dressing gown over the usual handy low branch, stood for a moment in her swimming costume, the cold grass soft beneath her feet, then took a deep breath, held it, and walked straight out into the water. 57 or 58 degrees, she thought, wading now, the fiery line of the water rising higher with every step, knees, thighs, privates, belly. She put both arms in, that was always a bad moment too, but now there was only the final push.

Breathe out, breathe in again, hold it, then lean forward into the freeze.

She swam fast at first. One's body was so very much against the whole idea of icy water; one must trick it a little, allow it some urgent escape-style action. Though not fast breathing; at this stage that would feel like panic, which could easily prompt the real thing.

"One gets used it," Edina had often briskly explained, when questioned; but really the whole business was much more active than that, more thrilling, as her body at a certain point seemed suddenly to acquiesce, to put temperature aside. Then the iciest water felt delicious, alive and sparkling on the skin.

She turned onto her back and kicked up a small triumphant fountain, then turned again and began her slow-but-steady Edwardian breast stroke, her arms deep beneath the surface, so that she made almost no sound. A shifting moiré pattern of tender little ripples continuously formed and softly broke before her fingertips. The rising sun shone a golden path onto the water, she swam along its brilliant dazzle. Halfway to the bridge, she told herself. Best not to overdo it.

On the way back, the sun behind her, she saw that one or two sheep had gathered on the far shore to nibble the soft grass of the bank. One was right beside the water, and and not for the first time she noted how much, from a distance, it might look to some like a person huddled there. One of the local rather pretty little black-faced sheep; or a ghostly dark-haired girl in a nightgown - which did you prefer to see?

She had been bemused, when first at Rosevear, by the sheer number of lake-stories, which were partly due, she thought to the depth and opacity of the water, but mainly of course to the grinding relentless boredom of rural life. Who wouldn't want to seize on any potential ingredient to cook up a little excitement now and then?

She eyed the sheep for a few strokes more, then turned onto her back and for a moment lay still. The water hurt her scalp, made her gasp again, but it was always worth it, on a day like this, to lie quietly for a while and look up at the sky.

For a few seconds she admired, and was also enjoyably aware of herself doing the admiring, of being sensitive to a beauty others barely noticed. At the back of her mind there was also a vague but satisfying idea that this conscious appreciation of blue sky, of a moorhen's delicate red beak, had lasting value in itself, was a solid virtue, now registered and safely banked away for keeps.

She turned back onto her stomach, saw that the sheep had wandered off again. Time she went too, she decided; her fingers were numb. But as she struck out for her bank her left foot touched something in the water below her, and it seemed to her straight away that this was not the passing slip of weed or waterlily but something more substantial. Then her whole left foot was suddenly enfolded in what felt like a soft insinuating grasp.

There was something horrible about being touched in deep water. Instinctively she kicked it away, but the softness touched her again, swirling, reaching up about her whole left leg, a filmy caress.

Edina threw herself sideways away from it, but the softness stayed with her, it billowed around her from the depths and stroked at her. For a long terrible second she knew it was the long-dead girl in her nightgown, come to embrace her, to show her that all the stories about the lake were true, and as this flashed though her mind she actually saw a shape clouding just beneath her in the water, a submerged and sinking paleness of soft drowned cloth, and gave a great shout of horror.

To her own ears the cry sounded more like anger than fear, and thus like the everyday, for as everyone who worked with her knew, Dr Edina Broughton was a woman much given to rage. Hearing her own familiar fury, Edina was suddenly her own competent self again, and not to be trifled with; at a disadvantage, perhaps, but still not about to give the idea of ghostliness a single moment's credence:

"*Total* nonsense," said Edina aloud, swiping wet hair out of her eyes. Now she was clear of the pale shape she must find it again for herself. She trod water furiously, feeling for the floating softness with her feet. But she could find nothing, so she duck-dived into the dim freeze, peering about her, circling until at last she made out a shifting cloudiness, kicked her way down to it, and fiercely caught at it, both hands.

Got you, beastly thing! But as she turned, trying to pull it upwards, it slid abruptly from her grasp, it was fastened down, she realised, or attached to something heavy. Gasping at the surface she trod water again, thinking.

It had looked like, acted like, felt like, material. Because that was what it was: a great deal of material. For a second more she thought about the way the stuff had felt in her hands, tried to recapture the sensation. It had been so thin, almost membraneous, cloudy in the water. Silky.

Edina turned and began to swim back to the bank as fast as she could, and presently staggered out breathing hard, her whole body bright scarlet. With difficulty, her fingers numb with cold, she tore down the icy grip of her costume, clambered shuddering out of it, then snatched up her dressing gown and wrapped herself, gazing out at the spot where the pale floating softness had touched her. Less than twenty feet away, she thought. Caught perhaps on an old tree roots, or some other submerged thing.

Never a nightdress, of course. But yards of pale material, moving because she herself had stirred the water, fastened down to something heavy. It was soft, thin, and silky. It had to be a parachute.

There was a dead man deep in the water, drowned in his harness.

The only other person awake at Rosevear at that moment was Minnie, who did the Rough. She was a large woman, increasingly heavy in middle-age. She was always hungry, always had been, and this was quite a trial these days, when, as Mrs Hawes the cook often pointed out to her, there were so many mouths to feed, and on so little.

In fact Mrs Hawes had gone to Dr Broughton some time ago and complained about Minnie's uncontrollable greed, and the nuisance of having to keep an eagle eye on her all the time whilst still getting her own work done. But the doctor had seemed uninterested, and said that if she sacked Minnie the Rough would still need doing, and who else did Mrs Hawes think she would possibly find to do that, around here, when anyone with any get up and go had already long ago got up and gone?

"Up to you, of course, it's your kitchen," Dr Broughton had said, very off-hand, and getting up from behind her desk, so that it was clear the interview was over.

Mrs Hawes had not argued. "I just thought as you should know what's what," she had said, but gone away fairly content; she knew she had planted the seeds. If any order fell short from now on, if a tin or two here and there went missing, suspicion would fall where it might, Mrs Hawes had thought comfortably, and that afternoon she had been unusually kind to Minnie, and let her scrape out the cake-mix bowl.

At this time in the morning the Rough involved coal-hauling, and Minnie, who had been awake as usual since just after five, had first made her own room tidy, before starting on everything else.

"Minnie might be slow, but she is thorough," her Ma had once said, and Minnie had remembered this praise ever since. Slowly but thoroughly she had stripped her bed, picked up the feather-mattress, thumped it soft, set it back again on the sagging bedstead, and re-made it with the slowly but thoroughly shaken sheets and blankets. She had swept the floor, given the bedside rug a good bashing against the wall outside through the open window, dusted the mantelpiece, wiped each photograph.

When she was satisfied she went out to the scullery, put on Ma's old coat, tying it tightly round her middle in a big bow with string, and pushed her hands into the stiff leather gauntlets. The coat brought her Ma back to her a little. It was always like visiting her, to wear it. She stepped out of her slippers and into her enormous and easily-discarded rubber boots, took up her buckets, and began on the long series of trips out to the coalshed and back.

All the coal scuttles, collected and lined up and given a quick rub-over the night before, had to be filled – if possible, there wasn't always enough coal - and left ready to be taken back again; then, when Minnie had put away Ma's old coat and gloves and boots and shaken out the buckets, she tied on the special sacking apron and carried each filled coal scuttle back to the right room, swept out all the fire-places – making sure first to light the kitchen stove well before six - laid the new fires all ready, and finally got the fire in the dining room going, when it was time to hang up the sacking apron, wash her hands, and take Mrs Hawes her cup of early morning tea, on the dot of ten to seven.

Minnie always made the tea slowly and thoroughly, but there was often something wrong with it.

"Are you sure the water boiled?"

"You know this milk's on the turn, don't you? Well, did you check?"

There were so many things to remember, so many pitfalls. Sometimes Minnie's hands trembled as she carried the cup and saucer along the corridor.

At Mrs Hawes' door on this particular sunny morning she bent and set the cup and saucer down on the floor, knocked neither too hard not too quietly, turned the doorknob to open the door just a little, carefully picked the cup and saucer up again and entered. The smell of the room hit her at once, it was so dense, so full of Mrs Hawes.

Balancing the cup and saucer in one hand she reached down with the other to switch on the bedside light. In the sudden circle of glare Mrs Hawes' head looked as usual surprisingly small on her pillow, the short hair ruffled into damp-looking clumps. At least today she was facing the other way; she still made the sticky fluttering noise with her lips, but not so that Minnie could see.

There were things on the bedside table that had to be pushed aside, not too gently not too hard, but carefully as they were Mrs Hawes' own special private things, and then Minnie could set the tea down, say "Good morning, Ma'am," neither too softly nor too loudly, and at last successfully escape, though of course quietly, and without banging the door behind her.

After all that Minnie really deserved her own tea, and often privately told herself so, in Ma's own voice.

"You just sit yourself down now, Minnie, my lamb."

But this particular morning, just as she was peacefully stirring in the sugar, the kitchen door burst open with a crash, and someone staggered in, dragged out a chair, and collapsed heavily into it, leaning her head on her hands on the table.

Minnie was too appalled to speak or move. After a little while it occurred to her that this was none other than the lady doctor herself, that distant deity! Minnie had never before shared the same room as her, let alone the same table.

Then she noticed that the lady doctor was quite wet. She was chattering her teeth together and quivering hard. She was wearing a tartan dressing gown (*that's seen better days*, said Ma, in Minnie's head) and there was a loop of bright green pond weed in her hair.

Minnie sat still, thinking, and presently remembered some long-ago frosty mornings, and Ma telling the bread delivery boy to come in and have a warm, and giving him a hot cup of tea. Stealthily she moved round in her chair, readying herself for flight, then from as much distance as she could manage carefully pushed her own cup and saucer across the table towards the lady doctor's bent wet head.

"I ent touched it," she said.

Rosevear House had never held so many women as it did that morning, at the absolute height of its wartime female ascendancy.

For the moment everyone is asleep, and most are dreaming.

There are three landgirls up in the small comfortless attic rooms once occupied by housemaids; the newest arrival, Phyllis, just turned eighteen, dreams she is at home again, helping her father pick the last of the peas in the back garden.

On the floor below the two resident midwives have a large guest bedroom each. Sister Lockheart has just found mice in her underwear drawer. She shouts at them, and they spill away over the carpet. Matron, Miss Nesbit, twitching in one of her lesser nightmares, is watching the butcher fondle cuts of fresh liver, while Amy the nursery nurse, in the smaller room on the far side of the second-floor bathroom, is presently a boy riding a bicycle. In the dream she can whistle.

The floor below is the hospital. This morning there are twelve patients and two newborn babies in the blacked-out peaceful darkness, along with Evie the night nurse, who sits leaning her head on one hand, her pen in the other, a half-written letter on the lamplit desk in front of her.

Softly, at this distance, Matron's alarm clock shrills on the floor above, and at the sound the very newest baby, nearly two hours old, and for now tucked into bed beside her mother, startles in her sleep. At her desk so does Evie, but neither of them awake. The baby slips back into fathomless sweet water, Evie carries on writing her letter as beautifully as a lark singing. In the dream she knows that when he reads it he will love her again. Meanwhile in reality the fountain pen sits at an angle in the slackened grasp of her right hand, its nib at the centre of a small round blot.

Downstairs on the ground floor Mrs Hawes the cook, in her bedroom near the kitchen, is slowly rousing, summoned not only by Minnie's knock and the cup of tea fragrant on her bedside table, but by the pain in her stiffened back and arthritic knees; and on the far side of the ground floor bathroom, Sam Keverne, the ancient gardener, currently Rosevear's only breathing male, is also floating nearer to wakefulness.

He turns over, careful even in sleep to leave room for his dog, warmly curled against him, and for the moment goes on walking home with two good fat rabbits, Cuff at his heels.

Sam paid no rent for his airing cupboard; he had noticed how under-used and roomy it was in 1941, and taken several careful weeks to dismantle the shelving and smuggle in various of his own belongings, a folding bed, a set of wallhooks, the bedside table neatly constructed out of fruit trays, his Bible, his almanac. Then he had quietly tacked a blanket over the tiny window, and moved in. No one has challenged him yet; he has almost stopped worrying about it.

Five minutes pass, and some dreams have vanished.

The land girls sympathise with one another's blisters and aching arm muscles, as groggily they climb back into yesterday's stiffened clothes.

Matron has knocked on Sister Lockheart's door to wake her, on her own way to the bathroom. A single hard *biff*, they are not even pretending to be friends this week.

Amy has jumped out of bed at once to kneel and say her prayers.

Evie yawns as she draws up the blackout blinds, barely noticing the lake outside glittering in the sunshine.

Ten heavily pregnant women, two of them already in early labour, try to ignore the light, burrowing beneath the bedclothes, hanging for dear life onto the last few seconds of doze, while in their warm continuing darkness most of the unborn go on sleeping, dreaming of rocking movement, of liquid space, of certain special voices, of music playing. One has roused a little, and is sleepily sucking her thumb. One is wide awake, listening raptly to the swish of his mother's heart.

Behind their screen the new mothers at the other end of the ward both seem peacefully asleep, though in fact they are dreaming similar inchoate horrors of blood and tearing flesh, and one is feverish. The newest baby is still floating, but the other one is beginning to stir, increasingly aware of a new and terrifying sensation of emptiness within.

Downstairs Mrs Hawes is critiquing her morning tea, today a touch too strong.

Sam has woken up, and remembered about Cuff again.

Dr Edina Broughton is shivering in her office, talking briskly into the telephone, an empty teacup in her other hand.

Norah was very happy that day, though this was something she didn't notice at the time. She spent the morning in the kitchen with Egg, who would be nine years old the following Tuesday.

"Lift it right up, let it fall. Bit more."

The tip of Egg's tongue protrudes, her whole body is tense with concentration.

"That's it," says Norah at last. "See, looks like breadcrumbs? Now the water. Just a little at first."

Egg picks up the old blunt knife to stir in the cold water, then at Norah's nod puts in her small inexpert hands and tries to press the mixture together.

"Tiny drop more, perhaps," says Norah after a moment, and makes herself stay still while Egg picks up the cup again. All is well, Egg tips in just enough, and eventually the flaking sticky mess in the bowl obliges, smoothes and gathers itself together into pastry.

While it rests beneath a dampened tea towel Norah has a cup of tea, Egg has milk with a dash of tea in it. Her feet do not quite reach the kitchen floor, she swings her legs. "Can I do the rolling?"

"You can start. I'll have to take over if it goes wrong, though."

It occurs to Norah that this exchange is very like one she herself had long ago with dear Janet, Mamma's kitchenmaid: I think of her every time I cut fat into flour.

"I learnt how to make pastry here, when I was a little girl," she says.

Egg looks startled.

"It was a very long time ago," Norah concedes.

"Did your mum learn you?"

Teach, not learn. Norah lets it go. "No, it was – someone else, who lived here," she says, deciding that Egg will have no idea what a servant is, or was, as she has almost certainly never seen one. It seems extraordinary now, thinks Norah, that Mamma at one time had employed such a crowd, cooks, chambermaids, gardeners, scullery maids, boot boys. Life had been so complicated. All that endless dressing and re-dressing, for mornings, for afternoon visits, for dinners, all those intricate hairstyles, and hats that had to sit just so, it made you feel half-suffocated just thinking about it.

"My mother didn't like me coming down here at all," she says. "Ladies didn't cook in those days," and she smiles; Norah is still young enough to be amused, surprised, by how distantly historical her own childhood now seems. "I hope we've got enough spuds," she says now, getting up. "How many are we tonight?"

Egg counts on her fingers. "You and me. Etta. Tom. And Percy."

The usual pang of sadness for Alice, who will perhaps never be counted here again. Going to visit her tomorrow, Norah reminds herself. "Seven, then," she says aloud. Egg smiles. It is a long-standing joke between them that each RAF trainee counts as two hearty eaters.

There will be just enough potatoes if she mashes them, Norah decides. And in any case the pie will fill any gaps, she thinks, as Egg takes up the rolling pin.

"That's it, very gently - " Egg rolls the flat sheet of pastry over the pin, lifts it entire, and drapes it over and onto the pie dish. She pricks it with the fork Norah hands her, and sets it to rest again while they do the apples. Barely a tablespoon of sugar, and a little honey. Then Egg rolls out the pastry, presses round the dampened edges, firming it into place, and exactly as Janet taught Norah all those years ago she holds up the dish on the spread fingers of her left hand, carefully turning it as she cuts away the excess in one thin neat continuous ribbon.

"Very good - well done!"

Norah is completely unaware of how little she usually praises either of the children in her care. She is generally critical, even stern, and has no idea how different she is in the kitchen. Even Egg has not noticed, not consciously. She just thinks she likes cooking. Norah thinks that teaching Egg cookery is simply sensible, and that such everyday practical knowledge is the one of the many essential freedoms she herself was denied in her youth.

"Look what you made, you clever girl!" Norah exclaimed last week to Egg, as she took a particularly successful bread and butter pudding out of the oven and set it down to cool on the rack. At this Egg had said nothing, but put her arms round Norah's waist, and hugged her tightly, pressing her head against Norah's bosom. Norah had been startled, but not displeased. She had briefly stroked Egg's hair, and noticed that the ribbon on one of her plaits was coming undone, and gently pushed her away to re-tie it.

"Very nice," she says now, as once Janet said to her, never quite noticing that as well as the basics of plain English cookery, Janet had also taught her a little maternal warmth. "Want to do some pastry leaves?"

"Ooh yes please!"

Norah thinks she has got used to the girls. She has got used to planning the days round them, keeping them well-fed and clean and respectable. Even now, she can look at Egg and think about what she is wearing, the full achievement of clean comfortable vest, knickers, petticoat, skirt, blouse, cardigan and socks, and feel the liveliest satisfaction at a difficult job well done.

This is partly because things had been so different the night the girls first arrived, nearly five years earlier, bundled onto a train south with lots of other Bristol children. Bristol had gone, was the word. Bristol was in flames.

"I think there's been some mistake," Norah had told the Welfare Officer. She was really Agnes Henty the optician's wife, local WVS organiser, village hall First Aid officer, and soon-to-be-manager of a small War Office manufacturing establishment near the railway station, except here she was on the doorstep with a bundle and a clipboard on a freezing evening in November. Two smaller figures drooped below her on the dark pavement.

"It's an emergency," said Mrs Henty.

"But I'm not even on your books," said Norah, "I don't know anything about children. I'm already an RAF billet."

"It's only for a night," said Mrs Henty. "We're desperate, to be honest. Nowhere else to go."

In the hallway, the heavy curtain back over the door, Norah had turned the light back on.

"I've got some night-things for them here," said Mrs Henty, dropping the bundle on the hall table and consulting the clipboard. "This is Henrietta-Maria and this - " she caught Norah's eye, warning her - " this is Eglantine. You're staying here for the night - say hallo and thankyou to Mrs Gilder, you two."

The children stood close together, hunched with cold, heads hanging; Norah was quickly aware that she could smell them, old urine, and the other sweetish greasy tang of clothes worn far too long.

"Hallo," said Norah, and the elder child, Henrietta-Maria, briefly raised her head, and gave Norah a furtive glance. Her narrow face was greyish-white, she had a cold sore on her lip. The smaller child only put up a black-nailed hand, and scratched about dully in her hair.

Horrified, Norah turned to Agnes Henty, but she was refusing to notice any unspoken messages, instead she kept up the official cheeriness:

"Just give 'em a quick bath and something to eat, alright? I'll be back in the morning," she said. "'Night all!"

There were at first some difficulties about the bath. Eglantine was too small to demur, Henrietta-Maria inclined to refuse outright. Norah was not used to house-guests who stank. Did dirtiness alter the basic rules of hospitality?

They had come directly from a very makeshift children's home, Agnes Henty had said; before that they had apparently been living with an aunt, one Marjorie Freely, their dead mother's sister, who was so far proving untraceable. She had been at work when an earlier raid began, according to the children. But they had not known where.

"Down the pub" was no use at all, said Agnes Henty, when there were dozens of pubs in that part of the city. All gone now anyway, blown to bits, like the rest of Bristol's medieval heart.

That first night Egg's grimy cotton dress was so worn that it gave way all round the neck when Norah unbuttoned it. Beneath it was a woman's woolen bodice, grey with filth, and beneath that a long flannel vest, its lower half stiff with the dried urine of several days. She smelt even with no clothes on. The back of her neck was dark with grime, her ears were black inside, each toenail was outlined, each toe divided from its fellow by a fat little sausage of black.

Neither child spoke much. Henrietta-Maria sucked her thumb and watched as Norah got to work with soap and flannel. Once she had taken her thumb out of her mouth for long enough to point into the water:

"Grandad one," she said.

"Yes," Norah had agreed, after a pause. "That one is very big." Was it dead, though, she had asked herself, as the large but happily motionless insect floated about in an eddy of scummy water. Did green soap suffocate them, or was it feigning, ready to scramble back home given the slightest chance? She had pulled the plug and quickly hoisted the child out of the water just in case. Got you, she had thought, as the grandad headlouse and many of its children safely hurtled out of sight.

Eglantine wrapped in a bath towel, Norah sluiced out the bath, started the taps again, and turned to the older child. She was belted into a grown woman's grey wool dress, someone had roughly scissored round the bottom of it by way of taking up the hem, and the front was held together with a safety-pin.

The air in the bathroom was suddenly thick with shame. Norah noted her own, told herself she would think about it later.

"Can you manage that pin? It looks a bit stiff," she said briskly.

Agnes Henty's bundle turned out to hold two pairs of boys' pyjamas, clean but with all the buttons missing or broken, and no ties to the trousers. After some thought Norah went to Joe's chest of drawers, and took out two of his soft white flannel work shirts. It gave her a pang of unidentifiable emotion to disturb them. Shaken out in front of the fire they made decent enough nightdresses. She tied Henrietta-Maria into her own woollen dressing gown, the sleeves well turned back, and knotted her thickest shawl round Eglantine.

"Dinner time now. Come along, girls," said Norah, for the first time.

Five years of saying that. Come along, girls. Goodnight, girls. Ready, girls? That's enough, girls. No, not like that, like this. Fork in your left hand, Etta. Your left. What do you say now, Egg, what's the special word? Time to get up, girls!

Etta always more trouble, a moody, sometimes almost baleful presence, rolling her eyes when corrected, slouching about with her shoes undone, careless with crockery, hard to get out of bed on school days. Or suddenly light and teasing, singing to herself as she runs upstairs.

"Grandad one", she had said, pointing, that first night, and Norah has occasionally reflected on the apparent composure, even sophistication, of this remark ever since. Yet such a dunce at school! At nearly ten Etta could barely write her own name, could hardly read at all, had attended Miss Griffith's remedial classes at Bishop Road Primary without any noticeable benefit, seeming to grasp certain essentials one day only to forget them all the next; it had been a relief for everyone when she had finally left school altogether.

Besides the children there has been a constant passing traffic of very young men in the house, posted to RAF Silkhampton three miles away. First there was David and Ted, then Peter and Jim, then Billy and another Peter, Norah generally found them easy guests enough, but soon almost impossible to tell apart.

Quickly she had grown used to the startling amounts of food they put away at night, and almost inured to their various habits. None were around much, they slept and ate and disappeared, but some left foamy stubble in the sink every morning, one or two barely used the bathroom at all; nearly all of them smoked, and filled the ashtrays, or didn't bother, so that every flat surface in the attic rooms, the top of the chests of drawers, the windowsills, the mantelpiece, was soon dotted or pocked with cigarette burns; one particular misfit could not be prevented from peeing out of the window into the square below; in defiance of house rules another had smuggled in a spirit stove, and made himself private cups of tea, dumping the used tealeaves into a wooden fruit tray balanced on the parapet, and several had - perhaps drunkenly - smoked in bed and scorched the bedclothes, though so far no one has actually set his bed on fire.

They look like schoolboys, thinks Norah, tall schoolboys passing through, learning their craft, their art. She tries not to think about what they are training for. They thunder up and down the stairs, and occasionally try to slide down the bannisters, they laugh and shout at one another, they tease Egg, the braver ones try to talk to Etta, they sing in the bath, drop cigarette ends in the toilet, leave the seat up and forget to pull the chain.

But also they whistle in the kitchen as they polish their boots, they volunteer to bring in the coal, to chop up firewood, to do the washing-up.

"Such sweeties," Alice used to say, at first.

Alice had adored them all, particularly the good-looking ones.

"Don't you agree Brian is the very spit of Ramon Navarro?" she had asked one evening over the washing-up.

Norah, drying, was lost. "Sorry?"

"Brian! Exactly like Navarro – such a physique!"

Norah could remember the silent film star Ramon Navarro and his magnificent torso, so often on display in the sort of lurid melodramas which involved him playing an almost naked galley-slave chained to an oar; while Brian was a stolid respectable youth rather prone (he had early confided) to indigestion. She had laughed, assuming Alice was joking, and gone on assuming this for the next few months, while Alice went on remarking, not always discreetly, upon more and more extraordinary film-star likenesses amongst RAF Silkhampton's more junior personnel.

"Freddie March's younger brother, don't you think?"

"So like dear Charles Farrell – such a fine open countenance!"

"Er, thanks, Miss Pyncheon." This was Gerald at breakfast, Gerald who had so delightfully reminded Alice of the very young John Gilbert ("such commanding features!"). Now scarlet with embarrassment, he opened the small parcel she had left by his plate. It was a pair of socks in fine re-worked merino wool.

"I knitted them myself, they used to be my very favourite cardie!"

"Thanks very much." Meanwhile Steve across the table was barely able to contain himself, Norah noticed uneasily. She heard them both burst out laughing as they ran upstairs later.

After that it was hard not to see how often Alice simply stared at Gerald across the table, her eyes greedily following his every move. You'd almost think she was in love with the poor boy, thought Norah, carrying on like that. Thank heaven none of the trainees stayed very long; Gerald and his relentlessly teasing mate Steve would be off for good in a week or so.

But two months after Gerald there was blue-eyed Robbie. Robbie was ravishingly beautiful, there was no getting away from it. Egg openly loved him at once, Etta sneaked wondering looks at him, even Norah found herself looking forward to mealtimes, to the small spicy luxury of having every reason to speak to him, to offer him largess.

"More stew, Robbie?"

"Thanks, Mistress Gilder."

His speech exotically Scottish, as he had been raised on some near-foreign island of the far distant North. Norah waited, a little warily, for Alice to tell her which antiquated silent film star he reminded her of, but she made no claims for ravishing Robbie at all.

Then one night Norah left Alice in charge of Egg while she went to Sewing Night, as the child had a bad cold, and ought to be early in bed.

"Etta's out at some girls' club thing," said Norah, "so can you just check at Egg's door now and then – make sure she's alright? She still wakes up sometimes, and doesn't know where she is. I won't be long."

The truth was (she admitted guiltily to herself later) that Norah rather enjoyed Sewing Night, and hadn't wanted to miss it, despite poor Egg's feverish shiverings.

The Sewing was of camouflage net, and took place a few streets away at the Bishop Road school's assembly hall. The WI had custody of the great black netting roll, as huge and unwieldy as carpet, and throughout 1940 set out stretches of it on trestle tables every Tuesday and Friday evening. If there were enough nimble volunteers there was sometimes another swathe spread out like a giant's wedding train on the parquet floor.

You simply brought your scissors and your own biggest darning needles, and your essential thimble, and you went to the two enormous reels of pale and darker green canvas tape, a giant's bias binding, snipped yourself the lengths of your choice, found a good empty stretch, and set to. You could sew your lengths into whatever shape you fancied, an L or a C or an S, anything, so long as from the air, from the distance, it blurred and coalesced into vagueness. Leaving an end free, stoutly sewn into place, was good: flapping helped.

The ladies and women of Sewing Night, none of them young and some of them hefty, also took up varied shapes, Norah had often noticed, curved upon the floor, or kneeling, or sitting sideways at the trestle tables or standing up and leaning over, one hand raised high from time to time, drawing up a particularly long thread. There was usually a low murmur of communal conversation, which was soothing after a day at the office, and though tapes and netting alike were stiff and refractory it was cleanly work, another pleasure, thought Norah, if you had also just spent a further hour or so dutifully sorting through cast-off clothing and blankets.

Occasionally she remembered the hours she and Mamma had spent on needlework in the days of her girlhood, quiet evening after quiet evening, on complicated tapestry cushions and firescreens, lacework tablecloths and delicately initialled handkerchiefs. Silks and fine woollens then, doubled waxed thread now, and a good stout well-knotted blanket stitch, to withstand any wind or weather.

"Defeating Hitler with embroidery," she said aloud once, and everyone had laughed. But often she had thought how tranquil Sewing Night seemed, a roomful of friendly cooperation and communal effort, the picture of peace; ironic that all this quiet constructiveness was to camouflage guns, and tanks, and aeroplanes. Death machines operated by men, and hidden by women.

This particular evening Norah had just completed a first letter C, and was selecting another length of dark green when she heard her name called.

"Mrs Gilder – someone to speak to you."

And there was Robbie, his face tense, there was clearly something wrong.

"What is it - is it Egg?"

"I just need a word. Please."

"Of course, just a moment - "

"In private."

He was sorry, he said, in the corridor. But he must look for other lodgings.

"Oh – but why? What's wrong?"

"You don't know?"

"Know what?"

Norah knocking on Alice's bedroom door. No answer.

"Alice! I know you're in there. Please open the door."

Silence. Norah turns the knob, goes in. The room is empty, tidy, the bed made, though a large indecipherable object lies on top of the counterpane. Closer to she sees it is one of Alice's mother's hats, an immense Edwardian confection of creamy stiffened tulle set with two slightly battered greenish feathers, lying as if discarded there, its special lined and padded hatbox open on top of all the others. Norah skirts the stack, and opens the wardrobe door. No Alice; just her few winter dresses, some of them dating back to a brief period of relative wealth in the early 1920's. The worn velours and jerseys turn on their padded hangers, saying *dingy*. Where was Alice?

As Norah turns to leave she hears a faint sound, and stands still, holding her breath. There, again: the faintest intake, panting, or a sob. She crosses the room, crouches down, lifts the edge of the counterpane, and peers under the bed.

"Alice?"

She has crammed herself all the way in next to the wall, lying prone, her head turned away. Norah's stomach turns over inside her, she begins to tremble, for even in the semi-darkness beneath the bed it's clear that Robbie was telling the truth, there's no point now trying to hang onto any ideas about honest bath time mistakes, or unfortunate lapses of attention. Alice is completely naked.

"Alice," says Norah as gently as she can. "I'm not angry with you. Honestly. No one is. Do come out, dear. Come out and - we'll have a nice cup of tea, Alice. Please."

"I shouldn't have laughed," says Alice, her voice muffled. She is shivering, perhaps with cold, poor thing. "He said there were elephants, small ones, they came up the stairs and looked at him over the sofa, and I laughed, I couldn't help it, I pictured them all in a row, their trunks and so on, and I laughed, and all the time he was despairing. Oh Freddie, I'm so sorry."

Since then, in the mental hospital at Sedan Cross, she has spoken often to Norah about Freddie's torments, and of how she had laughed.

"They were real all the time, you see."

"I don't think so, Alice."

"Oh yes! I know. Because – don't tell anyone will you - I've seen them myself, Norah. They'd finished with him, d'you see? So they had to find someone else. And they knew about me. They come up the stairs. They bounce rubber balls across the carpet. They hide in things."

Certainly Alice herself has developed a tendency to hide in things, behind the armchairs in the hospital sitting-room, behind doors, beneath her bed, beneath the beds of other patients.

"Everyone was worried about you, Alice, that's all. They just wanted to know where you were."

Alice had looked puzzled. "But I'm not really anywhere, am I," she said, in the tone of one explaining something obvious.

One afternoon, on what had so far seemed one of Alice's better days, she and Norah had been sitting beside the French windows when one of the nurses came round with a tea-trolley. She had given them a nice smile, and a cup each, and as she wheeled the trolley on Alice had leant forward and whispered:

"Norah - d'you think that young woman *saw* me?"

"Yes," said Norah after a pause. "I'm sure she did."

"So – can you see me too?"

"Yes."

"All the time?"

Meanwhile at Rosevear the hours pass, slowly for some, at lightning speed for others.

"You be careful with that teapot," says Mrs Hawes.

Minnie's tray is heaviest, she has the biggest teapot, muffled in its hand-knitted cosy and padded stand, blue and purple stripes. She follows Mrs

Hawes, who is carrying the smaller tray with one of her apple cakes on it, and the tea cups. It's a long walk over the gravel path and past the whole house, along paths Minnie rarely walked on these days, and she is further disturbed by all the faces watching them from the windows of the hospital ward.

They pass through the kitchen garden and out at the lower gate, and there is the haunted lake, that Minnie has largely spent her whole life trying not to see or think about. There is also a big lorry, a car with its doors hanging open, a farm tractor, old Sam Keverne leaning on a shovel, and lots of strange men standing about at the edge of the water.

As they get closer Minnie sees that one of the men is really the lady doctor again, tall in her coat with her hands in her pockets. There's a smell of crushed grass, and muddy ruts where the lorry had been driven backwards and forwards. Minnie tries to hide behind Mrs Hawes, and sees that there is something hesitant in the way even Mrs Hawes goes forward now.

"Gentlemen?" she says.

But it's alright, everyone looks very pleased. They take both trays and put them down on the back of the lorry, and Minnie pours tea while Mrs Hawes cuts the cake and passes it round. Minnie keeps her eyes down, she always has to concentrate very hard not to drip that particular pot, its spout was put on wrong, Ma told her once.

Minnie feels sorry for the pot. My spout was put on wrong too, she thinks to it sometimes.

The men are soldiers, or perhaps they are sailors. They are loud and handsome, with clean red faces.

"We meet again!" says someone, taking a full cup. It's a woman's voice, so Minnie dares to look up, and it's the lady doctor, smiling down at her. "You jolly well saved my life this morning," she says.

Minnie blushes.

Mrs Eltham and Mrs Driver, both in established labour, spend the morning walking companionably up and down the corridor, pausing to lean against the wall during pains, commiserating, rubbing one another's backs, occasionally wandering over to the window of the ward where the others are clustered, trying to make out what's going on down there.

"Any news?"

"There's a frogman!"

"No – where? Let me see!"

Lying next to one another at the other, post-natal, end of the ward the two new mothers neither know nor care what's going on outside or anywhere else. Fitfully they sleep the morning away until Sister Lockheart sets the screens around them and wheels in the babies for the next four-hourly feed.

Marjorie Johnson is quickly at a loss.

"She doesn't seem to want to," she says, her eyes full of tears. Who would imagine not being any good at this sort of thing! Who could imagine beforehand that it was even a thing a person might be good or bad at in the first place! All Marjorie's pregnancy daydreams had ended with a picture of herself smiling gently into a cradle.

But now her breasts, which for a decade or so – ever since their arrival, in fact – have been perfectly reasonable, even satisfactory, have all by themselves turned overnight into big hot mounds of molten swelling on her chest, they look like falsies; the baby seems to have absolutely no interest in their tense flattened nipples and who could blame her, confronted with something so much bigger than her own head?

"Make sure Baby's fixing on the lower third of the nipple," Sister Lockheart advises, and Marjorie at once nods seriously, and says "Right, right," as if she is perfectly accustomed to dividing her own nipples into three, as if she thinks everyone else does it all the time.

"Like so," says Lockheart, leaning over and firmly pinching Marjorie's tight left nipple between thumb and first finger. Rolling quite hard she works it into a point. Then she presses on the baby's little chin until the mouth opens, cups the nape of the little neck, and thrusts the child's head forward into position.

"There," she says. "Now she's properly attached. D'you see?"

The baby's small jaws work briefly, then stop. The stiffened wet flesh slips out of her mouth; she turns her head, and lets out a feeble wail.

Sister Lockheart has another go, brandishing baby at breast, breast at baby, firmly squashing the two together.

Baby Johnson will have none of it.

"Keep trying," says Sister Lockheart, getting up, and brushing down her crisp white apron. She turns an enquiring eye onto the next bed, but Mrs Salway seems to have gone back to sleep again.

Bronia Salway has spoken very little since arrival, as she went into labour during the bus ride from the station, and delivered only after nearly thirty-six hours, forceps, and a fairly severe post-partum haemorrhage.

Sister Lockheart knows all this, since she was on duty for a great deal of that time and assisted Dr Broughton at the birth, but she also suspects Bronia of being Jewish.

"Sit up now, Mrs Salway," she says briskly, picking up the bundle of baby. "We can't just lie about all day, can we!"

A pause, while Bronia translates the words, though the tone is clear enough straight away. She tries to struggle upright, but takes so long about it that eventually Lockheart gives in and helps her, stuffing pillows behind her back to hold her in place.

"She fixing on yet?"

Bronia looks down at the baby, and the baby looks intently back up. It's as if the baby can't get enough of looking at her, that gazing is really all she wants or needs. Bronia wants it too. She also wants to undress the baby and look at her all over, every bit of her. She is a little alarmed at wanting something so odd, so unexpected. There's no word in any language she knows for wanting to look at your baby all over. So it can't be normal or right.

Still she thinks she can now understand the difference between how she loved her parents and how she loves this child, like the difference between warm and scalding. Childbirth has divided her into two, she thinks, fearfully, dizzily. She is now both Bronia and the baby, though the baby comes first by miles. She smiles down into the searching gaze. "*Dzien dobry*," she says softly.

"Come along now," says Sister Lockheart, busily undoing the top buttons of Bronia's nightdress, folding back the cotton to expose the left breast. To Bronia both breasts are full of strange sensations like movement, an almost electrical sparkling within. Laid beside them the baby at once turns her little cheek, as if in yearning, and Bronia's left nipple drops into the beautiful mouth. The baby draws upon it, seeming to ask, and almost immediately the breast answers her, and gives.

"Good," says Sister Lockheart, straightening up, and the clear approval in her voice goes right into Bronia, warming and soothing her, a powerful medecine Lockheart herself is entirely unconscious of dispensing, though as she walks away she is aware of disliking the foreign one a little less than before. At least the girl is trying, she tells herself.

At the other end of the ward the women clustered round the window watch the tractor slowly moving forward, but by accident or design the lorry hides most of the action, though several catch a glimpse of a stretcher being carried down to the water's edge.

Another hour passes. Presently Sister Lockheart puts her head round the door, and says one word:

"German."

Then there is rather a sag in the air, a general lowering of spirits. The women move away from the window, disconsolately take up their books again, their letters, their knitting. The little flutter of excitement is over. There was a dead body; discovering anything about the living man, even that he had been the enemy, still makes him human, less like something out of a jolly old Agatha Christie whodunnit.

Further, the war has been brought home to them again. Even here, in the lying-in hospital, a special safe place deep in the countryside for pregnant women and newborn babies, even here, a foreign soldier has tried to hurt or kill them. And got close.

Before the clinic starts Edina goes out again.

The weather has changed, sky and water now a matching flat grey, and her beautiful bank is a ruin of mud, discarded bits of equipment, tangles of rope.

"Afternoon, gentlemen – how are you getting on?"

The two officers smoking beside the water throw their cigarette ends into the water (careless bastards, notes Edina) then turn and walk back to her, their boots squelching in the flattened grass.

"Miss Broughton?"

"Doctor."

"Sorry, doctor, we were just coming in to see you."

"You've finished, then?"

"In a way. The ah body's over there," says the taller officer, tilting his head towards the lorry. Edina looks, sees the shape in the back, wrapped decently in canvas, and tied about with ropes.

"A Stukka came down near here," she says. "Years ago."

"Could be. Probably later though. I don't know, sorry." His face says: more to come.

"Go on," says Edina.

"There seems to be – well, something else down there."

"Yes?"

"Our man here," he gestures at the canvas shape in the lorry, "he was caught on something. We think - there's a car down there."

"What? In the lake? Someone put a car in the water?"

"Can't be sure, not until we get a team in. Well, the police, I mean. But this car. I'm sorry to tell you this. But it looks as if there's someone in it."

Five o'clock.

In Silkhampton Norah runs cold water over the potatoes before peeling them. While Egg was safely out playing with the little girl two doors away she has spent another hour working on the child's birthday present, a new summer frock, made from a voluminous yellow cotton day dress she seized on weeks back in the clothing depot. The tucked bodice has taken ages, and she had to unpick the side seams twice, to fit the full skirt's gathers.

Perhaps Etta will be able to get her hair ribbons to match; I'll suggest it when she comes in, if she's in the right mood, Norah tells herself. They work her so hard in the factory. Perhaps I should go and have a quiet word with Agnes Henty. Surely she needn't choose Etta to cover quite so many extra shifts? The poor girl often comes home exhausted.

(Etta is meanwhile running along the field path towards the cliffs, her good shoes rolled in a tea towel under one arm, towards their special place, where they had first met. Lightly she jumps over the last stile and slows to a fast walk through the last cornfield. His name is Jem Whitacre, and he is eighteen and a half.)

At Rosevear the viewing angle is definitely better in the nursery. Amy the nursery nurse has been peering out of the window on and off all afternoon, the comings and goings, army lorries, police cars, the diver in his extraordinary rubber outfit, the laborious slow disposition of equipment and men, sheets of corrugated iron, sandbags, lengths of heavyweight chain.

In the cradles beside her baby Johnson and baby Salway lie damp and scarlet-faced in a frenzy of unmatching full-throated screaming, but Amy takes no notice of either of them, sitting rapt as the tractor heaves forward, and the chains begin to move.

"D'you think it's odd they're going to so much trouble?" Nesbit asks, as they put their coats on.

"They can hardly leave it there," says Edina. "Not if there's someone in it." But she knows what Nesbit has not said. "This is England," she says. "The law still matters. If it doesn't, what have we been fighting for?"

Outside they can hear the tractor engine straining already as they hurry towards the makeshift fence, guarded by a police constable.

He salutes them. "That's far enough please, ladies."

Edina stares at him. He is young, pink-cheeked, a delicate flower of a policeman, thinks Nesbit, in a hat like a bluebell. Carefully she looks away.

"Are you addressing me?" asks Dr Broughton, tremendously.

He quails. "S'not a nice sight. For ladies."

"Don't be ridiculous," says Edina, and pushes past him.

Nesbit hurries after her, pretending to have seen nothing, which is her usual method of dealing with Eddie's more overbearing moments.

They reach the first parked lorry, and edge round it. There is a deafening noise now, not only the shuddering thunderous tractor engine but a terrible grinding noise of chains passing over iron, a raw scraping rising slowly in pitch to a something like a human shriek.

Christ, thinks Edina, and then there is a sudden lessening as something gives in the water, and the tractor surges forward, the dripping chains rising freely behind it.

The police camera flashes as the tractor slowly passes the camera stand, the chains lengthening out of the water as it gains ground. The men stand ready on either side with grappling hooks.

"It's coming," says Nesbit, clutching at Edina's arm.

And the back of the car, the small smashed back window, breaks through, rises clear in a torrent of water, and a sudden black stink of sludge. The rounded roof, the boot still with its natty little chromium handle, the bumpers, break through the water, and what were once tyres at last find solid ground again.

"Steady now, slowly!" yells someone.

Finally, just after six in the evening, as the light fades twelve hours after Edina Broughton's last morning dip, the drowned car sits streaming filthy water on the ruin of the bank, all spoilt fittings, splayed collapsing rubber, still recognisably an Austen Seven. The farmer turns off the tractor engine, and in the sudden quiet all the people gathered about can hear the swift churning as the level inside the car drains and gurgles away.

As it empties, all is clear enough.

That evening Norah and Egg and Etta went to pictures, and saw *This Happy Breed*. Tom and Percy, that month's lodgers, went to RAF Silkhampton's chosen local, the Tinner's Arms, where Tom played the piano well enough to be bought two pints of beer. Mrs Hawes listened to the radio and wrote about the findings in the lake in enjoyably gruesome detail to her sister, currently landlady of the Bull Inn at Minehead. Minnie polished the silver, her favourite task, Sam Keverne, cosy in the airing cupboard, read his Bible, and upstairs four of the patients played Whist.

Sister Lockheart looked after Mrs Driver, whose daughter arrived safely just before midnight, and Mrs Eltham, who did less well; Edina was scrubbing her hands to intervene when the baby suddenly descended anyway just as he was, and was born facing upwards, only the third time

Sister Lockheart had seen this phenomenon in nearly thirty years of practice.

Edina sewed up the resultant complex vaginal tears and was back in bed by two, but it was hard to sleep and as soon as she did the parachute touched her foot, the water seethed with bony fingers. Just before five she knocked very softly on Nesbit's door.

"You're bound to be upset," said Nesbit, as she climbed back into bed on the cold side. "Anyone would be."

"So feeble of me," said Edina, lying down. "I keep thinking – suppose there's *more* down there!"

"It's a shame. You loved that lake."

At this Edina's face twisted, and Nesbit took her in her arms. "My poor darling," she said. "I'm so sorry."

A long pause.

"Oh, Marion," said Edina at last, "whatever would I do without you?"

Soon she fell asleep, but beside her Nesbit went on lying wide awake, as she had been already, when Edina first knocked; because of all the souls born and unborn then at Rosevear, only Nesbit had known the man to whom the drowned car had once belonged, the man whose hardened soapy remains had been sitting behind the steering wheel all these years.

Best place for him, thought Nesbit now. Crying shame he'd been found.

She had dreamt of him often, always had; in his clotted blood-soaked apron he had haunted her nightmares for years.

Sometimes, he tells her cheerfully as he pulls and twists the heavy steel forceps, *one has to apply a certain force,* and all the while she cannot move or speak, cannot so much as begin to stop him, though she knows all the time that she must. That she should.

Strange, unnerving, to think that she had been working here at Rosevear all this time, right beside the water. She'd even paddled in it once or twice, one hot summer, but never mind about that now, Nesbit told herself. The real question was how much she had to worry about. Was she open to any charge of collusion?

I merely suspected, she reminded herself. For all I knew he really had gone to Rhodesia or somewhere. I didn't care. So long as he never came back.

On Sunday morning everything changed.

Norah and Egg went to church, as usual, leaving Etta in bed, also as usual. But after the service, in the little gathering at the church porch, there was talk, and plenty of it.

Had Norah heard? About the bodies? Not one, but two! Yes, there, in the lake, my goodness! One a Jerry of course. Still in his harness! So you know what else they found, then? So shocking! But the car, now. Someone's nephew in the police had already given out the make, and - you remember, don't you? That was the doctor's car, wasn't it? All those years ago! What was his name again?

Several recent newcomers had not heard about the mysterious disappearance of Dr Philip Heyward, and were told all about it now; how the doctor had gone out one night on a call and never come home again – took his passport with him mind – old soldier – did a lot of fine work - presumed run off somewhere, maybe Africa, and now all the while it looked as if -

"You feeling alright, Mrs Gilder?"

"Just a headache," said Norah, relieved and surprised to find how normal her voice sounded, despite the horror, the quaking turmoil within. She took Egg's hand, and felt strength flow into her from it.

"Let's go home now," she said, but it occurred to her as they crossed the road towards the Square that she would never feel at ease again, at home or anywhere else. Her heart went on pounding. What she was feeling, she thought with a painful surprise, was already a sort of nostalgia, a sense of loss, for the dear old days of five minutes ago, when she had worried so much about whether there was enough oatmeal to do porridge for five tomorrow, or how Egg would manage whilst having her shoes mended when she didn't actually have another pair to go out in, small things, manageable things, that all the same had gone on simmering away nicely in the foreground, useful distraction from the black everyday everynight background horrors of what the War was doing, how it was doing, and lately about the advancing Allied forces, bombing their way across Europe towards wherever Barty lay helplessly waiting for them; where after all these years in prison he might yet die by accident, killed by his own side, his own friends.

So now there was still all that. And there was the car.

The car was found, the body was found. Get used to it, Norah told herself as harshly as possible, as she and Egg walked through the garden to the back door.

"I'm just going to have a little lie down," she told Egg, who immediately looked terrified, she saw, at this unprecedented announcement. "I'll be down in a minute," she added.

"Shall I do the potatoes for you?"

"No. Tell Etta to. You're not old enough," said Norah flatly, and closed her bedroom door.

Etta of course was out; she had gone to meet Jem again, because after that they wouldn't be able to see one another for a whole week.

She waits now, trembling with nerves in her best dress and her good shoes, her plimsolls hidden in the hedge, her lips freshly painted, a little early in their special place on the cliff top, where they could sit together on a flat white stone. Theirs now for nearly four whole weeks.

She had been escaping some tiresome errand, had told Mrs Gilder that she was too busy to do something or other, sort out a bundle of newspapers or a box of empty bottles, something like that, and then had had to leave the house to back herself up. But it had been a nice clear Sunday evening, and she'd decided to walk moodily along the clifftop path, like a heroine in films.

Of course real heroines didn't usually walk moodily along country paths for long before encountering someone or something dangerous or at least interesting, and Etta had been feeling more and more fed up, pointing out to herself that she could hike up and down the bloody path all night, there'd still be a fat chance of her encountering anyone even slightly more interesting than the dreary old bags in Mrs Gilder's Knitting Circle, when she had suddenly come across a boy in uniform, a young soldier sitting looking out to sea all by himself on the big flat stone near the cliff edge, an actual Yank!

Etta had more than once been told by several different authorities that she must on no account talk to American soldiers, let them talk to her, or allow them to approach her in any way. Ha!

"Hallo," she said. "What you looking at, there something down there?"

The Yank jumped to his feet, looking caught out, and swiping off his hat, as if she was a lady, and looking so frightened that she'd had to laugh. "What's up with you? I won't bite," she added, feeling this was perhaps a bit too daring, but knowing that was the sort of heroine she wanted to be.

He had smiled, still uneasily, but so sweetly that Etta's heart had turned right over in her chest at the sight, it had thudded away inside her, it knew right away that here was someone special.

"You at the Wooton camp?" she said.

"Yes, Ma'am." So American!

"Zit true you ride motorbikes up the stairs?"

"Pardon me?"

"That's what I heard," said Etta. "And driving tanks about in the shrubbery. You ever driven a tank about in a shrubbery?" As she said this she began to laugh, and so did he, for a while they could hardly speak for laughing.

"I sure wish I had," he said at last.

"Me too. I can think of a few places I'd like to drive a tank through."

"You know Wootton, Ma'am?"

"'Course, I do" said Etta airily. In fact Mrs Gilder had taken her and Egg there several times, years ago, in the school holidays. The last time had been really boring, they'd had to trail from room to room while Mrs Gilder wrote things down and poked about in the rubbish in every corner, and the biggest room, which was whopping like a cathedral only empty, had thick black stuff growing high up on the walls. Mrs Gilder had gone on and on about it, said she'd once been to a ball there, of all things, though Etta knew balls were only in fairy stories, and for Cinderella, not actual people.

"Haven't been there for ages," she added, because of course that had been before the Yanks had arrived at all. "Which bit you in?"

He shook his head. "Never been inside, Ma'am. Not the house. Officers only."

"Typical," said Etta. "Where do you live, then?"

"We got huts. In the garden."

"The grounds, you mean. What's your name?"

"Jem."

"That short for Jeremy?"

He looked startled, ready to laugh again. "I don't think so."

85

"What, don't you know? I'm Etta," she said, and held out her right hand, half-remembering some of the stuff Mrs Gilder was always going on about - though come to think of it her ladyship would probably have died rather than ask a strange man what his name was, you were always supposed to get someone else to introduce you, and if there was no one to do it, too bad, you just had to bugger off home without talking at all, fat lot of good that did anyone.

He hesitated, then stepped closer, and they shook hands. His was slender in hers, warm and delicate.

"Short for Henrietta," she said.

"Hi, Henrietta."

"Hi," Etta had said back, for the first time in her life.

————A week goes slowly by.

Norah barely sleeps or eats but still serves thirty-five breakfasts and dinners and ten lunches, goes to visit Alice, puts in three afternoons at the offices of Bagnold and Pender, sorts laundry, cleans, gardens, shops, queues, attends her weekly Knitting Circle evening (which has replaced the lost pleasures of Sewing Night, overtaken long ago by mass-production) does two late ARP shifts, goes to a WI meeting, bakes and as far as possible decorates a birthday cake for Egg, and finishes the new summer dress.

On the Tuesday Etta's present for her little sister is an entire bar of American milk chocolate ("Come from one a the girls at work," she explains), and her usual birthday picture; this one shows Egg with her nose proudly in the air, carrying an enormous pie, with the heads of several blackbirds peeping out of the crust. Egg laughs with pleasure. Tom and Percy give her a new skipping rope; Percy, who is a mechanic, has somehow contrived turning handles from short lengths of bakelite piping, set with tiny metal washers to make them jingle. Egg takes the skipping rope to bed with her, she loves it too much to leave it downstairs all night in the toybox.

Everything, in short, goes as well as it possibly could. But when Egg first sees herself in her pretty new dress in the mirror all Norah can manage is "Decent fit," because all the time she feels as if she might explode with tension, her hands tremble, she is waiting, waiting, without any clear idea what it is she is waiting for.

Egg herself is far more trying than usual, she finds.

"What's the matter *now*?" she asks crossly, when later in the week Egg starts whining about some vanishingly small childish concern.

Etta at least has the sense to keep out of the way.

If only there was someone to talk to, to consult!

Not Lettie, alas. Poor Lettie, and her little sideline. Of course it was because of her that I was there at Rosevear that night in the first place, thought Norah, but then again, I wanted to be there. I wanted to help.

Barty. If only she could talk to him! Not a word from him now, for months. But even if she could talk to him, she didn't really know how much he knew. He had seen something, that was clear, turning up early that morning, the morning of the car, with bread for his grandmother. Did he know how Dr Heyward had died? It was another of the many things she and Barty had never talked about. Whatever he had seen, poor boy, it had been enough to make him get straight back on his bicycle and race home again to summon Joe.

Oh, Joe. Joe would have known what to do, how to behave, how to stay quiet. She remembered following his gaze that morning, as he noticed the tracks in the grass all across the front of Rosevear House, dewy tyre marks in the soft spring grass, leading straight to the water. He had seen them, sure enough. And said nothing.

Sometimes, lying awake at night, it occurs to Norah that she has continually made assumptions, seen patterns. Years ago, with Lettie, she had committed certain crimes, consciously broken the law, and the violent excitement of this, the thrilling despatch of her own behaviour, had prompted other bold actions; had essentially made it possible for her to discard shyness and shame to court Joe Gilder. Crime had brought rewards: an inner freedom, a new life, and love.

So it had been extra hard when the baby had died before he was born. It had felt meant, like retribution, even though she had long ago consciously thrown out such Old Testament ideas. She had still seen the pattern: sin was punishable. Often, it was punished.

When Joe fell ill, when he suffered, when she had to lie to him on his deathbed, when he lovingly called her by his dead wife's name, all that felt deserved, a just punishment, that she was losing everything she had gained, it was vanishing away like fairy gold. When Joe died she could think only of stepping into the cold embrace of the water herself, joining her victim, and completing the punishment.

Then she had saved the German pilot, not just by chance, but by a long unlikely chain of them.

Now – sitting alone in the drawing room at night, nearly a week after the car was dredged up from the depths – she works out that since the German pilot she has allowed herself to feel that her various actions have cancelled one another out: if before the war she hid a murder, since then she has in turn concealed a beyond-the-call-of-duty rescue, a life saved.

Saving the pilot made everything alright again, that was the barely-examined notion. Barty's glorious postcard arriving so soon afterwards had been one of those strange coincidences, she thought, that crop up now and then to muddle the credulous, but the German boy really did owe her his life, and hardly anyone knew about it or ever would, and these facts had made sense to her. Whenever she felt tired, she only had to think of his face as he thanked her to feel renewed and strong again.

It was simply more nonsense, she thought now, this almost-unconscious shepherding of facts, a mere human habit of seeing patterns and retribution and balence, when life was really just haphazard. She remembered the camouflage netting she and the other ladies of Sewing Night had spent so many quiet hours working on. You chose the shapes, you made strips of canvas into letters, C or S or L or T. But the shapes were really about breaking up and hiding reality. The patterns concealed the truth.

There is nothing to link me to the car, that was the main thought Norah usually ended up coming back to, after a lot of circular anxiety. And it was surely a nine-days' wonder; everyone in Silkhampton might be going on about it now, but no one anywhere else cared, and soon enough other things, other perhaps more pressing or terrible things, would come along and take its place, even here.

Reaching this most hopeful point in her thoughts once more, she decides to try going back to bed again, and on the way stops for a moment outside Etta's door, which stands ajar. Then very quietly she goes inside.

Etta a dark shape in the bed. Etta has been a frankly difficult wartime duty, an unrewarding child, sullen with adults, spiteful to her little sister, prone to sudden outbursts of fury, equally sudden withdrawals, and only occasional exuberant joys. For a while, when all efforts to find Aunt Marjorie had failed, Etta had claimed that she had a father in the army; he was not Egg's, she said firmly, just hers. Though it seemed she was not entirely sure what his full name was, and eventual recourse to a copy of her birth certificate showed no official paternity at all, just a blank space.

"Henrietta is so moody," complained Mrs Griffiths, the Remedial teacher.

Though once -

Norah smiles to herself in the darkness: just after the girls arrived, when they both slept in Barty's old room, she had hoped to settle them a little by reading them stories at night. It hadn't been something they were used to, as it turned out, and it had been some time before she could persuade them simply to lie still and listen, especially as the books she had tried at first, childhood favourites of her own, hadn't worked at all – Etta soon bored by *The Wind in the Willows*, both of them baffled by *Treasure Island*.

But then she had chanced in the library upon Richmal Compton's William books, and they were almost too successful, violently exciting rather than soothing. There were nights when at the climax of the story – when William ruined the village fete, or feasted on spoilt greedy Herbert Lane's party food, or inadvertently kidnapped the wrong cat, Etta had bounced wildly up and down in her bed, shouting with glee. Her fierce delight had been touching, it was so rare. Why had she so enjoyed those stories of small-scale subversion, when her own short life had been one terrifying wreckage after another?

Sweet dreams, Etta.

Norah crosses the landing to Alice's old room, now Egg's. Egg has always been the easier guest.

"I can't keep them," Norah had protested to Agnes Henty that first morning, when Agnes had turned up quite early with extra coupons. "The little one's too young for school – she's a baby - I have to work, you know!"

Of course, of course, said Agnes Henty, no one expected Norah to keep them for good, poor little orphans! But – surely she knew about the Council nursery in the church hall? Open all hours! No, volunteers. So mothers could still do their bit, see, be part of the war effort - and cheap as could be; drop the baby off on your way to work, then pick her up on the way home, meanwhile little...Eglantine, wasn't it? would have been playing all day long with the other children, do her the world of good, after everything she'd been through, poor little mite! And so much better for her to stay with her sister, as long as she could! Keeping the two of them together, Mrs Gilder. That was going to be the difficult thing. Maybe not possible, long-term. So - could you just manage another couple of days, please, Mrs Gilder? Maybe even a week?

Norah bent now and carefully pulled the child's eiderdown back into place, catching a faint smell of Egg herself as she did so, something faintly milky, and for a moment experienced an odd longing to lie down in the bed beside her.

She remembered the time she had had to take both children with her to Rosevear, and caught the afternoon train, and it had been full of soldiers on some exercise, and two of them had given up their seats, one for Etta, one for Egg and herself, though what with all the kitbags there had still been so little room that Egg must needs sit on her lap cross-legged, Norah holding her fast in place.

"Sorry I've had to fold you up like this," she had murmured lightly into the child's ear, and to her surprise Egg had answered seriously, straight away:

"I love it."

Curiously impressive, the passion of that answer. Norah had not known quite what to make of it, regarding herself as more the girls' teacher than anything parental. The long-suffering Mrs Griffiths for reading and writing, herself Remedial personal cleanliness, tidiness, household routine, and manners.

Well, Etta is surely old enough now to take charge now, thought Norah. If she has to. If. When.

If I am arrested, but why should I be? There is nothing to connect me to the car, Norah told herself for the hundredth time.

The thought makes her heart rock again. She stands still for another few minutes, breathing in Egg's quietness, for as long as she can.

She was finishing a quick tidy-up of the kitchen before she went to work after lunch the next day, which was a Tuesday, when there was a sudden hard knock at the door. She hardly needed to glance up at the pavement outside, she knew straight away. For a second she leant breathlessly against the kitchen table, then sank onto into a chair, feeling floppy all over, boneless with fear, unable to move at all; she could only breathe in and out, panting, as the knock came again, harder, louder.

Thoughts seemed very slow. An idea came to her from a long time ago, that fainting could be averted by lowering your head, and she leant forward as far as she could in the chair, while her heartbeat seemed to pound throughout her whole body, noisily shattering thud after thud.

Some moments passed. More knocking.

Then she managed to rise, and holding variously for balance onto things as she passed them, chairbacks, the doorway, the bannister rail, she got herself shakily upstairs, and there outside were the policemen, two in uniform, one in a raincoat, serious grim-faced men, come to take her away.

And the actress she had no idea was inside her steps into place, her role patent innocence, she draws breath, she holds Norah's head up, and appears a little surprised to find three policemen on her doorstep, surprised but not, of course, in the least alarmed.

"Mrs Norah Gilder?"

"That's me," says the actress, innocently. "What can I do for you?"

Jeremiah Wainwright, eighteen years old, troubled virgin, his mother's adored only son, knows far less about Etta than he thinks he does, and several of the things he knows aren't true.

He thinks she's alone in the world, for instance, an orphan, living with a maiden aunt, who is very strict, and won't let her go to public houses or dance halls. He knows that in July, when she turns seventeen, she means to join the ATS. He knows she can draw; once as they sat on the cliff top she took out a thin book, an old school exercise book, and drew his portrait in soft scribbly pencil.

He had sat still on the grass, trying to pretend he wasn't thrilled, trying to seem like someone who'd had his picture drawn any number of times before.

"Can I see it?" he had finally been unable to stop himself saying.

"Only when it's finished. And if I like it."

But she had liked it.

"There you go." She turned the book round, and there he was, all soft cheeks and soulful eyes, with the beginnings of a smile, a picture his mother would love, he was at once delighted and horrified. It was hardly a man's face at all, he looked like a girl with a guy's haircut. He couldn't think of anything to say.

"It's, it's - "

"Lovely," said Etta.

He had looked up, and seen that for once she was serious. They had looked into one another's eyes, falling, falling, the plummeting sensation inside him almost more than he could bear. He had leant forward, and very gently they had kissed for the first time, and it had been so sweet, so wonderful, that for a moment he had forgotten all the myriad things he was afraid of. He had even – significantly, he thought afterwards – forgotten desire. It had been there, of course. But it had seemed not so much resistable as beside the point, unimportant, not as engrossing, anyway, as Etta so close, so slender, so funny and so wildly exotic, breathing his breath, in communion already.

This afternoon they sit side by side on the warm grass, nicely private between two stands of flowering hedge, talking, laughing, still constantly surprising one another. He can't quite believe she's never eaten a hamburger, or ridden in an automobile, she's never even sat inside one, not once in her whole life. She couldn't believe he'd never seen the sea before, until the day he got on the troop ship.

"Can't get enough of it now, though," he told her once, and the next time they met she gave him a picture she'd drawn, not a portrait then but a cartoon, of himself as a grinning merman with a fish's tail, playing in the waves. He's never met a girl who made him laugh so much, though sometimes even now he can hardly follow what she's saying, the words all bent into foreign shapes, and so fast and teasing, full of phrases he can't understand, Taking the mickey, Bob's your uncle, How's your father.

"It ain't half boring." That was her job, at some kind of munitions factory near the railway station.

"So – it's boring, then?"

"'Course it is, I just said so."

"No, Ma'am. You said, It ain't *half* boring," he says in her voice, and they both laugh, end up kissing, vital kisses that seem as refreshing as food and drink.

Then he looks at her in the sunshine and thinks that with the lipstick kissed away she looks about fourteen years old, a thought that goes no further. Though eventually it will come back to haunt him, and in some ways will do so for the rest of his life.

"I got to go now," says Etta now, sitting up straight, brushing at the sleeves of her blouse.

The aunt is particularly strict about chores. Jem understands that sort of thing all too well. His mom is no different, so he finds the aunt reassuring, for all that Etta herself is often so disrespectful about her. He is sometimes a little shocked by Etta. Now and then she strikes him as unladylike, coarse, even ungodly, though she's so foreign it's hard to tell. Would his own sister Marie boldly make friends with a boy she didn't know, the way Etta had?

On the other hand he knows that Etta is pure, that she's never had a boyfriend before. Sometimes contemplating Etta's physical purity is almost more than Jem can stand, he lies on his bunk at night wondering if he can hold out much longer. He fears that Etta herself may not help; he can't quite trust her to stop him. Without thinking about it at all he is sure that to do so is Etta's moral duty, and none of his own. If, of course, she really is a nice girl.

He has found too that in Etta's own unpredictable presence the Old Testament phrases that normally weigh down his sexual imagination seem to lose some of their insistent gravity. She seems far more real than most of the things that have happened to him in the last few months. Her smile makes his heart thud with pleasure in his chest.

"I could get here some time next Thursday," he says. "You free any time Thursday?"

"Not until four."

They stand close together, smiling into one another's eyes. Hers so blue!

"Hey," he says.

"Hey yourself."

The news arrived at Rosevear early, via the postman, and was reinforced later by another visit from the police, who wandered down to the lake and back again, taking measurements and writing notes. Mrs Hawes the cook enjoyed it most. She had no particular reason to think badly of Norah Gilder, with whom she had exchanged cordial greetings and remarks about the weather for many years, but the idea of someone she knew to talk to being had up for murder was deeply thrilling.

"'Course I barely know the woman," she said to her sister-in-law, who came in weekly to help with the laundry. "But she got a cousin in the loony bin at Sedan Cross."

"Bad blood will out," agreed Mrs Hawes' sister-in-law.

Mrs Hawes lowered her voice, so that Minnie scrubbing pots at the sink behind them could not hear. "They do say, the cousin, as how she likes to run about in the buff!"

"In nothing but a great big hat, I heard," said the sister-in-law, and they both laughed.

The landgirls were agog, but also prone to amusement. They had often glimpsed Mrs Gilder carefully wobbling up and down the drive on her bicycle, they knew she was plummy and middle-aged and respectable; the idea of her being involved in fatal villainy was almost too much for them. Though Phyllis the youngest one kept the gossip out of her letter home that afternoon. Mum was worried about her enough as it was.

Sister Lockheart was also pleased, on the whole. It seemed to her, looking back, that she had always had her suspicions about Mrs Gilder, had known all along that there was something unwholesome about her. She had, of course, married beneath her, and that was distasteful in itself.

"Everyone says it's got something to do with that Wainwright girl," she told Evie the night nurse at tea-time.

"How d'you mean?" said Evie.

"Well, I don't think she killed herself. I never did."

"What, they think Mrs Gilder done it? Threw her over?" Evie was at once appalled and thrilled. She herself had sat drinking tea with the woman, many a time! "What about the doctor, then, in the lake and all?"

"The talk is," said Sister Lockheart, dropping her voice, "that it was her husband all along."

"No!" said Evie, scandalised. "You mean Joe Gilder, the baker - isn't he dead? Why would he, anyway?"

Sister Lockheart's face implied she knew a great deal more, but that some facts were too indecent for Evie's innocent ears. "I don't like to speak ill of the dead. But between you and me," Sister Lockheart whispered, "well, Miss Dorothy Wainwright – I think there was immoral conduct."

"You mean..."

Sister Lockheart nodded. "Heaven *knows* what was going on."

The police had wasted Edina's whole afternoon, traipsing about with tape measures and cameras and asking her the same questions over and over again.

"Showed me a picture of him. Heyward, I mean," she said chattily, as she and Nesbit went out together for a breath of fresh air after dinner. "Rather a good-looking chap, wasn't he, if you like that sort of thing. Big and beefy. And of course a war-hero. Got himself parachuted into France. Set up field hospitals. Very well thought-of, apparently."

Nesbit made no reply.

"What did you think of Detective Inspector Thouless, the murder squad chappie?" said Edina. "Shocking colour, I thought. Tubercular, if you ask me."

Nesbit shrugged.

"Shipped in from somewhere more civilised to take over, apparently," said Edina. "Though someone else swears he's local."

They neared the ruined bank. The passage of ten days had not made much difference to the deep ruts left by the tractor, Edina thought. "Apparently he was actually here that day" she said. "Joe Gilder, I mean. Norah's husband. Came racing over, the morning after Dr Heyward was last seen alive."

They stood where the sheets of corrugated iron had torn and flattened the tender grass. The water was grey today, shivering with little ripples in the wind.

At last Nesbit spoke. "Who said that?"

"Oh, I don't know. Some woman who used to work in the bakery. Apparently."

"Hearsay," said Nesbit, "gossip."

"Yes, yes, heated talk of all kinds is everywhere," said Edina, "except between you and me."

There was a pause.

"Didn't you know him? Heyward, I mean? Work with him?"

Nesbit looked away.

"Poor sod," said Edina. "Fellow medic after all. War hero and so on. Bashed on the head and chucked in the water. What was he *like*, Marion? And this Dolly Wainwright person everyone's talking about. You must have known her too."

"Yes. I knew her. We worked together. But she committed suicide, Eddie, it was awful. Of course I don't want to talk about it. Is that so surprising?"

"Heyward, then?"

"I don't want to talk about any of it. If you don't mind."

"I do mind," said Edina. "I think you're keeping secrets."

"Yes, I am. You have some of those too, I expect. Don't let's quarrel. Please."

They were standing in full view of the back of Rosevear, of its many long windows. Nesbit, her hands deep in her coat pockets, turned away a little, as if scanning the tangle of rushes on the far side of the water. Face still slightly averted, she said: "I'm taking your hand. I'm holding both your hands in mine. I'm looking into your eyes."

Edina looked across the water too. "Go on."

"And I'm saying, Eddie, please leave me alone about this. Please just trust me, as I trust you. And love you, with all my heart."

For a moment longer Edina stared in silence at the far side of the lake. "I embrace you," she said.

Presently they turned, and as if casually strolled back towards the hospital.

Detained. The word itself made Norah's insides weaken. Don't fuss, she told herself. As an innocent person she would have nothing to fear, had only to wait for the police themselves to understand what a blunder they were making. She merely requested that the children in her care – foster care, yes, evacuees, motherless, poor things, with her for years – be told where she was, as the younger girl at least would worry, expecting her to be at home as usual when she got home after school.

"We'll let them know," said WPC Hendricks, indifferently.

The detention cell had been painted pale brown a very long time ago, but was clean enough, and smelt strongly of disinfectant. There was a creaking straw mattress on a wooden shelf, with one pillow inside a clean case, a thin blanket of different-coloured knitted squares and in the corner a bucket with a sort of rough sketch at a toilet seat set onto its rim, two thick curving strips of something that looked like compressed sawdust.

They would leave imprints, thought Norah, as carefully she perched upon them, hoping that no one would suddenly open the cell door and catch her in the act. The pee sounded extraordinarily loud. There was no toilet paper, and after some thought she sacrificed her handkerchief, afterwards tucking it out of sight behind the bucket for next time.

I feel better now it's started, she told herself. Like dreading the dentist. And I think I'm doing quite well so far. But there would be more questions.

Would they throw poor Lettie's name at her? She must be prepared for that, she thought. Don't think of dentistry, that's no help, don't think of the sound of the drill. Think of a game of cards. The police have a hand; so do I. Is Mamma's brooch a trump card?

I think not, Norah tells herself. And I have some valuable cards of my own. One is being an honest landlady who can barely recall one Miss Lettie Quick, once her lodger, after so many years. We parted on perfectly amicable terms, officer. Long ago.

But don't bring Lettie up unless they do.

Light-fingered Lettie, who had helped herself to more than Mamma's sherry; who had also at one time helped herself to handsome Dr Heyward, despite poor Mrs Heyward and the three little children. It was still hard to believe someone as energetically alive as Lettie was dead. But the telegram had left no room for doubt. Not an air-raid, but a car crash, in the blackout. Why Blackpool, Lettie? What were you doing there? What were you up to?

Dear Lettie, I still miss you. You needn't have stolen the brooch. If I'd known you liked it I would have given it to you, gladly.

Through its clean pillowcase the pillow smelt oddly, though quite pleasantly, of boot polish, and if the knitted blanket was thin, the cell was not cold. I have slept in much worse places, Norah reminded herself, and strengthened by this thought was able fitfully to sleep a little.

The following morning she was given a basin of luke warm water to wash in, but no towel, a cup of tea and a slice of bread and margarine. Feeling very frowsy she followed WPC Hendricks back up the stone stairs and into another room, where she was told to wait. After a few minutes alone the door opened, and Hendricks came back in again, but this time with Etta.

"Etta! How lovely to see you!" Norah got up, suddenly near tears, she was so pleased, even lifting her arms, as if for an embrace.

Etta looked slightly startled at this unusual warmth. "Brought you some stuff," she said, and she swung the household shopping bag onto the table. Norah turned to Hendricks, who nodded.

Inside the bag, neatly folded, her nightdress, her blue blouse, clean underwear (so Etta must have rifled through her chest of drawers, but think about that later), her toothbrush and flannel, her comb, two clean handkerchiefs, one of them with a sliver of soap wrapped in it, her entire knitting bag, squashed and folded in on itself at the bottom, and best of all her newest lipstick, which Etta must have taken from her handbag.

"Oh, Etta, thank you!"

"Egg done it," said Etta, shrugging. Then she felt about in the pocket of her coat, and took out a rolled-up cellophane packet, which turned out to be a pair of nylon stockings, lavish, American, perfect. "Got you these," she said.

"Etta, no – you should keep them - where on earth did they come from?"

"Friend at work," said Etta. "Gets 'em all the time. They're for you."

"Well, thank you," said Norah. "And please tell Egg how grateful I am."

"When they letting you out?"

"I don't know. It won't be long, I'm sure, it's just a mistake. Did Egg get off to school alright?"

"Yeah. Going home with some mate of hers for dinner."

"And the boys? Do they know?"

"What, that you're in clink?"

"I'm not in clink, Etta."

"What's this then?"

"I'm just - being detained."

"Yeah, in clink," said Etta. "You got a lawyer?"

"What?"

"You should have a lawyer."

"Time's up," said WPC Hendricks. "Come on you," she said to Etta, "hop it."

"Good-bye then, Etta. Thank you so much."

Etta looked stern. "'Bye, Mrs G."

Left alone again Norah sat down, trembling a little.

She felt very ashamed, involving innocent children in her disgrace. Egg would suffer at school, coarser types would tease Etta at work. Part of her mind also tussled feebly with the possibility that whilst foraging in her underwear drawer Egg might well have come across one or two intimate items of black silk lingerie, long unworn, but which she had not been able to bring herself to part with, as Joe had been so fond of them. Further she was aware that Etta despite looking unmoved as usual had called her Mrs G.

"Hey, thanks, Mrs G!" Etta's tenth birthday, opening her present, a clean new sketchbook all to herself, and a pencil box; it had been almost the first time Norah had seen the child smile. Mrs G was rare; a treat. Largely Etta called her nothing at all, scorning Egg's *Aunt Norah*, or *Auntie*; there had been some painful difficulties very early on, when Egg aged four had asked if Norah was now their mum. Etta had answered for her:

"'Course she ent! Mum's dead, right?"

But Egg had forgotten their mother. She could for a while remember an Aunt Marjorie.

"We ent kin at all," said Etta.

At the time Norah herself had been nonplussed. Usually of course her lodgers called her Mrs Gilder, but these were hardly usual lodgers. And Etta's feelings were understandable. Indeed, they were correct, Norah thought.

"Sometimes people have pretend aunts," she had offered eventually. But she had stayed Mrs Gilder to Etta. Usually.

So thoughtful of Egg, she thought, working out exactly what was needed; and how typical of Etta, to ignore practicalities and instead bring her a extravagant present!

Unusable too, as it had been some time since Norah had stopped bothering with stockings; socks were so much warmer and easier to darn, and it had been a relief to abandon that particularly sorry item, her last working suspender belt. She smoothed out the cellophane packet of nylons, there was a picture of tremendously long female legs on it, from the back, in very high heels. It was cheering, somehow, she thought. It said, *future*.

Thank you, Etta.

Late that afternoon Etta caught the bus out along the coast road, and discreetly (she didn't want any gossip getting back to the devout aunt, she had explained) met Jem on the cliff path on the other side of Wooton House. Jem brought two chocolate bars and two small slabs of fruitcake, Etta brought a bottle of ginger beer.

The sun shone; below them to their right the sea was flat calm, turquoise, clear, and beside them to their left the long boundary walls were topped with flowers. Every so often a fresh skylark rose singing from the fields as they passed.

"Never been this far before," said Etta. Ahead the path now dipped steeply down to another low point. There would be a stream down there, she thought. Perhaps they could stop there for their picnic.

"Truly? You don't know what's on the next rise?"

"No – what, then?"

"Come see," he said.

"This better be good," she said to him, as they toiled up again through the heather and gorse on the other side of the valley. There had been such a nice little grassy flat bit, too, beside the stream; he'd gone straight past it. And she'd got her feet wet getting across the stream. In her good shoes, too.

"We nearly there?"

Yes, they very nearly were. At the long flat top of the rise, where they could at last walk side by side, and thus hand in hand, the short grass was soft and glossy in the sunshine.

"There. See?"

"What is it?"

On the seaward side, nearer the cliff edge, Etta could now see what looked very like the roof of Mrs Gilder's chicken house, sticking out through a scrub of prickly bushes.

"C'mon," said Jem. "We can go inside!"

Inside what? Baffled, Etta followed him down an incline towards the cliff edge, it wound backwards and forwards, always going lower, until they reached rocks he had to clamber down. He turned to help her down, and then she was on a stretch of the wiry clifftop grass, in front of a small wooden building close to the edge of the cliff, made of thick wooden planks, with shuttered windows on either side of a split door.

"What is it?"

"I kinda thought you'd know," said Jem. "It sure ain't like the others."

"What others?"

"Those concrete look-out things. We went past one."

"Oh, those," said Etta, going closer to the small door, "those are pill boxes. For when, you know, when they thought the invasion was going to happen, only they didn't know where. For soldiers to shoot out of."

"Sure, but this is something different, isn't it?"

"I don't know. Is it locked?"

"No, ma'am," said Jem, and he undid the wooden hasp, and pulled the door open.

It was dark inside, perfectly dry, the floor was hard sand. There were two more planks set sideways inside, like seats on a train. Jem opened the shutters, there were big wooden pegs holding them shut. Light streamed in.

"It's like a little house!" said Etta.

"With fine sea views," said Jem, propping the door open with a stone.

"Look. Look at this." In the slanting light she could see a sort of writing on the wall. Kneeling on the seat she traced it with her fingertips, it was carved there. It read *SW 1848*.

"Guess it's not a pillbox then," said Jem.

Suddenly they could both make out dozens of them, sets of initials and dates all over the walls, and even on the broad heavy beams of the ceiling.

M Mc C 1872, that one was very deeply carved, curly writing, artistic. "Must have taken ages," said Etta.

QP 1906 had been more slapdash. *Sam was here 1910* had been carefully inked; *Bill B* had only brought a pencil, but pressed very hard with it some time in *1915*.

The earliest they found was on the ceiling, HH, carved with a flourish in *1790*; the most recent *RW*, messily scratched in *1941*.

"Picnic?" says Jem.

The story that Jem will tell his children, his grandchildren, and then directly and indirectly many, many other people about the Second World War is set not in England, which he will often visit in dreams for the rest of his life, but in Tennessee, where he did some initial training.

"Eighteen years old. I'm eighteen years old and stupid, I guess. Innocent. Think I can do what I want, if I work hard enough. Make something of myself. Make a career. Be somebody. I enlisted to get to college. Before I had to. I was no conscript. Growing up where I did. I had some crazy ideas. But. No one had ever called me nigger to my face. Maybe they thought it. You knew when they thought it. But having a officer say it to you, giving you a command, ending it with nigger. That was hard. That was real hard to take. I ever tell you about the prisoners, in Tuskagee?"

Yes, Daddy, you did, Jem's young son and daughter will think to themselves, many a time, though never say out loud.

"Me and a coupla buddies are out on a evening pass. We go to the diner, everyone says it's the only decent place in town. But when we get there what do we find? It's Whites only. The uniform don't count: we can't go there. And while we're standing there, a troop of white guys go by, US soldiers, and they got prisoners with them, German POW's. The ones we're fighting, over in Europe. And they're talking and laughing together, real friendly. And they all go into the diner, the fancy diner that won't serve me and my buddies. They serve Nazis. They serve enemy personnel. They serve the people killing their own children over in Europe. But they won't serve me, an American soldier, because I am a black man."

Long long after Jem has bored his teenaged children with this, the story will achieve a different status, become over many decades something he is requested and required to bear witness to, by various religious and social and political organisations, in person, on radio, on television, on film. People will listen then not with affectionately concealed impatience but with respect, with furious reverence, with tears in their eyes. Jem will live long enough to see the story become evidence, become an instrument of truth.

Right now though, in the strange little wooden hut on the clifftop with Etta, the hurt of what happened was only months ago. The wound is still raw. Etta soothes it, with her fearless blue eyes. Not a white girl congratulating herself on being unafraid, not a white girl being self-consciously unprejudiced. But a white girl who without irony thinks he looks like Jimmie Stewart.

"But you do! Just like him – I bet everyone says that, don't they?"

No, Etta. They don't.

It's as if Etta herself is a doorway into a different just-about-imaginable world, where coloured people are not invisible or menacing but simply the same as everyone else.

Etta, though, is a doorway made of astounding ignorance. It's taken him weeks to discover how profoundly she misunderstands everything American. His America, everything that he is. He can hold her hand, he thinks, and at the same time be aware of the whole wide Atlantic ocean between them. They cannot possibly meet across it. Not really.

It's true that all the time, in the camp, whatever he's doing, he finds himself thinking about Etta and wondering what she's doing and whether she's thinking about him, and working out how long it is until he can see her again, because he keeps wanting to see her face, to gaze at her, it's as if he can't ever look at her long enough.

Noticing these thoughts he tells himself though that he is only playing at being in love. It's a pleasant make-believe, a game or pastime, with a sweet but impossible girl, in a country far more foreign than he had thought it would be. When any day now he might be sent away to the fighting, perhaps to his death.

"Picnic?"

Etta is not playing; she doesn't know there's any game to play. Though she feels almost ill with nerves before every date with Jem, in his company the fear dissolves at once into dizzying happiness. She thinks Love is always like this, and that it will last forever. Name Romeo or Juliet to Etta, and she'd say, Who? Those two certainly got a mention at school, but not when Etta was listening.

She likes the fact that Jem is different, that he's not only a Yank but even more extraordinary, even better, a *tan* Yank. Her friend Debbie at work is going out with a tan Yank too, called Sam; lately Debbie has confided that she is considering Going All the Way. Etta is not quite ready for that, she implies to Debbie, though in fact she is not entirely sure what Going All the Way entails, or rather, is not able fully to imagine the process; it seems so unlikely, so unwieldy; and if you're unlucky you can get pregnant. Etta has no idea that contraception exists, and she fears pregnancy more than she fears death.

On the other hand she has complete faith in Jem, who is perfect. She is his, and he is hers. Which means that one day soon she knows she will also own the rich promise, the freedom, the generosity, of America itself.

Though right now she is aware that this afternoon feels different. Everything has felt different, in fact, ever since she'd come home after work the day before, and Mrs Gilder hadn't been there. The house had been odd without her, she was always there, fussing in the kitchen, banging pots around, ordering people about, telling them off, there was always something she was going on about, someone not hanging their coat up or not washing their hands properly or not bringing the coal in.

"Where is she then?"

The trouble with Egg was, she was so drippy. You only had to look at her and she started snivelling.

"D'you think something's happened to her?" All woebegone.

"Pete's sake. She's out shopping or something. She's always going out."

"No, she's always here when I get back from school. She always is."

"She'll be back in a minute, then. Oh for crying out loud," Etta had added, seeing Egg's eyes fill with tears. "Grow up, will you?"

But then there had been a knock at the door, and that awful Hendricks woman.

"She's helping police with their enquiries," Hendricks had said, and the idiot Egg had stopped bawling, no doubt imagining her precious Auntie Norah actually helping coppers, thought Etta, pointing out clues they'd missed, maybe, or kindly explaining complicated bus timetables.

"She under arrest?" she had asked awful Hendricks, who had a behind like a bus in those trousers, and Hendricks had made a face at her, which said Not in front of your sister! though out loud she had said,

"Of *course* not!" in a sickly smiling voice, as if Egg was a baby, when she was quite big really, in fact the same age as Etta herself had been when

when

In Etta's thinking there was often a gap. She had arrived at it then. On the other side of the gap were a great many things it was best not to consider. So she did not consider them.

"She will come back though, won't she?" That was Egg, eating bread and marg Etta had without much difficulty swiped from the British Restaurant on the High Street. "And we'll stay here. After the war. Won't we? Etta?"

Etta had simply told her to shut it. But while she has vague but spectacularly different plans herself, some part of her keeps warning her she's on the verge of something bad, it feels like something weighty in her stomach, that buzzes and shakes. The RAF had whipped Tom and Percy out of the house pronto, as if the reputation of the entire service was at risk, and at night the house feels so big and empty with just the two of them in it that for once she doesn't mind when Egg comes running into her room and gets into bed with her, even though she kicks so much.

Twice now she's had the old dream, the one that wakes her up all shaky and sick-feeling, the one with the train on fire.

The slab of Eighth Army fruit cake is stuffed full of raisins and sultanas and candied peel. The buzzing inside Etta lessens while she's eating it, but when it's all gone she suddenly feels sick, she ate it too fast, she tells herself, but suddenly she's shaking all over as well, and her heart's beating really hard, she can't breathe in this nasty dark little hut-place, she gets up but her legs have gone all weak, they can barely hold her.

"What is it, you ok?"

Outside, the swinging air hits her, revives her. She sits panting on the grass, strokes it, tries to take slower breaths.

"Etta? Honey?"

"Dint like it in there," she manages at last, trying to smile. It is the first, very first warning attack of something she will not be able to name for decades. It's going to get a whole lot worse before it gets better; perhaps luckily, this is one of the many other things Etta doesn't know about.

Barty is on a train between Exeter and Silkhampton. He even has a seat. This is because he looks so ill; earlier, a young enlisted man had seen him standing in the corridor, and pretended he was getting off at Newton Abbott.

"There you go, mate," said the young enlisted man to the grey-faced shambling wreck in the corridor, indicating his empty seat as he stepped off the train, before nipping smartly along the platform and getting back on again a carriage further down.

Barty had nodded his thanks, sunk down, closed his eyes, gone to sleep immediately, like the very old man he suspected he was. He is twenty-six now, and, barring two brief abortive escape attempts, has spent the last five years in prison, and most of the last four months walking under armed guard, first in snow, then in mud, sometimes in huge baffling circles, sometimes on streets lined with friendly faces offering bread and fruit, sometimes through ruins, through towns empty of all signs of life.

At first, walking was better than the barbed wire. But not for long. A hundred and twenty men, trailing along, nearly always damp, getting huge crippling blisters, catching colds, trying to sleep in cellars, in barns, under hedges, in open fields, with no idea where they were going and not enough to eat.

For one day, in the second week of the march, when they were still walking in snow, dragging their belongings and precious Red Cross parcels along behind them on sledges made from broken-up prison bed frames, his group had been joined by a hundred or so other prisoners, not British or American, quickly rumoured to be Russians.

They had barely looked human. They were starving men in rags, their feet in bundles of rags, their staring eyes on the ground as they staggered along in the snow; all of them looked near death. Three times Barty had been marched past one of their number made to kneel by the side of the road, then heard the shot, then watched the guard hurry on by him, catching up with his mates. They left three murdered men lying in the snow, just in that one afternoon, before the Russians were all hived off again in the evening, marched away in another direction.

For the rest of his life Barty will never speak of this.

"I say, I think this is Prague!"

That was Butterfield, something of a friend of Barty's, though after the march finally ends they will make no attempt to see one another again for nearly thirty years. At the time they were limping half-starved through a long series of deserted cobbled streets, in a freezing shuttered darkness.

"Delightful city," says Butterfield, and no one has the energy to tell him to fuck off. Several days or weeks after that they began to hear American aeroplanes somewhere overhead, and once one strafed them, diving down and letting fly with what sounded like machine gunfire. No one was hit, but shortly afterwards Butterfield produced an enormous Union Jack, which he had been keeping folded very small into an inner pocket of his greatcoat. They were able to spread this out on the ground smartish, whenever anyone shouted that he could hear a distant engine coming. The guards had stopped caring by then, in fact they got quietly among their prisoners until the planes had gone, everyone doing his best to hide, as there was no knowing how visible the flag was, or how trusting the pilot might be.

After a while they had arrived in Germany, and took a long time reaching a state farm, where they were fed gruel of some kind, and for a week or so slept in a cellar. Then they went on again, with different armed guards, and with less and less to eat, sometimes going a whole day with nothing. It was hard to sleep at night, no matter how tired you were. The weather was better, though.

"Look at that blackthorn," said Butterfield. "I adore April, don't you?"

"Yeah," said Barty, after a while.

At last came the strangest day of all, when they were halted somewhere at a stone bridge high over a deep wide river. There were five guards by then, none of them inclined to be friendly. They didn't speak to one another at the bridge, so Barty was able to work out later that they had already decided what they were going to do, which was swiftly set the bridge with explosives, run across it, blow it up up behind them, and disappear.

They were free: it was incomprehensible. There was no one to tell them what to do. No one pointing guns, barking orders, directing the day, guarding the night. It occurred to Barty that he might be the ranking senior officer, but he felt too tired to say so. Like everyone else he sat down in the weak sunshine and had a rest, and after a while several men said they thought they'd go off this way, or that way, and presently the ragged crowd began to drift apart, in little groups, as they chose.

Barty and Butterfield and three others risked using their unmistakeably accented German on a passing farmer, who let them sleep in his barn, where they spent the evening baking big potatoes in a bonfire; he also gave them a hunk of cheese, which they carefully divided into five. The memory of eating the salty cheese with the hot fluffiness of the potato was to stay with Barty for the rest of his life; for sheer tear-inducing pleasure no other meal will ever come close.

The next day they argued in a dispirited sort of way about what road to take, and spent the afternoon hiding from a German tank convoy. The day after that they made their way across the just-about navigable remains of another bridge and were cautiously approaching what looked as if it might be a fairly large village when someone shot at them, a bullet struck the ground just in front of Butterfield, Barty felt the wind as another passed closely over his head.

From the wet freezing depths of yet another ditch, they shouted.

A silence, then voices, absolutely real, American voices, shouting back.

"Oh hurrah," said Butterfield weakly, "it's the Seventh Cavalry."

Sitting dozily on the train between Exeter and Silkhampton Barty thinks he's recovered from all that. He's fine now.

Well, he's still limping a bit, and a couple of stone lighter than he ought to be, and badly hungover, obviously. He'd got into Victoria station the day before, from an airfield somewhere in Kent, where he and dozens of other ex-POW's had arrived via a fleet of Lancaster bombers, and been given tea in an aircraft hanger.

A motherly type in a pinny had put a plate of bread and butter in from of him, said "Alright, ducks?" and he had been completely unable to reply; it had been years, he told himself, since he had heard a woman speaking English. So it was only to be expected. He was fine. On the train to London he had stared out of the window at hedges loaded with hawthorn blossom, trees in new leaf, a meadow full of schoolkids playing, hopfields, orchards, telling himself that it was beautiful, that it was home, as if he had to keep reminding himself; some part of his mind seemed convinced he might after all be back in Germany somehow, on a train taking him God knew where.

At Victoria he tried to to telephone Jess. Hers was the only London number he had by heart, he'd dialled it so often once. Though long ago; he'd been someone else then, perhaps. There was no answer, so he tried making a trunk call to his step-mother Norah: no answer there either. He tried Jess again, but
 then why should she be in, at five in the afternoon? She'd still be at work anyway. Or on her way home, maybe. He had pictured her coming in and picking up her mail in the narrow hallway, finding his postcard. She would know he was on his way, at least.

He tried to ring her again, from a booth outside the Underground, and this time a woman's voice answered, and told him that the line had been disconnected. His bag felt very heavy, suddenly almost too heavy to carry, but he decided to go there anyway, take a chance, all the while trying to remember exactly when Jess had last written to him. He kept coming up with a year.

Not that he could check. Once he had thought he would keep all her letters forever. But he had lost the lot, and with barely a glance back, somewhere on the long trek round Germany. Her photograph too, that he had cherished all those years. He had put it for safe keeping in his precious copy of Palgrave's Golden Treasury. But one morning he had found he'd stopped caring about Palgrave's Golden Treasury, and just left it behind when they set off, as mere extra weight he didn't need to carry. He had forgotten the photograph inside until it was far too late. Couldn't nip back and fetch it. Had he cared much, at the time?

No, he thought now. Not really. But he still wants to see her, doesn't he?

Once or twice he stopped for a rest, putting the bag down on the pavement, waiting for his heartbeat to slow down a little. But when he turned at last into her road, the whole street of houses had gone. Instead of tall matching terraces, there were two high banks of orderly rubble on either side of the road. After the first shock he had sat down on the left-hand rubble-bank and tried to think. He would know, wouldn't he, if she were dead? Someone would have let him know somehow, wouldn't they? But the only person who had doggedly gone on writing to him all this time was his step-mother Norah, who knew none of his friends. Had known none of them, he reminded himself: five years was a long time.

Eventually he had got up and limped to the nearest pub, where he sat trembling on his own for a while until someone he knew slightly came in, and said Christ, is that you, Gilder, how are you, old man, good to see you, what are you drinking?

Barty couldn't remember the man's name, and didn't think to say so until it was too late to ask. But the man he knew slightly at least knew what had happened to Jess, which was that she was really doing frightfully well these days, living out in the wilds of Hampstead, did Barty know her husband at all, decent chap, worked in the Foreign Office?

Barty pretended he had known all about the wedding, and also that he had known about the land mine on her old street, whilst simultaneously coming up with plausible ways not to need the man's name. It was all quite a strain until he got too drunk to care.

He had spent the latter part of the night in a shop doorway, it felt like old times, sitting shivering on his kitbag, waiting for the sun to rise, except that this time no one had a gun on him. Or any kind of plan for the next day. Eventually he felt capable of movement and winced along the unfamiliar streets until he came to a kiosk outside a park, where he bought himself a cup of pale brown liquid billed as coffee, an elderly bun, and best of all a pristine morning newspaper, smelling deliciously of clean fresh ink.

He found himself an empty park bench in the slowly strengthening sunshine. What a ferment of luxury this would have seemed six months ago, he thought, as he sat down. Today's newspaper, his alone, to read with a cigarette in the sunshine! Why didn't it feel luxurious now, why did it just feel a bit nothing much?

It was Jess, he decided, he was bound to feel low. I'm glad she's not dead. Glad she's doing frightfully well living out in the wilds of Hampstead. Glad he's a decent chap. Bastard.

He went on turning the pages, not seeing anything much except the advertisements, nice little drawings of people enjoying Ovaltine or telling one another about new shampoos, they were very soothing. There were one or two blokes he could look up, he thought. The war wasn't even bloody well over yet, there was probably something they'd find for him to do once his leave was up.

But what – wasn't that - He stared, but the picture went on being Rosevear House, and in a national newspaper, how extraordinary! And a story underneath: the German airman. The car they had also found in the lake. The second body, of a murdered man, which had been identified as that of Dr Philip Heyward, missing these thirteen years. The local woman, who was helping police with their enquiries.

That didn't mean Norah, did it?

"Oh fuck," said Barty aloud.

Presently Hendricks took her back to the same room as yesterday, the same battered table. They will make you wait, she reminded herself, and to keep up her spirits turned to Tennyson, her usual resource when in the dentist's chair. She got to her usual sticking point at the third verse, after *Now lies the Earth all Danae to the stars/ And all thy heart lies open unto me, Now* something something about a meteor, when the door opened and the three of them came trooping in again, it's Wilson, Keppel and Betty, thought Norah from nowhere, and had to turn away and disguise her startled giggle as a cough.

"You alright, Mrs Gilder? Get her a glass of water, Hendricks, will you?"

They sat as before, Davey scribbling shorthand, the silent Hendricks standing behind Thouless to one side.

"So, Mrs Gilder. Let's start right at the beginning. Tell me about Rosevear House."

Opening gambit, Norah told herself. Concentrate.

"Very well," she said. "It was built in 1747, and hasn't really been lived in for decades. For a long time it was an orphanage; then it was a sort of private ad hoc lunatic asylum. And now it's a mother and baby hospital, since ah, 1940, that was the year we really got it going."

"Who got Rosevear hospital going, Mrs Gilder?"

"A group of very wealthy patrons in London. Mostly rather grand ladies, in fact," she added. Possibly too grand, her tone implied, to be fully comprehensible to the likes of *you*, Inspector Lower Lower Middle. At the back of her mind the shade of Mamma, whose favourite tone it had been, for once gave a tiny smirk of approval. While the two policemen, thought Norah, wore their faces rather tighter than before.

Stop that, she told herself. It might be fun. But it's not going to get you anywhere. She went on, trying to sound straightforward:

"A good many donors preferred to remain anonymous, but I'd be happy to furnish you with the list of names as it stands. It was a patriotic act - to fund a hospital where anyone, no matter their circumstances, could give birth in relative safety. Especially if they'd been bombed out. This was in 1940, things were looking very bad at the time, as I'm sure you remember."

"So why Rosevear?"

Norah shrugged. "It was one of a number of possibilities. Rural, isolated, not too far from a railway station."

"Must've given *you* quite a turn," Davey put in.

Was this a trap? Bit obvious, thought Norah. "Why do you say that, Sergeant?" she asked.

"Tell me about the lake," said Thouless.

"What is there to say? It's a lake. It's very deep. There are stories about it. It's supposed to be haunted. I don't know what you want me to say." Slow down, she told herself. You sound anxious.

"Haunted", said Davey, rubbing at his neck. He had some sort of rash there, just above his collar, she saw. Bad diet. Possibility of boils, if his wife wasn't careful. Or more likely his mother.

"Some of the lake stories go back a long way," she said more slowly. "There's an idea that the Black Death killed everyone in a village that used to be there, a place called Rozver. It's in the Domesday Book, apparently, but no trace of it anywhere else. So sometimes - at dead of night of course - the villagers of Rozver are supposed to come up out of the water. And there's some poor girl in her nightie, who drowned herself, any number of otherwise rational people claim they've seen her standing in the reeds. There are other stories, if you like that sort of thing. Which I don't."

"Keeps people away, though, that stuff, dunnit?' said Davey, looking up from his shorthand.

"Hardly," said Norah. "It's perfectly easy to avoid a lake."

"Wouldn't want to swim it yourself, then." Thouless taking over again.

"I wouldn't dream of it, it's so cold for one thing. And muddy." The mist rising, some special nights, whether there was anyone there to see it and marvel or no.

"Dr Broughton thinks otherwise."

"So it seems," Norah agreed.

There was a pause.

Got some funny ideas, said Lettie in Norah's memory. But she's good, Eddie Broughton. And tough. Tough women doctors, that's what we need.

"How often do you go to Rosevear, Mrs Gilder?"

"About once a month," she said. "For the accounts. There are other meetings I sometimes go to. And I'm on good terms with the staff."

"Bit of a step."

"I cycle there.'

"But you've been going there a long time, haven't you?" said Thouless. "Long before the war started."

For a moment she forgot to hold back: "Yes. You must know I work for Bagnold and Pender. I'm office manager there, have been for years. The leasehold and the running and the upkeep of Rosevear House has always been our responsibility. I am probably the most frequent long-term visitor the place has ever had. Do you really imagine that any court will allow a single witness to put me there on one particular night fourteen years ago?"

There was a short silence, before he smoothly replied.

"Oh, at this stage, Mrs Gilder, we can imagine all sorts of things."

Fear of enclosed spaces, Jen told her, was called claustrophobia. Etta was impressed with herself for having a condition with a name, especially such a long one. She cheered up quickly as they walked back along the clifftop path.

There was an opposite fear of open places, said Jem, called agoraphobia. People had all kinds of phobias with crazy names. They were afraid of storms and blood and clouds and chickens.

"Chickens?"

"Alektorophobia," said Jem, and they both laughed, Etta a little shakily, but feeling almost herself again. There was still half an hour to go, so they climbed over a stile into a meadow, and sat down on the soft damp grass, hidden by in the corner of stone walls.

"Sorry about – that. The way I was," said Etta.

Jem shrugged. "I took you there. I'm sorry too."

They look into one another's eyes, which is essential and at the same time hard to bear, it makes them both feel dizzy. Neither can speak at all afterwards, they can only kiss. After a few minutes Etta lies down, and with her eyes tells him to lie down too.

They lie in the tender grass, kissing.

Is Jem an oddity? He worries that he is, because he cannot make Etta into *women* in his head. When the other guys talk dirty, about *women*, he feels miserable, always has; ashamed of them, but ashamed also of himself, for not being able to join in. He has tried to be a real man, laugh with the other guys, accept the fact that no matter how distinct and individual Etta seems in the flesh, she is in fact only *women*. He can almost do that to her, in camp with the others, carrying out the dim routines required, or lying on his bed.

In her company though she is too much herself. Desire comes mixed with other emotions. He touches the chestnut gloss of her hair with something like awe.

The teachings of his mother and her church are also alive and well in his pounding heart. At least part of his mind informs him that he is lying in a field with a maiden, enacting Leviticus, and makes vague but powerful suggestions of death by stoning.

She will stop me, replies the other part, lost in urgency.

He turns, lies almost on top of her, her slender strength stretched out beneath him, all alive and perfect and holding him closely to her. She will stop me soon. She will stop me. Stop me, Etta. Stop me.

"Oh!"

He lurches sideways and sits up, appalled at himself, as acutely overwhelmed as Etta had been in the strange dark little hut.

"Sorry!" He scrambles to his feet, turns his back, quickly unzips and inspects and tries to mop himself up with the end of his shirt.

"You alright?"

Etta sounds puzzled, a little hurt. It will not occur to him for several years that she genuinely does not fully understand what has just happened to him.

He tries to control his breathing. "Sure. Just got a little.... carried away there."

She's sitting up, her skirt rucked up about her knees, her blouse partly unbuttoned.

He understands that they have at least avoided the sin of fornication. Is she disappointed, surprised, pleased? It does not occur to him to ask her. His only desire now is to regain his own picture of himself as someone in control.

But then she jumps up too and embraces him from behind, presses herself against his back.

"I love you," says Etta.

He closes his eyes. He loves her too. Should he say it, when she is also impossible? After a little while, he turns round.

At Rosevear now, there are eleven newborns crowded at night into the nursery, for the medical thinking of the time dictates that new mothers need their rest more than they need their babies. Of the current batch there is only one patient left to deliver, a young woman whose fiance is somewhere in France.

Despite her unmarried state the other patients are tender with her, in fact the atmosphere in the wards is extraordinarily warm and loving, even with the background noise of crying babies. Excitement over the discoveries in the lake has been forgotten, expunged by greater, more personal, dramas. The women are all of different social classes, ages, standards, religions, even nationalities, but they have shared this strange childbirth experience in this enclosed place, they have undergone the ordeal and survived. For a few days more, they speak gently to each other, they give one another tentative advice and kindly warnings, they laugh softly as they tell self-deprecating stories, they tiptoe around the ones who are sleeping, they enquire about one another's pains and wounds, they exclaim admiringly over one another's babies.

A postnatal ward can be like heaven, for a little while.

Downstairs the cottage hospital is in full everyday swing. A fisherman has caught his elbow in a winch, a housewife has lavishly cut her thumb opening a tin of sardines, a little boy has fallen out of a tree and broken his collarbone. Towards lunchtime a large young man wanders up to the counter where Nesbit is busily scribbling notes.

"I see the doctor?" he asks her without preamble. "Feeling proper ill, like."

Nesbit looks up at him. The skin around his eyes is dead white, two startling circles of pallor standing out in his flecked scarlet face. He looks like an albino panda, she thinks. She takes a showily deliberate step backwards.

"You don't need to," she tells him. "You've got the measles."

"Oh. That's what Mum said. What do I do, then?"

"Go straight back home. Don't talk to anyone. Go to bed. Stay there."

"Was that entirely necessary?" says Sister Lockheart reproachfully, as they hurry down one of the corridors afterwards. This is a reversal of their usual roles; Nesbit can see at once that Lockheart is relishing being the overtly nice one for a change.

"He was infectious," she says flatly, as she steps into her office. She slams the door behind her and leans against it for a while. Despite the busy morning's work every time she shuts her eyes bits of last night's familiar dream come back to her, Heyward as she once had seen him in reality, in a white apron soaked all through with blood, some of it sliding in thick smeared clots towards the hem, his hands still busily at work, turning, twisting, pulling

"sometimes," he says to her, his tone conversational,

complete

"sometimes one has to apply a certain force," and he pulls, and twists, and here is the sound again, a tap on full gushing straight onto the floor, no, no, that's her lifeblood -

complete procidentia

Nesbit closes her eyes, trying to banish the butcher's shop image, the groaning woman whose uterus he has by hellish accident drawn out inverted through her legs. Long ago, Nesbit tells herself. That was all over years ago. After a while she opens them again and sits down at her desk to roll herself a cigarette.

It has been a luxury, she thinks, not-thinking about Dr Heyward. Thinking about him used to take up so much of her day. He had been such a puzzle. It had taken her years to understand that he was not simply incompetent. She had assumed for too long that his impatience, his rough handling, were the results of an all-too well-founded professional anxiety.

"But you hated them as well, didn't you," says Nesbit aloud now, to his shade, wedged deep underwater in his drowned car these thirteen years, and at the same time intimately beside her, near her, within her. "You hated your patients. You hated us all. I'm glad Joe Gilder did away with you. I applaud him for it. I wish he'd done it earlier. I wish I'd done it myself."

All the same she feels like crying again.

She knows the shade of Dr Heyward can still smirk at her: blackmail is consensual, it reminds her. If you had reported my mistakes, I would have reported your perversions. That was the choice I gave you. And you kept quiet, so I kept working. You had your chance. You didn't take it.

Nesbit stubs out the wretched cigarette half-smoked, glances as she gets up at Norah's neat empty desk across the room.

Norah: I hope to God you get away with it. But oh, I wish you'd hidden him better.

"Let's talk about Dorothy Wainwright, shall we?" said Thouless. "Miss Dorothy Wainwright, deceased. Remember her?"

"Of course," said Norah. "Of course I do."

"She was a nurse attached to Dr Heyward's practice, am I right?"

"Not quite. She was a midwife."

"Ah. So she was. Friend of yours then?"

"An acquaintance, rather."

"Must have been a shock for you though, finding her dead body like that."

"Yes, it was. A very great shock."

"Tell me about that."

"There's not much to tell. I'm sure you've seen the reports. I went for a walk along the beach, one morning. And – there she was. Lying at the foot of the cliffs."

"On the rocks below Wooton House?"

"Yes."

"You know how far those cliffs are from your house, Mrs Gilder?""

"A few miles."

"Nearly five. You often walk that far on your own?"

"No, not often - "

"Yet you gave the alarm, it says here," and he touched the file in front of him on the table - "before nine am. You must have made a very early start."

I was so unhappy in those days, Norah remembered. It was not long after Mamma died. I was so lonely, and sleeping so badly. I just had to get out of the house. If I say any of that, will it sound convincing? Or just seem more fishy still?

Thouless spoke again, very gently: "You knew she was there, didn't you, Mrs Gilder? You knew already."

That was a real shock. "What? No, I didn't!"

"It's what people do," he said coaxingly. "Go back, and check. Maybe just making sure it's real. Was that what you were doing? Making sure it really had happened?"

"No! I just found her. It was awful - she killed herself, it was suicide - "

"So you say."

"So the inquest said."

"See, we're not so sure about that any more. The way we can't help looking at it now, is this. We've got two dead people, maybe died just months apart. Miss Wainwright, friend of yours, yes yes alright an acquaintance of yours, found dead at the bottom of the cliffs. Then there's Dr Heyward. Disappears for years on end, then turns up in a place where you go all the time, dumped in the lake."

We didn't *dump* him, part of Norah's mind protested in horror. We were just *hiding* him. The other part saw the danger, and floundered in more panic - had the foolish protest shown in her eyes?

"You're most frequent long-term visitor at Rosevear, you said so yourself. Two dead bodies – I'm leaving out the Jerry - that's two dead bodies in a little place like this. We can't help wondering what they had in common, d'you see? From where I'm sitting, Mrs Gilder, it looks as if that might be you."

"It's a small town," said Norah. "Lots of people knew them both."

Thouless ignored her. "The other person they had in common," he said, "these two dead people, was your husband. Joseph Gilder. Also deceased. Am I right?"

Norah stared at him. "I don't know what you mean."

"You known your husband long, when you married him?"

"I beg your pardon?"

"You knew he'd been bound over to keep the peace, did you? 1921, this was."

Calm, calm, she told herself. One thing at a time. "Yes. As a matter of fact I did know that." Innocent. Act it.

"On account of, he'd been going around town saying things about Dr Heyward. Slanderous things."

"So Dr Heyward may have claimed," said Norah carefully.

"You know what he was saying, then?"

"Well," said Norah. "I didn't know anything about it at the time. But later on. I knew Joe blamed Dr Heyward for the death of his first wife. She died in childbirth. There were a number of other similar cases, and Joe thought - "

"I'm talking about your husband's first wife. Name of Grace Dimond. And eventually Dr Heyward had to threaten to take him to court, protect his good name. That correct?"

"I - "

"Him and his mother-in law. Mrs Violet Dimond. Both got solicitor's letters, 1921. Warning them to lay off. That right?"

"Well, - "

"But it wasn't only Dr Heyward who looked after Grace Dimond, was it? She had a midwife too. D'you know who that was?"

"I – well, for heaven's sake, there were only two of them - "

" - so you knew it was Dorothy Wainwright, did you? The midwife who looked after Grace Dimond. In that most unfortunate case, ending sadly in that young woman's death. That's Dr Heyward, and Dorothy Wainwright."

"This is crazy - "

"I haven't finished yet. D'you know who was the housekeeper at Rosevear in those days, Mrs Gilder? At the place where Dr Heyward was murdered. Remember the name? Leasehold and running and upkeep's always been your responsibility, so I expect you do."

"Yes," said Norah, hearing herself sounding breathless. "It was Mrs Givens - "

"Old Mrs Givens, that's the one. Beatrice Givens. Who was Violet Dimond's sister."

Twin sister, part of Norah's mind put in. Violet Dimond, Bea Givens, once the legendary Kitto twins; everyone in Silkhampton who still remembered them knew they had looked exactly alike all their lives, and that they had hated one another like poison.

Concentrate, Norah. Innocent. Act.

"Are you suggesting that I – that we - "

"Why don't you tell me what happened, Mrs Gilder? That night. Dr Heyward goes out on a call, sees a patient. Then. He's seen driving away, setting off for home, but he doesn't get there. He goes to Rosevear instead. Late at night. So. Why would he do that, Mrs Gilder? Why would he go to Rosevear?"

"I really don't know."

"Well, we think he went there because someone had called him. Someone had asked him to come. I mean, no one lived there. Except the old housekeeper. But maybe that night, there was someone else. Maybe your husband Joseph Gilder - old soldier, wasn't he – was waiting for him."

Norah tried to breathe slowly. "My husband was an honourable man. What you are suggesting is monstrous."

"Mrs Givens to tidy up afterwards," Thouless went on cheerfully, as if she had not spoken. "And you. You're there too. Helping with the car, maybe. Dropping your little brooch, that was careless. But maybe you didn't know what was going to happen. Maybe it was all a mistake. What happened, exactly? Tell us."

It sounded quite convincing, she thought. A complete edifice. The sort of thing any judge or jury might find perfectly credible. She could almost believe it herself.

"I should like to speak to a solicitor."

"Well, that's up to us, at present. Defence of the Realm Act, Mrs Gilder. We're going to hold on to you for a little bit longer. Of course that might have implications. I understand you have responsibilities."

Norah briefly closed her eyes. "Etta is looking after her sister while I am away," she said, after a struggle.

"I'm not sure either of those kiddies can left in your care," he said, getting up, moving towards the door. "Under the circumstances. Looking a bit pale, Mrs Gilder. Perhaps you'd like a cup of tea. I get you one?"

At Silkhampton station Barty pauses for a while, getting his bearings.

His father has been dead for five long years. He had shed tears when he first heard, that was fair enough. More than once, in fact. Toasted him, privately, on his birthday, at Christmas. Thought about him too, often for no reason at all. Remembered him: his good moods and bad, his accent unaltered by decades in Cornwall, his resentful membership of the Labour party, his constant grumbles about its leadership, *bunch of wankers*, his robust loathing of the war, his half-meant railing at Europe's most despicable nation, *bastard French*, his pride in the best bread in the county, his occasional glooms and drinking bouts, his gentle face, his laugh. Several times in the first year of Barty's imprisonment he had appeared in dreams, in his old armchair among the bunks, not saying much, just sitting there quietly with his hands clasped on his walking stick.

Obviously, Barty tells himself, arriving at your old home town after so long is bound to be difficult. He's pleased with himself for coming up with that word, difficult, and repeats it to himself as he walks along the platform. The familiar streets outside will be difficult. They will be full of his father; that will be difficult.

Nothing from Norah. He's tried several times to put a call through. But the lines are often down, he knows that. And she works all hours. Anyway it's not necessarily Norah, he reminds himself, who is helping police with their enquiries. And then immediately thinks: but who else could it be?

I only need to say something if they charge her, whoever it is, he tells himself. Meanwhile, meanwhile, here is a pub, and hallelujah it is still open. The Railway Tavern, not one he can remember ever having visited before. Inside, the usual dim smell of old beer and tobacco smoke, a flag floor spread with sawdust. Not classy. He shoulders the kitbag and limps up to the public bar, where someone is wiping the dark wooden counter, and as he draws breath to ask, the barman looks up, not quite at him but past him, and says, "Closed."

Barty looks round in surprise. Several men are sitting or standing nearby, each with a full glass in front of him.

"What?"

"Get out," says the barman.

Barty actually looks behind him, for the person the barman must be talking to. But there's no one there. He turns back.

"Why?"

The barman finally looks him in the eye, speaks in a low voice, discreetly. "Look, just fuck off out of it, will you? We don't serve your sort."

Barty is still too baffled to be anything else. "What d'you mean?" he asks, but the barman simply turns and goes out through a door at the side, and disappears. After a few seconds Barty turns round too, and limps out again.

We don't serve your sort. What sort was that? On the pavement he puts the kitbag down and tries to think, tries to see himself as the barman saw him. Not at his best, obviously, unshaven, not clearly in uniform, perhaps looking as if he'd slept rough, which, of course, he had. Perhaps he looked like a criminal, an unsavoury character. But the pub was hardly the Ritz. He should go back in, he told himself, and ask the barman for an explanation, preferably after blacking one of his eyes.

At the thought of offering violence though Barty feels cold rather than hot. I can't be bothered, he thinks. What do I care if some four-ale shithouse won't serve me, I'll go somewhere else. As he decides this someone comes up behind him, stops dead, and speaks to him. He turns, and for a moment there's a nasty echo of the night before in London, and the man he knew slightly, who had known about Jess; but this time the face in front of him suddenly becomes entirely familiar, becomes Bill James, oldest of his old school friends; they had sat next to one another for years, at the Bishop Rd Primary school. Joyfully they shake hands.

"Bill! Good to see you, how you doing?"

"All the better for seeing you, mate! Thought you was dead!"

Without fuss Bill takes the kitbag, and refuses to give it back, as he shepherds Barty away, talking, talking, soothingly, about himself.

Married man these days, respectable, got a little girl too! Nah, joined up in '38. Nice little expedition to France, camping out, boat trip home. Then he'd thought he fancied a bit of a change, somewhere hot, had himself another jaunt to foreign parts, all the way to Egypt this time.

"Dint like it though," says Bill James. "Too much sand."

So – he'd seen some action, then?

Bill pretends to consider this, then deadpans: "Had some tough times with the Aussies down in Cairo."

They reach the High Street, and come to a stop, partly because Bill has noticed how hard it is for him to keep up a normal walking pace, partly because there is a startling messy gap halfway along the street; one, no, two of the tall shops in the right-hand terrace have gone. Wooden beams crudely buttress the next building along.

"Copped a good few raids early on," says Bill James. "Dunno what they thought they was playing at, bombing a shoe shop. And a Gentlemen's Outfitters. Though they say Goering's very strict on tailoring."

The Square is unchanged, littered as ever with market detritus, stalls folded flat under a tarpaulin. There's his father's bakery, someone else's now. There's the stone soldier on his pedestal in the centre, head bowed. At the sight of him Barty has another bad moment, his heart pounds, he can't quite breathe properly.

"Nearly there," says Bill.

They reach the far side of the square, and Norah's house.

"Thanks." He's fine now. Absolutely.

Bill nips up the steps, leans the kitbag against the front door, comes down again, looks at him, seems to make a decision:

"You do know about - your step-mother, don't you?"

Barty nods. So it's true, he thinks.

"There's talk," says Bill, "it was your dad done him in. With her in on it. Accomplice. Sorry, mate, I know it's bollocks."

Afterwards it will seem to Barty that he was not in the least surprised. The information feels unreal, but then so does everything else, including himself, not-real Barty Gilder, walking about in this imaginary half-ruined home-town.

Even so he can respond correctly. "He didn't do it."

"'Course not," says Bill.

"Neither did she. She didn't do it either." Saying this suddenly does feel real; Barty hears his voice break a little, and shuts up, in case things get worse.

"I know," says Bill. "Look, when you've settled in, come and have a jar with me – George and Dragon?" and then he is gone, and Barty must face the house full of ghosts alone.

"...Looking a bit pale, Mrs Gilder. Perhaps you'd like a cup of tea. I get you one?"

By this, of course, Inspector Thouless means, "WPC Hendricks will get you one," for he has never made a pot of tea in his life, wouldn't know how. As a standard lower middle class mid-twentieth century adult male he has never in fact made his own bed, dusted anything, washed any of his own clothes or ironed or folded them or put them away; he has never set or cleared a table, cooked anything, worked broom or mop or vacuum cleaner, shopped for groceries, or planned a menu.

At one level he is unaware that any of these tasks actually need doing, and only notices them if his wife for some reason fails to carry one of them out properly, when eventually he may, or may not, become vaguely aware that something is different, and not quite right. At another more conscious level he knows that they are entirely his wife's business, her part of their joint concern, Mr and Mrs Thouless.

Expanding concern, in fact. He wonders if he can call her again yet, or whether it's too soon, and he'll just get on her nerves. She keeps saying she's fine, but what does she know?

It's hardly rational, he knows, but this morning's talk of midwives – of Dolly Wainwright, for instance, found dead at the foot of the cliffs – has upset him a great deal. He feels midwives ought to be decent serviceable middle-aged motherly types, respectable, dutiful, expert but retiring – in short, the last sort of people who would ever fling themselves off cliffs. Or get themselves flung.

So he needs to hear her voice, too soon or not, and for privacy nips out of the station to the kiosk on the corner.

"Hallo, love. Me again. How you doing?"

"Not bad, thanks. What about you?"

"I'm fine. Your mum get there alright?"

"Yes, she's right here. Want a word?"

"No! Thanks. What you been up to today?"

"Nothing much. Double-dug the garden. Fixed a few roof-tiles."

"Funnycuts. You seen the doctor?"

"That's next week. I'm just a bit tired, that's all. Every time I drop off he gives me a right kicking. Or she does. How's the case going?"

"Pretty well," says Thouless.

"What's your digs like?"

"Alright."

"That bad, eh? Locals friendly?"

"Bit too friendly," says Thouless.

"How d'you mean?"

"They're coming forward. Volunteering."

"What's wrong with that?"

"It's fishy."

"You think everything's fishy."

"That's true," says Thouless.

By the time she's collected the cup and saucer and locked the prisoner in again the late afternoon post has come. With a sigh WPC Hendricks sits down at the desk and makes a start on it. She is not quite aware of how low she is feeling.

Truth is, the job that promised so much has turned out to be mainly skivvying, domestic service in a different uniform. Worse, because she has no way to identify or even fully to notice it, the police station is full of male atmosphere and inclusiveness. She's not quite the only female officer but this is a man's place. The voices are male, there is a general tendency to stride down corridors, biff on doors, make boisterous remarks and utter stentorian laughter.

Hendricks has done her best to fit in. She can stride, up to point. She can be a lot louder than she usually is. But the effort is strangely tiring and doesn't always come off anyway. She feels self-conscious a lot of the time, and ungainly: part of her knows she is being false to herself, and protests about it.

The afternoon post is humdrum, mainly forms. She sorts it into the relevant piles, then turns to the last large battered-looking envelope, addressed merely *Police Station Silkhampton* in inked capitols, inserts the paper knife and neatly slices it open. A little type-written note at once slips out and flutters to the floor. Hendricks picks it up, and it reads: *Ask Mrs Heyward about Dollys hair*

What?

An anonymous note.

Carefully Hendricks takes a clean handkerchief out of her pocket, picks up the envelope, uses it to shield the edge of what seems to be a large photograph inside and draws it out with a gasp of horror; for a second she can make no sense at all of what she sees. It's a blonde woman with no clothes on. A nude woman, all bent and folded up, and yet smiling right back at her. And recognisable: from the file, Hendricks at once see that this is the woman who killed herself long ago by jumping off the cliffs at Godrevy: it's a picture of Dorothy Wainwright.

Hendricks has never seen pornography before, barely understands that it exists. Also she has been brought up to believe that the human body, male or female, is in itself a sort of obscenity, a constant fount of all kinds of barely-constrainable filth, and that the only way to cope with this inherent dirtiness is to hide it: clothes are decency. There are certain parts of Hendricks that she herself has never looked at. The parts are dirty; looking is dirty. Touching, for any reason other than dutiful hygiene, is unthinkable. At night Hendricks undresses in order, putting her ankle-length nightdress on before she takes her trousers and knickers down, so that nothing is ever on show, even to herself.

The photograph of Dorothy Wainwright makes WPC Hendrick's whole self jump and blur all over with shock. She breathes fast as without in the least wanting to (but it is your duty, she tells herself) she peers further into the envelope, and pulls out two more dreadful photographs. Everything, every bit, is shamelessly visible.

She swings quickly sideways, to retch into her own waste-paper bin. Then Hendricks puts all the pictures back into the envelope, still carefully, still not touching them. They belong in the incinerator. But she knows she must give them to Thouless.

Ask Mrs Heyward about Dollys hair

These horrible things are about the Heyward case. These horrible things are about murder.

The first change is the smell. The hall smells like a stranger's house, somewhere he'd never been before. I lived in Germany longer than I lived here, he reminds himself. But at the time it had felt like forever. Fourteen to eighteen.

Warily he puts down the kitbag. There are oddly-sized coats on the row of hooks and at once he remembers the evacuees, that there are two of them, two girls, a big one and a little one, both with funny names.

Dear Egg made a very nice if heavily bespectacled angel, he remembered from Norah's most recent letter, which she must have written just after Christmas.

So Egg was the weepy little one. Etta the big grumpy one.

He picks up the post, three letters for Mrs N Gilder, adds them to the disorderly pile on the hallstand, notices under several envelopes his own last postcard, the one he sent from the airfield in Kent. *All well, back soon, will telegram, love Barty.*

He goes downstairs to the kitchen, and there it's as if a loud continuous noise has suddenly stopped at last. It's peaceful here. His hand recognises the handle of the kettle, with a sort of gratitude. The same gas stove, lit with a match. The same battered silver-gilt tea caddy with the same metal spoon stuck into the tea inside. Using all these remembered things is deeply soothing, posits the theory that he has merely been away, and has now come back: it's that simple.

Only when he has poured the tea – no milk, there isn't any - does he notice his father's small sagging armchair at the window at the back of the house. It was one of the few things Joe had taken with him when he and Barty moved out of the flat above the sweetshop, to live here in the worn gloomy splendour of Miss Thornby's house.

"Not room for the three of us in the flat," Joe had said, reasonably enough. "You can have your own room now, son."

Don't want my own room, he had thought. But not said.

Silence had always been his weapon of choice, he thinks now. Against his father, and especially against his step-mother. He sits down in his father's armchair, takes in the view his father had been so keen on, mainly vegetable beds just cleared for planting, the two apples trees just coming into blossom, the fine high walls set with espaliered pear and cherry.

"Morellos make the very *best* cherry-brandy," says Norah from long ago, pouring his father a tiny ruby glassful. His father complacent, taking it. Barty had seen the glance pass between them, almost felt it, like a blow.

It was the fucking, he thinks now, sipping his tea. I was fourteen. The last thing I could bear to think about was my dad fucking anybody. Let alone snobby Miss Thornby of the Square, Miss Thornby the old maid.

Miss Thornby the recently-notorious Local Woman. *Local Woman Finds Body,* he could still see the headline. Just before Heyward disappeared, wasn't it?

Just before Heyward died.

I would be dead but for him, thinks Barty, his eyes unseeingly on the garden. No: I would never have lived at all. His Nanna Violet had more than once told him that old Dr Summer would have let him die unborn. Then Grace, his mother, might have lived.

"That's what they done in the old days," says Nanna Vi in his memory. "They let the most innocent go to His Mercy."

But Dr Heyward had pulled him, Barty, from his mother's body, extracted him and saved him, and so Grace had died. It had been quite something, knowing that, when you were a kid. When you saw Dr Heyward in the street, tipping his hat to a passerby. Driving past in his shiny car. You saw him and you went quiet, because he had made you live, and made your mother die.

"Lay off, Vi," says Nanna Bea sharply. "He dint kill her on purpose."

Barty checks the bread bin. It's empty, but that doesn't matter, he thinks, because he's not in the least hungry anyway, not really. Perhaps he's tired. He is unwilling to leave the quiet kitchen, and spends a few more minutes prowling about opening drawers, the old mismatched kitchen cutlery all as it was, the glass cupboard full of tumblers, Norah saying "Would you like some lemonade, Barty?" tentatively, on a hot summer's day, when he was fifteen.

On the dresser he comes across the studio portrait he had had taken of himself three years later, in uniform, complete with an almost-respectable moustache. It gives him a curious shiver now. It makes him think of the photograph in Norah's drawing-room upstairs, of her long-gone brother Guy Thornby, who had died on the Western Front.

Barty's own soft child's face, very pleased with itself, smirks back up at him from within the silver frame. It's fair enough that it reminds him of Guy, he thinks now: it really is a picture of someone who died. He puts it back in its place on the dresser and makes himself go upstairs, hauling on the bannister. Heavyweight Edwardian bathroom, as before, except untidy, hung with alien stockings drying on a string tied across the bath. Beside it, his old room, the door closed. His hand hesitates on the dented familiar doorknob. It's not going to look the same, he tells himself, not after years of shortages, and dozens of people coming and going.

All the same he shuts his eyes and pictures the room he left at eighteen, the walls painted Norah's choice of pale blue, because of course when urged to say what colour he would like his new room to be he had answered with a very slight shrug, and the shelves his father had put up for his books, and the desk at the window where he had written so much homework, reams and reams of it, he had worked so hard, because all the time all he wanted in the world was any access of any kind to the glory that was aeroplanes.

"What you going to do when you're a man, my lovely?" says Nanna Bea coaxingly, knowing already what he will say, wanting to hear him say it again. He is eight years old.

"I'm gonna fly, Nanna!"

Barty opens the door, and finds the room now clearly belongs to someone else, though the bed, the desk, the shelves, even the colour of the walls, are all more or less as he left them. The room smells different, feels different; tidy enough, the bed roughly straightened, a dark blue dress laid across it. A small pair of worn brown slippers akimbo beneath the bed. A coil of pale blue hair ribbon on the bedside table. A comb.

Does the room belong to the big one or the little one?

Cautiously, one of the Bears in Goldilock's house, he trespasses across the room to the window, the floor boards creaking just as they always did beneath his feet, and sits down at the battered desk, brought from home, once his mother's, to check on the view, once gazed at so often from within quadratic equations and irregular French verbs. Garden, wall, tower of St George's, other rooftops, sky, all present and correct. Chicken coop at the far end of the garden: that's since his time.

They were supposed to be at point of lay, but they are hardly bigger than blackbirds. The children have named them, which is of course exactly what one is exhorted not to do. Egg most suitably called hers Snowy, but Etta insisted on naming the other one after a certain notorious American lady. So every now and then she remarks casually that she can see Mrs Simpson scrabbling about in the compost heap, or preening herself on top of the garden wall.

He had actually read that bit out to Butterfield, he remembers.

The desk holds nothing but two pencils, one of them broken, and a school exercise book, the same sort he himself had used as a child. He remembers suddenly that he used to keep his mother's three short stories, all she managed to finish before he himself had come along and killed her, in the secret drawer hidden within the molding. That he had left them there. Carelessly. As if they hardly mattered. Are they still there? Suppose Norah didn't know they were there, and the room's new owner discovered them, and hadn't known what they were, just flipped through them carelessly, discarded them with a shrug, used them to light the fire!

He gives a little groan at the thought. He wants to read his mother's works again. He needs to. Urgently he searches out the tiny nail which locks the secret drawer in place, scratches at it, but it won't budge, it always was a sticker. He worries at it with finger and thumb until at last it shifts, and he can pull it free, and the drawer at once slides open, and there inside is the remembered buff envelope, full of his mother, of her own handwriting, her own thoughts. He pulls it out, breathing fast, and holds it to his chest, rocks to and fro a little, his eyes closed.

Presently he notices that he is close to tears, and wonders ashamedly what's wrong with him. He tells himself to grow up. He tucks the envelope inside his jacket, buttons it in safe, then leans back in the chair, takes a deep sighing breath, and picks up the school exercise book. The label on the front says *Property of Bishop Rd County Primary School*, with a empty space for a name.

He flips through it. It's almost full, of drawings. He puts it down and opens it more carefully, at the first page, where a small girl is skipping, the rope flung in a narrow arch high above her head, her plaits flying, she's on the next page too, not so successfully, abandoned, face missing. He keeps turning the pages, seeing children playing in a street recognisably part of the Square, playing a game he suddenly, seeing the picture, remembers playing himself, creeping up on the one who has his back turned, chorusing *What's the Time, Mr Wolf,* then – he sits back, gives a little gasp – a serious intentional portrait. It is of Miss Pyncheon, that rather odd Miss Pyncheon who had run the Silkhampton Picture Palace, who had turned out to be some sort of relative of Norah's.

My dear cousin Alice has come to stay while her house is being redecorated, he vaguely remembers, and then later on something about *rest in hospital.* Had there been any more? He can't remember.

The portrait is curiously touching, Miss Pyncheon perched on the arm of an unfamiliar chair, as if she had just alighted there. She wears one of her long droopy frocks, her endless strings of beads. Her head slightly tilted, her entreating smile: it's her, he thinks. It's good. He turns the page, and there is a cartoon of Norah; absolutely unmistakeably Norah, as he had seen her many times himself, sitting up very straight in her armchair by the fire, knitting hard. Except that in this picture she is knitting something that looks very like a Sherman tank. It hangs from her needles by the barrel of its cannongun, the size of small dog, almost complete in her lap.

"Who the hell are you?" says a fierce voice behind him.

Barty starts so violently that he almost falls off the chair, he leaps up and spins round, the book dropping from his hand.

"Well?" A smallish skinny girl with her hair in plaits. Is it the big one or the little one? His heart pounds, he feels dizzy with shock. She is holding the poker, he notices. He takes some breaths, as slowly as he can.

"I'm Barty Gilder," he says at last.

She snarls at him. "No you aint!"

"Yes," he says feebly. "I am. Honest."

She comes forward, scowling, the poker raised. "How'd you get in?"

"I know where she keeps the spare key."

There is a pause. She lowers the poker, still staring hard at him. "You looked at my book."

"Sorry."

"You come in my room."

"It used to be mine."

"Well, it's mine now. You can fuck off."

This is so surprising he snorts with laughter. She grins too, unwillingly.

"Are you Egg?"

"No!"

"Etta. How d'you do." He holds out his hand.

She swops the poker into her left and takes it, bitten fingernails, hot little hand: "How d'you do, Mr Gilder," she says stiffly. Then in a different voice, with a tilt of her head towards the stairs: "Come on."

Obediently he follows her down to the kitchen where she taps on the pantry door, talks to it: "It's alright, you can come out now."

A second child, her small face streaked with tears, opens the door and timidly emerges; definitely the little weepy one, he thinks.

"It's him," says Etta.

Egg has the sort of glasses that make her eyes look like headlamps. She dares one look up at him, then turns to her sister. "He's too old," she says, more decisively than he would have expected.

Etta shrugs.

Egg stares back up at him: "Have you come to get Aunt Norah out?"

"Yes," says Barty, after a pause.

"Told you," says Egg triumphantly to Etta.

"He hasn't done it yet," says Etta and turns again to Barty. "You got any money?"

"Why?"

"We're starving," says Egg.

"No we aint," says Etta irritably. "It's just today."

"It's a different manager on Fridays," says Egg, in the tone of one explaining something.

Is this Friday? Barty asks himself. He has no idea. He's not even sure what month it is. I'm really hungry too, he suddenly understands.

"Is the fish and chip shop still open, the one on North Rd?"

Etta nods.

"Can you go? If I give you the money?"

"We'll both go," says Egg quickly, and the girls exchange a hard glance he cannot begin to interpret.

He hands over a ten bob note and they're almost out of the door again before he remembers something from the long yearning list everyone had ceaselessly compiled in the prison camp.

"They still do pickled onions?"

"They're awful," Egg tells him gleefully. "Eyeballs in a jar!"

"Just one for me then," he says. "Please."

She answered the door herself. A tall pale slender woman, with auburn hair swept up in the modern style, curling in front, a slash of scarlet lipstick, and a little silk scarf knotted jauntily at her throat. She was still very striking, he thought.

"Mrs Heyward? I'm Detective Inspector Thouless. This is WPC Hendricks. May we come in, please, have a word?"

"I'm afraid it's not convenient, Inspector. I'm just about to go out."

"We won't be long, Mrs Heyward. It's important."

"Well, if you must - "she stood aside. "Do please wipe your feet," she added sharply. She led them down a long hallway, her heels clacking on the tiles, saying *sophisticated*. From the floor below, from the kitchen presumably, thought Thouless, came the sound of radio dance music.

Mrs Heyward showed them into a rather beautiful sitting-room at the back of the house, with tall French windows opening onto a garden full of twilit blossom. "Do sit down," she said. The radio went on cheerily saxophoning.

"Well, now, Mrs Heyward. I'm sure this has been a very difficult time for you."

"Yes. It has," she said coldly. "And I have already spoken to your Sergeant at some length, Mr Thouless."

"I know you have, and I'm sorry. But something's has come up, and I need to talk to you about it."

She looked at her watch, a tiny gold affair. "You'll have to be quick," she said.

He left a pause, to let her know who was in charge. Then began: "Thirteen years is a very long time, Mrs Heyward. Without a word from your husband - you must have suspected that something had happened to him?"

"Yes. As I have already said. Though of course I couldn't be sure. Until now."

"You never attempted to have him legally declared dead, though. Why was that?"

A shrug: "I didn't need to. My father's death left me comfortably off. I had no wish to remarry."

"You were married for what, twelve years? And you had the three kiddies. How old are they now, Mrs Heyward?"

"My daughter is nineteen. She has just joined the WRENS. The boys are still at school."

"Would you say on the whole that it was a happy marriage, Mrs Heyward?"

"I don't believe that's any of your business, Inspector. We were happy enough."

"But when he first disappeared, you assumed that he had left you for another woman."

"What else was I to think? As I'm sure you know already, he took his passport with him. And he had been making enquiries about emigration. All this has been documented."

"Had he been unfaithful to you before?"

"I imagine no wife can be altogether certain about that, Inspector."

Mine can, he thought. "A wife can suspect, without being sure," he said. "Did you suspect him, Mrs Heyward?"

"Possibly. I really can't say - this was all a very long time ago, Inspector."

"Well, the thing is, Mrs Heyward, we've been sent some photographs."

She became very still.

"By post, this afternoon. Anonymously. The pictures are ...of a particular kind," he went on. "Obscene, in fact. Unlawful. Of different women, but similar enough in themselves to make us think they were probably all taken by the same hand."

"I don't see what this has to do with, with - "

"I'd like you to take a look at one of them for us, please."

"No. Certainly not!"

"Only the face," he said. "Thank you, WPC Hendricks. Here, Mrs Heyward. This one. Recognise it?"

Hendricks had covered the photograph in office paper, a square cut out to show the head. He held it out across the low table, the soft young face, the loose hair.

"This is you, isn't it?" he said.

Mrs Heyward gave a little cry, and sagged back in her easy chair. It was as if had knifed her, he thought. He leant forward, and in a different voice said, "I want you to know – listen to me, Mrs Heyward. Are you listening to me? Really listening?"

She managed a nod.

"I want you to know that WPC Hendricks here is the only other person who has seen the photographs. She opened the envelope herself, didn't you, WPC Hendricks?"

"Yes sir."

"And very properly she brought them straight to me. No one else has seen them. Or will. Alright? Mrs Heyward?" To Hendricks he said, "Go and put the kettle on, will you? Or find someone who will. Discreetly."

"Sir."

"So," he went on, as the door closed, "there were pictures of three different women all together. One was a known common prostitute at that time. There's the one of you. And there's one of another local woman, deceased, used to work with your husband, I expect you remember her, a nurse called Dorothy Wainwright."

She whispered: "You don't know what he was like." She was crying now, the tears sliding down one after another.

"No. That's true. I don't."

"He made me do it."

"How did he do that, Mrs Heyward?"

She made no answer.

"Was he violent to you? Did he hit you?"

Her face twisted, and he felt a surge of familiar irritation. These women, always refusing to stand up for themselves, and then blaming the man!

"I was very young," she said. "I didn't know - "she swallowed - "I didn't know there were others. I thought it was a private thing. For my husband."

"So. You agreed to pose for him."

"I didn't want to do it, he talked me into it!"

"You agreed."

"Yes."

The door opened, and Hendricks stumped in with a tea tray. With his eyes he told her to pour out, and keep quiet. And the radio had stopped. Perhaps she'd told the skivvy to can it.

"I'm going to ask you again, Mrs Heyward: why did you assume at first that your husband had left you for another woman?"

She sipped her tea. "I knew he was having an affair. At the time. Just before he disappeared. I knew there was someone else."

"How did you know?"

She wiped her eyes. "I always knew," she said, "because he was different. He was nicer. So I knew."

"It was something that happened often, then, was it?"

"Yes. I got used to it."

"I see. Did you have any idea who he was having a love affair with, at the time of his disappearance?"

"Not really. I thought it might have been the new midwife. We met her once in the street. I saw the way he looked at her."

"What was her name?"

"A Miss Quick. He introduced her. It was just a feeling – I might have been wrong."

"Very well. These photographs. Not the sort of snaps you take to Boots. How did your husband get them developed, Mrs Heyward? You know where he went?"

"He did that himself."

"Where?"

"Here. He had his own dark room."

"You mean, in the house?"

"No, it was in the old stable-block, behind the house. It was always kept locked – there were so many dangerous chemicals in it, he said. You know, dangerous for the children."

"You ever go inside?"

"Not until he'd gone."

"Oh?"

She put the cup down, clearly made a decision. "Someone sent me a note, I don't know who. A week or so after he - left. I kept it. Just a moment." Getting up she went to the desk in the corner, opened it, took a keyring from her jacket pocket, and unlocked a small inner drawer.

"This is the envelope it came in."

She held it out. He took out his own handkerchief, shook it unfolded, and shielding his fingers in it carefully took the envelope from her. Cheap everyday paper. London postmark. March 23 1932. Inside a slip of paper, of similar dimensions, he noted, to the one that had recently accompanied the photographs, though he could tell at once that it had been typed on a different machine, one with a smudge on the letter e. He read it without taking it out of the envelope, without touching it:

hes never coming back. look in his dark room.

"You show this to anyone?"

She shook her head.

"So, Mrs Heyward. What did you do?"

The faintest shrug. "I looked in his dark room."

"You had a key, then?"

"No, I didn't. I couldn't find one. I had to file through the padlock."

"I see," he said, trying to. It would have taken her hours, he thought. Perhaps over more than one dark night. The children in bed. Her arm aching. Gloves to spare her pretty hands. "So you got it open."

She nodded, and he saw the padlock bolt finally sheer through, the bold sliding open. She would close the door behind her before she put the light on. His own ideas of what a dark room might look like were vague. No windows. Laboratory fittings of some kind, a little clothes line to peg wet pictures on as they developed. A special red light?

"There was a filing cabinet," she said. "With pictures in it. He had said it was a private thing, between him and me. But it wasn't. It wasn't just me."

"You looked through them?"

"I saw what they were. Hundreds of them. Different women. Different – poses."

"Did you recognise any of the women?"

"I didn't *examine* them!"

"What did you do with them?"

"I burnt them. Everything. There were rolls of film. Files. Negatives. I burnt everything that would burn. His cameras and so on. I took them with me bit by bit on walks,I threw them in the river. The chemicals I put down the drain. Everything in that room. Every stick of furniture, I burnt. I had the stable block demolished. It's a rockery now. Look, you can see it through that window. Are you going to arrest me?"

"What for? What d'you think we might charge you with, Mrs Heyward?"

"I don't know. The photograph? Murder? D'you think I killed him? I didn't, I swear."

"We have no reason to think you had anything to do with your husband's death, Mrs Heyward."

"And the, the one of me. My children. It would destroy them. Please."

"We will keep it quite safe for now, Mrs Heyward. One more thing, and then we'll leave you. Hendricks?"

The picture of Dorothy Wainwright was disturbing even in its modest paper frame. The expression on the face was so dreamy, the eyelids drooping in langour.

"You knew Miss Wainwright quite well, didn't you? It would be very helpful to us, if you'd take a look at this and tell me, if you can, how long ago you think it was taken. I mean, a long time before she died? Or a short time?"

Out of the corner of his eye he saw Hendricks sit forward a little, and allowed her a tiny glance of complicity. Yes, said the glance. Let's first see what she says unprompted.

Mrs Heyward winced as she took the picture into her hand. It was a while before she could speak. "Well, I really don't see how - "Then she started suddenly, and spoke in an almost lively voice: "Oh, actually, not that long before, I think! Because of her hair, you see. She used to wear it long, in a bun, ever so old-fashioned. I remember her talking about getting a marcel wave. She talked about it for months before she went ahead."

"And when was that, Mrs Heywards, can you remember?"

"Not really - "

"A year before her death? Six months?" Did hairdressers keep records?

"Not more than six months. It was short at Christmas."

"But long the Christmas before that?"

"Yes. But. That means - "She broke off, the faint animation in her face suddenly draining away.

Yes, thought Thouless. It means your husband was still seeing Dolly Wainwright at the time of her death. Aloud he said: "Thank you, Mrs Heyward. That'll be all for now."

"Alright, Hendricks?" he says, as they cross a road on their way back to the station.

"Sir."

Briefly he imagines her innocently opening the post, the nasty shock of the dirty pictures falling out, and gives her a sidelong look, noticing once more how pitifully unattractive she is, so round and thick in the middle, and yet with no bosom to speak of, worst of all worlds.

Thouless thinks this judgement is entirely private; he has no idea how easily Hendricks reads it in his every glance. To be fair, Hendricks herself has no idea how clearly she is reading it either; doesn't even notice what it is that she is reading; wouldn't trust her own judgement anyway, if she did. In Thouless's company she feels even more anxious and sheepish than usual, and blames herself for this, because everyone else says he seems decent enough, as bosses go.

"You planning on staying in the Force, after the war?" he asks her now.

"I think so, yes, sir." Her heart leaps at this sudden show of interest.

"Well. You just remember what I said back there. If so much as a hint of those pictures gets out, I'll know it was you spread the word. And that will be that, for your career, my girl. Finito. Got it?"

"Yes, sir."

There is no Ladies toilet in the police station, so Hendricks as usual has to cross the street to the village hall, where there is a women's public lavatory. Safely locked at last into a cubicle she does not after all weep, as she had thought she would.

She had been pleased with herself, for putting on such a brave face, for not making a fuss. If she had wept and said she wanted nothing more to do with the photographs he would have been contemptuous; but she had been cool and professional, and he was contemptuous still.

Though she feels the injustice of this Hendricks can put none of it clearly to herself, and does not try. She knows only that she wants to hide away for a while, putting herself back together again, trying to find the small hard nugget of self-belief still inside her, and trust it again. She stays for as long as she dares in the narrow dripping peace of the cubicle.

While across the road in the police station, Thouless has shut himself into his office, thrown off his coat and jacket, loosened his tie.

All the while he was talking to Mrs Heyward, respectable widowed mother of three, he had known what she looked like in her youth with no clothes on, and bent into a deep inviting curve, her eyes half shut as if in ecstacy. Her bottom, a peach. He had followed her down the corridor in her own house, heard the businesslike clack of her high heels on the tiles, all the time knowing about the peach inside her skirt.

It wasn't the pictures, he thought, that were so disturbing. He'd seen far worse. But never before had he seen pornography featuring someone who had later drunk a cup of tea with him, a woman who looked as virtuous as his own wife.

In fact he is disgusted with Mrs Heyward for allowing herself to be photographed, disgusted with himself, for noticing peachiness, and particularly disgusted with Hendricks, who has not only seen the pictures herself, but seen him seeing them. He is partly aware that he has been a bit rough on Hendricks; partly sure that she had it coming.

He sighs as he sits down at his desk. Tells himself: Heyward is hardly the first utter shite whose murder he has been required to investigate. Being a shite is not a criminal offence. Though it seems Heyward committed a few of those too.

It strikes him that the detectives in the whodunnits his wife enjoys so much are often investigating the death of someone horrible, selfish tyrannical old men, cruel faithless women, cynics, frauds, drunks. But they keep going. M Poirot never says, You know what, I don't care who killed this miserable old git, let's just forget the whole thing. Jane Marple never says Dear me, what a nasty piece of work Mrs Gilmore seems to have been, no wonder someone bumped her off, good riddance!

Sadly Thouless half-smiles to himself at the thought. Pictures his sweetheart sitting on the other side of the fire deep in her library book, her feet up, her poor swollen ankles; and he longs, longs to go home.

Friday nights

He can surely find the factory easily enough. She's said it's near the station, and as far as he knows there's only one of those. She won't be there, and maybe that's just as well. He knows her work time table well enough, and she doesn't do late shifts on Fridays, she always has Friday evenings free.

And of course he never did, not usually.

"No. I can't swop, Etta. I won't ever have leave on Fridays, ok? Because the white guys do."

"What?"

"We get Wednesday-Thursday. They get Friday-Saturday."

"But - why?"

"It's better that way."

"What d'you mean? Why is it?"

Her puzzled questioning evidence in itself. She had no idea what she was asking. She was impossible.

Tonight, though, was the exception. The camp was moving on, even being abandoned, said the rumour. Tomorrow the Whites could say their farewells in turn, and the next day everyone would be gone. Somewhere. France? Germany? Home? No one knew.

He's left the other guys in one of the good places, the George and Dragon in the square. Legend said that years back when the camp was new, a white captain name of Bell had come in with four or five of his buddies and seen three coloured infantrymen in the Snug, and told the barman what he thought of him, serving coloured guys, letting them sit in the same chairs as Whites, drink out of the same glasses.

"Get the hell outta here," he had ordered the coloured soldiers, and they had started to their feet, naturally enough. But the natives, the locals, had told them to stay right where they were. Just a bunch of regular old guys in the pub, they had ganged up on Bell and his buddies, they'd asked him what side he thought he was supposed to be on, in the war they were all fighting. Told him straight out he was a Nazi.

"I am their superior officer!" Bell had hollered, and the landlord had said, Not in my pub you aint, and thrown him out along with all his mates, and given the coloured guys a free round.

Locals maybe think that's the end of the story.

Still, you can relax in the George and Dragon. He'll go back there when he's done what he's come to do, which is leave the letter. He crosses the market square, cobbled like the pictures in books of fairy tales, where folk are dismantling market stalls in the gathering dusk. Passes the stone soldier in the middle, the little alleys of shops he had written to his mother about, and crosses the street towards the church.

It rained all day. I mean all day, Mamma, it did not stop for a moment. People still real friendly, though. When we went into the church an old lady in there, she comes racing up like we're kin, shows us all around, takes us up the spire. Albie did not want to go up that spire, he hates heights, but she marched him up there, you went through this real small door, like it was for dwarfs, and it was a spiral staircase made out of stone, I'm thinking, how does this thing stay up, and how'd they build it in the first place, there's nothing to hold onto, you go round and round and higher and higher, it's all dark, like a tunnel on end, the steps are narrow, and worn, and then we get to the top of the tower, the spire goes on up, and but there's a place you go out on, a balcony all round the tower, and you go all the way round it, see for miles, green everywhere, and the streets all crooked...

That was the sort of thing his mother would like, he thought, and he had taken care to give it to her. He had also tried once or twice to write her about the sea, about the first time he had walked along the clifftop path and come right to the edge of the world. How he had closed his eyes, listening for the waves turning on the beach below, asking their question over and over. Opened them on the great sweep of colour and sparkle, changing shade all the way to the immense darker line of the horizon, one of the splendours of the world, that he had always known about and read about and seen in films, but now he was seeing its magnificence for himself, smelling it, feeling its glory. And it had always been there. Looking like freedom.

No, he could not write any version of that to his mother. Not one he could bear to sign. After lots of screwed-up paper he had let it go altogether: *Sure is nice to be close to the ocean.*

Of course he's never tried for one moment to write anything to anyone about Etta. Not even the guys in camp know about her. Not even his best pal Albie. He has let them all laugh at his lonely clifftop walks, his much-annotated pocket edition of *Wildflowers of Western Europe*. He has carefully kept her a secret, as she has kept him. Or so he thinks.

The railway station forecourt appears suddenly to his left, people queueing at a bus stop there. Somewhere near here, then. All he has to do now is find the place. He crosses the road, notes the Railway Tavern.

Some places the locals crowd in being friendly, saluting Allied soldiers, eagerly shaking hands. Some places you could wait a long long time to get served. Some places it was hard to tell. Once as he sat with friends in a tiny pub outside town a very old lady with straggling white hair and no teeth had hobbled over from her seat by the fire and told Albie that he and his friends were lovely fellows, and also - it took several repetitions of what she was saying before they could catch her drift, so mysterious were her intentions, so gnarled her accent – that in all her life she had never touched a blackamoor's hair, and would he be so kind, sir, as to let her have a feel?

At this point in the evening they all had quite a few drinks inside them, though not, as Jem had pointed out afterwards, as many as the very old lady, who had clearly been drunk as a skunk.

"Sure," Albie had said, and she had reached out her hand more smartly than any of them had expected and rubbed his head hard all over.

"Soft as kitten fur!" she had told them all, in triumph.

Was that friendly? Or the opposite?

"Not unfriendly, I guess," Albie had said on the way home.

Whereas the Railway Tavern was a known bad place, straight down the line Whites only. Some of the British were like that too.

"They got their own Coloureds," said Albie. "They got Empire."

On either side of the Railway Tavern are several shops, all shuttered and dark. He keeps going, in the direction of the town, until he reaches a corner, and there it is, big plate glass windows on two sides, evidently closed already, a painted sign in old-time writing, *Henty & Sons Ltd.* It's a small factory, Etta has said, used to be an Optician's shop, then a little place that made glass bits and bobs for the people who test your eyes. Now they make other things she's not meant to talk about, though point of fact, she says, she couldn't talk about them anyway, so indescribable in themselves are the items she helps in some way to produce, or possibly pack, or maybe it's just clean up after.

"War work," says Etta. It ain't half boring, he remembers.

As he scans the door for the letterbox he catches sight of someone inside, a woman sitting at a desk making a phone call. She looks weighty and respectable. She wears a hat he is dimly aware is called a toque, with stiffened ribbon sewn into several loops on top. Is this Etta's boss, the much-mocked Mrs Henty?

Agnes Henty, widow of the Silkhampton optician Mortimer Henty, son of Alfred Henty, who had first thought to make his own optical equipment, and then expand the business to supply others; Agnes Henty, for several years now in full managerial control of a wartime military manufacturing unit, hidden in plain sight, employing not three skilled craftsmen, as in the days of Alfred, or eight, as in the days of Mortimer and the peace, but thirty-three, mainly unskilled women, in a series of hastily-erected outbuildings crammed into what had once been wasteground at the back of the original factory.

Few of the thirty-three unskilled women know precisely what it is they are making, especially as the product is carefully packed and loaded and taken away in a state well short of completion. They assume that it is vital in some way to the war effort, which helps with the boredom, makes them all into Gracie Fields singing on the radio: *I'm the girl that makes the thing that drills the hole, that holds the spring, that works the thingummy-bob that's going to win the war.*

Agnes Henty, wartime factory manager, mother of two serving soldiers, one of them a prisoner of war somewhere in Java, spending what small free time she has in the green uniform of the Women's Voluntary Service, has had another in a long unbroken passage of very hard days. Towards the end of a taxing telephone conversation with one of her more unreliable suppliers, she looks up at the sound of someone tapping on the glass of the office door. She makes a gesture with one hand: Go away. Closed.

The tapping goes on as she says her irritated goodbyes. Looking more closely through the reinforced glass she makes out the pale American uniform, the dark face.

Agnes Henty has no time at all for the nonsense of racial prejudice. She was disgusted by the Americans' decision to segregate their own soldiers, to insist on separate leaves, on particular areas – in England! as it were fenced off for whites or blacks, and even more profoundly disgusted by Authority's feeble acquiescence to such alien iniquity - on British soil! - in the first place. At the same time she is appalled by the Americans' ludicrously high military wages, and cannot understand how these two phenomena – the race-nonsense and the opulence – can possibly be combined. She wants simultaneously to approve of the dark young face at her door, on grounds of decency, libertarian thought, and the warm respect due an Allied soldier, and at the same time disapprove strongly of the ridiculous amount the young man – who of course has yet to see any military action whatsoever - is earning. While her own child suffers abroad.

And her feet hurt. Agnes Henty ought to wear soft flat-soled shoes. Best of all would be trainers, give her poor old bunions some room. But it's 1945, and instead she forces her swollen feet into ancient stout-heeled leather pumps with buckles on the front, and every step pains, especially now, at the end of another long day.

"We're closed," she says sharply through the glass.

"Please," says the young man. "I won't keep you. It's just a message."

A message?

Warily Mrs Henty unlocks the door, allows him in, since it is, she now notices with some extra annoyance, raining.

"Beg pardon, ma'am," says the boy, taking off the funny little hat, and this soothes her, she doesn't get called Ma'am very often. There's nothing classy about Agnes Henty, and she knows it, and she doesn't care. But the occasional *Ma'am* still goes down nicely.

"Well? What is it?" she asks, with slightly more warmth.

"I was wondering, Ma'am, if you would kindly give someone a letter for me. I don't have her home address."

The warmth vanishes. Mrs Henty has heard a great deal about the sex-mad American soldiers, their unhesitating use of their absurdly inflated wages, their vile corrupting blandishments of nylons and perfume and cigarettes. And here was one of those very soldiers, apparently expecting her, Agnes Henty, to act as some kind of go-between for himself and one of her own workers - the bare-faced cheek of it!

"Certainly not," she begins to say, but he already has the envelope in his hand, and one glance down at it tells her who it is for. For an incredulous second her mind races through the roll call of her employees, looking for someone, anyone, else, who might by rights call herself Etta; finds no one.

Etta, Henrietta Maria, the saddest-looking little girl that Agnes Henty ever set eyes on, sitting ragged and verminous in the school assembly hall that long-ago night beside her equally-neglected baby sister, waiting for someone, anyone, to come and take them home. Every other child on the train had been found a place to go to, every child but them.

Now Etta, decently housed and fed and looked after properly these five years, given honest work – despite what the school had said about her, poor girl – now Etta was transformed, become someone able to seize on the fresh chance fate had dealt her, fate, that is, in the form of Agnes Henty herself, who all those years ago had thought of recently-widowed childless respectable Norah Gilder, and set the thing up, helped it work, made it happen.

Etta is Agnes' deep secret pleasure, her project, her pet. A job well done.

"What's in this letter?" she demands.

He looks startled. "It's – well, it's goodbye, I guess. We're moving out real fast, see, so I - "

"Goodbye to *what?*"

"Pardon me?"

"Let me get this straight," says Mrs Henty dangerously. "You saying you been *walking out* with Etta?"

"We - "

"Etta as works here? Etta Marshall?"

"Well, Ma'am, I - "

"You know old she is? *You dirty bastard!*"

Jem's mouth drops open in shock. For the moment he hears only the last thing she said.

"You miserable git!" says Agnes Henty.

"Now, wait a minute, Ma'am, I - "

"You get out my office right now!"

The contempt in her voice cuts right into Jem, opens some very old wounds, and a few more recent ones, and further abrades them. He takes a step back, sees her horrible yellowish face under the battered black toque, the jowls quivering, the hairs on her upper lip, snaggle teeth, a down-at-heel white woman calling him names. You dirty bastard.

"Get out, go on! Get lost!"

Frantic with anger and distress Jem looks about him, and some part of him, perhaps the part of his mind responsible for dreams, notices a small occasional table sitting beside the door holding a fair-sized pot plant. It has stumpy wrought iron legs and a heavy round top of pinkish marble. Without thought he raises one foot and gives it a shove, and at once with a spectacular crash it falls over sideways. The marble cracks in two, and the pot hits the tiled floor and explosively shatters; bits of earthenware and pot plant shoot across the floor almost as far as the counter.

It is the most violent thing Jem has ever done in his life, and he is almost as shocked by it as Agnes Henty is. After a second's paralysis he turns and makes a run for it out into the rain and away, while behind him after a very short pause Mrs Henty bobs out on her swollen feet to yell from the doorway, "I'll have the law on you, you dirty bastard! You get back here!"

In his mind's eye she is shaking her fist, like someone in a cartoon, and this is how he will for some time remember her, until at last that image fades and vanishes with the years. But he will go on dreaming about the occasional table and the pot plant for the rest of his life, especially when anxious or unwell. It was a Swiss Cheese plant, its deeply-cut leaves very similar in outline to the loops of stiffened ribbon decorating Mrs Henty's toque; a fact the waking man will never quite notice.

Meanwhile Jem keeps running, the letter still in his hand. The rain eases off, the streets fill, he has to dodge and weave his way past couples and threesomes arm-in-arm strung across the pavement, sorry, excuse me, thank you. Someone laughs as he dashes by, a voice calls after him, Husband come back early, did he?

He turns a corner and slows down, breathing hard. Normal sensible concerns come to mind at once: can she identify him? Did he introduce himself at all? He's almost certain she didn't give him time. Idiot, you idiot, he tells himself. He is ruined, he thinks. He will wind up not at college but in prison. How good it had felt, though, the stupid bandy metal legs, the huge crash, the skittering fragments! He has fought a little table and won, and thinking this he laughs out loud, doing a fast walk now, turning a corner, then another, understanding suddenly that he is lost. Well, it doesn't matter. Sure, it's a part of the town that he hasn't seen before, quiet, the shops all closed, but the place is tiny, he's bound to find his way before long.

He stuffs the letter into his pocket and sets off again, still grinning, making his way through the darkening streets. He has barely noticed a certain familiar smell of frying potatoes on the air, when stepping into the gutter to get past the queue at a telephone box when he sees something astounding.

Jem stops short, steps backwards, and hides in the nearby deep shop doorway, for coming towards him on the pavement he has glimpsed a girl who looks extraordinarily like Etta, as if she were Etta's little sister, a thin scruffy child with her hair in two braids, and carrying a worn straw shopping basket. From his hiding place he watches as the girl who looks like Etta walks right past him, with another even smaller girl who is hopping along beside her carrying a skipping rope.

"Not here, you berk," says the girl who looks like Etta, in Etta's voice, and he darts out to watch the two of them from behind as they turn the corner and disappear. Etta's walk. At last he understands that this is not resemblance, but the real thing. That was Etta herself walking past.

You know how old she is? asks outraged Mrs Henty in his head. You know how old she is, you dirty bastard?

His own memory answers him: with the lipstick kissed off, he remembers, she looks no more than fourteen.

At a short distance he follows the two girls easily enough. They turn another corner and the little one begins to turn her skipping rope on the pavement, her own braids bouncing. He is close enough now to hear the rise and fall of their voices, but not what they are saying. They come to a dark broad empty place and he realises that they have arrived at the market square again, at the far side from the George and Dragon. This time he remembers the rainy dispiriting Wednesday afternoon a few weeks back, when he and Albie had wandered between the stalls, looking for something, anything, that might be worth buying amongst the squalid junk set out for sale; it had been the first time he had understood that British people despite being white and in charge of an Empire could still be dirt-poor; that the bad teeth and old clothes weren't necessarily down to six years of war.

But there is Etta and the little girl – the *other* little girl, he bitterly corrects himself - disappearing into one of the tall old houses.

Jem leans against the unlit lampost just outside the house, and tries to think.

You know how old she is, you dirty bastard? Well, Ma'am, now you come to ask me, yes I do. I can guess. Or rather, he understands, he had known the moment he saw her in the street with her hair in braids. A hairstyle – that was all it had taken to fool him. That and a little warpaint, of course.

That was why he had hidden, why he hadn't just run joyfully over to her, shouting: "Hey Etta, slow down, it's me!" Briefly he tries replaying the scene that way in his head. What would she have said, done? What lies would she have told? And though her hair was very different, frizzy and blonde, hadn't the *other* little girl had an obvious look of Etta, a family look? Etta, who was all alone in the world, apart from that devout and domineering aunt, who stopped her going to pubs and parties and dances.

Jem heaved a great sigh. He had been so stupid, so gullible, he thought. Etta could not come to pubs and parties and dances because anyone with any sense would take one look at her and see that she was underage. He has been dallying with a child. Thinking unclean thoughts about her. Had very nearly sinned with he, lain with her in a field, known her.

It's 1945, and the word *paedophile* lies quietly dormant in dictionaries for most people, certainly for Jem, so it does not occur to him to apply it to himself, or to worry that anyone else might. He is deeply shocked at Etta, for telling him lies, and at himself, for believing her. Embarrassed, too. Where he comes from sex with fourteen-year-old girls is something only trashy types, of either race, go in for. With trashy fourteen-year-old girls, is the corollary. How easily though it might have happened! This, he now sees, is how young men can be ensnared. If they are at home, anyway. Though not, of course, if they are hopping out of town tomorrow, out of the country. Maybe out of this world.

He remembers the letter, the one he had tried to give to Mrs Henty, and thank God she hadn't let him! He had taken such guilty care with it, trying in the brief interval between being told they were moving out and catching the truck to town for that farewell visit, to do Etta justice, as the sweet but impossible girl who had so enchanted him. He had told her how much he thought about her every day, that he knew he would remember her always. That this was still to say Goodbye. That he was sorry.

Which was all true enough, but what a relief all the same, to end the thing so cleanly!

We're from different worlds, Etta. I don't think you realise how different they are. For a little while I stepped across the ocean and held your hand. But time's up now. Goodbye, Etta, and take good care of yourself. With love, Jem.

No address, of course. No town, no state. He's home free, as she is. Thank God they never -

Unconsciously shaking his head at his narrow escape, Jem gets up, and as he walks back across the square towards the George and Dragon where his friends are gathered, takes the letter out of his inside pocket, tears it into several strips, and as he passes a dustbin stuffs them deep inside.

Unbuttoning his jacket in the attic room Barty was startled for a moment by the strange noise of crackling paper coming from his own chest. Christ, really going dotty; how could he have forgotten his mother's stories so fast?

He sat down on the small sag of the camp bed, the envelope in his hand.

"I was saving it for when you were grown up," his father had said. "But then I saw you were."

He had not dared to read the the stories for years. They were all he had of her, all handwritten, so that he knew she had touched every page, every line, every single word: they were precious in themselves, as objects.

But of course there was more to it than that, the stories were fiction, they were early attempts at fiction; perhaps not even a diary could be more revealing of her self. And some of the revelations might not be true, might not reflect her reality at all. The writing would hold some version of her, and he had nothing else to go on, no countering memories of his own. He was afraid of how much he would suffer. If the work was admirable, there would perhaps be even more pain in the loss of her gift. If the writing was shallow, banal, there would be a different sort of added pain, an unendurable tenderness, and pity.

I'll never be grown up enough, dad, thought Barty now. Though he had in fact read all the stories at once, and for the first time, the day the RAF acceptance letter had come, and he had been seized suddenly with the idea that he was not after all likely to live much longer than his mother had.

But here he was after all, the war as good as over, alive and kicking. More or less. He slid the stories out of the envelope now, and laid them gently on the bed beside him. Hallo again, mother.

"She was good, wasn't she," was all he had said to Joe at the station in 1938, as the London train drew in, the day after he had first read the stories, the day he left home for good. "If she'd lived - she'd have been really, really good." If I hadn't come along and killed her, he did not add,

146

though he thought it all the same. Timing it so there was no chance for Joe to reply, except with a moment's bewilderment – who are you talking about? And then his startled nod.

For a long time *The Giant*, the first story, had been his favourite. It was so clearly autobiographical, perhaps even a memoir, though there was no way to find out; it was about a little girl going to a fair, and meeting the giant, the professional freak, and sharing an exquisitely uncomfortable moment of understanding with him, for the little girl, unlike everyone else she knows, is brown. The second was about identical twin girls, who play a special game together, called Mirrors; to make other children laugh they sit opposite each other and pretend to be one another's image; they are very good at making exactly the same movements, being an old lady putting her hair in curl papers, blowing her nose, plucking the bristles out of her chin; it's all rather jolly until when they grow older one of them gets a job in service and goes away, and the lone twin left behind has only her real reflection in a mirror to talk to, to pretend to.

That one had been acutely painful to read, for Barty knew Grace had taken the idea from life, from her adopted mothers Bea and Violet, his own dear twin Nannas. He had seen them play that game himself, though he had never found it funny, rather the reverse: almost alarming. But writing about it was the clearest shared statement his mother could possibly have made, and the fact that she had not planned to make it to him, that she had just written it anyway, without reference to him, long before he was born, and simply to please herself, was painfully, wonderfully, like meeting her at last, meeting her and finding her lovable, for the story was tender, and affectionate, and funny.

The oddest story, Barty thought, was also the longest, and the last Grace had finished. It was called *Vanishing Act*, and it was about a boy with his own name, a little brown eighteenth-century boy called Barty Small. At the beginning of the story he was eight years old, and a servant, or pet, acquired from the West Indies by a wealthy English household. The great house where he runs errands and sits now and then on his mistress's lap to be caressed and made much of was recognisably a picture of Wootton Hall, just a few miles away along the coast, which disconcerted Barty Gilder almost as much as the use of his own Christian name. Clearly it had been a name his mother just liked, he had thought; and then had to put the typescript down for a while, unable to read further.

Later Barty Small, soon growing too big to be a lady's little brown pet, steals away one dark night, runs all the way through an eighteenth-century Silkhampton to the sea down at at a small dirty non-artist-thronged version of Porthkerris, where he talks his way on board a fishing boat, progressing thereafter by slow degrees into the Merchant and then the Royal Navy, serving under Nelson himself in HMS Captain at the Battle of Cape St Vincent; coming home to Silkhampton at the age of thirty-five with prize money to invest in the coaching business, and in other local property. He is strong and clever and hard-working, and soon marries a decent local girl. Time passes. His children have children. And in the space of barely a hundred years, Barty Small has vanished as if he had never been. One of his Edwardian descendants, little Rosalinda Small, looks askance at Grace Dimond in the school playground, tosses her blonde ringlets, and tells her with distaste that she is a darkie.

Barty Gilder sits on the twanging camp bed in Norah's attic, reading *Vanishing Act* through again. The story now seems full of messages, and for him alone. He remembers something, and quickly flips through the written pages, peers into the empty envelope, and there it is, the little slip of paper torn from a book, with a pencilled scribble on it, not his mother's best handwriting like the stories, but in her everyday ordinary hand. It is a furious acceptance of the realities of her life, a declaration, a boast:

I am the Silkhampton darkie.

"Spanish, are you? Italian?"

What has Barty said, idly questioned thus?

He has shrugged, letting his shoulders say, *Yeah, something like that.* Because he's just wanted the fastest end to such questioning in the first place. But now he sees that he has been complicit. He has been helping his mother Grace to disappear.

A sudden hard knock on the door makes him jump.

"We're back. You coming down?" It's Egg, bringing an almost palpable smell of fish and chips with her up the stairs.

"Just a sec," he says. His hands are shaking too much for him to put the stories back in their envelope, he has to abandon the attempt, and instead hides them under the bed, then smokes a cigarette out of the attic window until he's fairly sure he no longer looks as if he's been crying.

Afterwards he got the boiler going for them and set off. He felt much better for eating, except that every now and then he found himself troubled by the idea that he wasn't really in Silkhampton at all, but lying on his prison bunk in Germany imagining the whole thing, even the pickled onion, a game his mind seemed to have started playing all by itself.

It was nearly nine by then and the streets were packed with airmen and soldiers, different uniforms, some of them American, he realised, in fact, overflowing the pavements, spilling out onto the streets, clustered shouting and laughing round every pub doorway. He had to push past several to get into the George, it was standing-room only in the bar, he couldn't stick this, he was thinking, when over the smoky tumult of voices and someone pounding on the piano he heard his own name called:

"Barty, over here, mate!"

Bill James just visible in the corner nook, two full pint mugs on the little table there.

"Bloody hell," said Barty, as he sat down. "Where they all come from?"

"The Yanks? Wooton."

"You mean Wootton Hall?"

"Since '43."

"Wooton's an American army camp?" said Barty again. The idea seemed impossible. He thought of the American army camp just behind the lines in Germany. He and the Butterfield and the others had been loaded into a truck, driven there at breakneck speeds, and tipped at once into a bewildering luxury of hot meals, hot water, cigarettes, soap, elastoplast, clean dry socks, a bed to sleep in, friendly strangers. Want some more coffee, sir? Eggs over easy, or sunny-side up?

Could that sort of lavish plenty exist at Wooton Hall, so grand and so bleak, perched high on the windy cliff top overlooking the sea? Or was he just thinking now of his mother's eighteenth-century version in *Vanishing Act*? Barty took a long swig of his beer. Try to think straight, he told himself.

"Did you get to the police station?" Bill said.

"Yeah, but - " The police station had been under beery siege, the foyer crammed with harrassed auxiliary constables and shouting soldiery. "They wouldn't let me see her," Barty said. "She doesn't even know I'm back."

"Someone might have told her."

"You think so?"

"Don't think you ain't been clocked." As if to prove Bill's point someone came over just then, pushing through the crowd, and carefully set two more pints down on the table.

Barty looked up, saw the landlord. "What's this?"

"You Barty Gilder?"

"Yes."

"Your money's no good here, my lad," said the landlord, giving him a level stare, which did not feel particularly friendly; for the first time Barty understood that other people, especially other men, might sometimes have rather mixed feelings about coming across one of the Few.

"Thanks very much."

"You're welcome," said the landlord, with a nod, then slowly made his way back behind the bar.

"Enjoy it while it lasts," said Bill. He'd noticed all of it; he'd always been sharp, thought Barty.

"So," Bill said, after a while. "What you going to do?"

"Make a stink, first off," said Barty. "Get her a solicitor. I can't imagine why they're holding her in the first place, she's hardly a danger to the public."

"Public might be a bit of a danger to her."

"What d'you mean?"

"You know what people are like. Say anything. Believe anything."

Norah, imprisoned somewhere deep in the police station, perhaps in some underground cell, where she could hear some of the drunken racket in the foyer, the shouting and swearing. Was she safe in there, really?

"She's innocent," said Barty, but as he picked up the glass he knew that he was in fact lying wakeful on his bunk in the prison camp, imagining all this. The illusion was so swift, so complete, that it took him a second to persuade himself that he was really sitting in a noisy crowded pub back home with a pint of beer in his hand.

The second of confusion was frightening; while it lasted neither reality felt true.

After a little while he could listen again, and soon realised Bill was in the middle of some story. Anxiously he looked into Bill's face for clues, trying to guess whether the end was going to be funny or not. But somehow it was at this point he noticed something astonishing, and interrupted:

"Hey – the Americans. Are they *all* coloured?"

For all the American soldiers crowded three-deep round the bar, talking and laughing and some of them singing, were brown. There were British soldiers, British airmen, clearly one or two Poles, but all the American soldiers were brown.

"They are tonight," said Bill. The camp at Wootton was a double one, he said. They liked to keep things separate, did the Yanks. So one end White, one end Black. Different nights out.

"Why?"

Bill shrugged. "You heard the joke? *We love the American soldiers, they're all such gents. So friendly, so polite, so well-behaved. Pity about the White ones they brought with them.*"

Barty smiled tightly, no, he had not heard that joke.

"Right bumptious bastards, some of them. The whites ones, anyway. Takes all sorts, of course. But some of them don't half carry on, boasting, going on and on about bathrooms. Sneering, you know. British plumbing not up to standard, apparently. Well behind in the bathroom stakes. But the coloured ones aren't like that at all. S'funny – they're more like us, really. You know, like English people. Not so full of themselves. Not so flaming *loud.*"

"Oh?"

They are of different shades, Barty noticed. Some as light as he is himself. Most darker. A thought strikes him.

"They welcome everywhere?"

"'Course they are," said Bill, indignantly. "We're not like that, are we? I mean, what's the war about?"

We don't serve your sort, said the barman in the Railway Tavern, but of course Barty had not then understood that, perhaps for the first time in his life, he had been correctly identified. "Spanish, are you? Greek?" Not this time. The War has educated the barman of the Railway Tavern, thought Barty.

"You remember what you said me at school, that first day?" he said.

Bill shook his head, grinning. "I know we had a fight."

"You told me that my mother was a darkie." And I hadn't known what that meant, except that it was insulting.

"What?"

"Don't you remember?"

"No! Why would I say that?"

"It was true," said Barty. "She was. Coloured, I mean." He nodded towards the soldiers at the bar. "Like them."

"What? Nah," said Bill. "What you on about?"

"Don't you remember?"

"I remember getting a fat nose," said Bill.

Barty remembers his hand lying beside Bill's on the desk they had shared at school, his own always browner, except in summer when Bill's caught up. And the wedding photograph, of his father Joe all young and skinny, and his pretty little mother, a picture Barty had seen over and over again for years until at the age of ten or so he had suddenly noticed that the faces were different colours, and thought of Bill James' baffling long-ago playground taunt.

"Was she a darkie, dad?" he had asked.

Trying to get his dad to answer a straight question. Silence had been his armour, thought Barty.

"I never called her that. I never called her anything, lad," Joe had said at last, before suddenly deciding it was time to nip off to the pub.

"I'd know about it, wouldn't I?" said Bill now, "if she'd been like that lot. You know, coloured. I mean, everyone would know."

"She's been dead a long time," said Barty.

"People wouldn't forget a thing like that," said Bill.

You did, thought Barty. It had taken a hundred years for Barty Small to disappear; Grace had vanished much faster, and I have helped her do it. He went for a pee, and when he got back there was another free pint on the table.

"Gotta go," he said, after it, because suddenly he could hardly keep his eyes open. Outside the fresh air made him stagger. The streets were still more crowded than he had ever seen them before, though the Americans were already disappearing, military Cinderellas well before midnight, climbing into a series of waiting lorries; one roared away in front of them as they crossed the road, young men waving out at the back.

"Talk is they're off," said Bill, amiably waving back. "Leaving Wootton, the lot of them."

"What? When?" Barty watched the lorry disappear into the darkness. They were leaving? It gave him a great pang at his heart to think that he had largely missed them, all these young men who had looked like him. Like his mother.

I am the Silkhampton darkie, she had written. She had been the only one, and then she was gone, vanished. Forgotten by nearly everyone who had known her. Now all these last few years the streets of her adoptive home town had been thronged with people like her, and she had not been there to see it! I wasn't there to see it either, thought Barty. Except the once. Just one night only, in the George and Dragon, mother, we were all there, in company.

"Alright, mate?"

"Pissed," said Barty. "Night, Bill."

Norah's house in darkness. He fumbled for some time with the key, then couldn't get the front door to close properly, and got into more difficulties on the stairs, which seemed more narrow and twisting than he remembered. At last he reached the attic and fell onto one of the camp beds, which turned as he closed his eyes into his own familiar bunk in Germany. It was all he could do not to reach up and to touch the upper bunk over his head. He knew it was there, though. Butterfield asleep in it. The other men breathing, breathing, the stove ticking as it cooled. For a minute or so more he lay wake trying to catch these familiar sounds, and then he slept.

The last baby in the cohort caused no end of trouble; poor little beast no doubt beginning as it meant to go on, said Dr Broughton later. The case was Lockheart's, the mother the young woman whose fiance was somewhere in France. Everything went very nicely, especially considering how late the baby was. Lockheart was perfectly relaxed as delivery drew near. Longitudinal lie, LOA, heartbeat steady, spontaneous rupture of membranes, clear liquor, a steadily progressing second stage – nothing to ring any alarm bells at all.

And yet.

And yet the baby, descending, slowly revolving through those tight curving passages with what looked like text-book precision, came into the world cyanosed, oxygen-starved, bluish-white with death.

Dr Broughton listened to the baby's little chicken chest.

"Was there meconium?"

"None, doctor."

"Hmm. What's the matter with you, little fellow?" Edina asked the baby, and to the girl in the bed said: "Baby seems absolutely fine!" whereupon the silly chit at once began to sob aloud with relief, making a real exhibition of herself, thought Lockheart disgustedly; if they had been alone she would have sharply told the girl to lay off, but as it was she merely gave her a hard quelling look, which worked almost as well.

"Ah, here's the clue," Dr Broughton went on cheerily. She had turned the baby over, and as she spoke, shifted the little bottom over towards Lockheart. "See this?" It was sticky with vernix; the doctor gave it another swift wipe with the blanket, and Lockheart saw that spreading over the buttocks was what looked like a dark purplish bruise.

"Mongolian blue spot!" said Lockheart later to Amy in the nursery. "Wasn't cyanosed at all - just mixed blood, see."

"Why ain't he brown, then?" said Amy, wrapping the new baby up again.

"He will be. It just hasn't started yet," said Lockheart grimly.

"Is she keeping him?"

"That's what I said. You wouldn't believe the look she gave me."

Post-natal ward tranquility faded with dissent.

One camp said: Carrying your young man's child out of wedlock was perfectly reasonable, given the times, but some lines simply should not be crossed. Camp Disapproval felt that it had been deceived: the mother had seemed a perfectly nice girl just like everyone else, but look what she had done, look what she had been, all this time, and never a hint dropped! And as for the baby, poor little thing, what sort of life was it going to have? Neither side would want it.

Camp Laissez-faire was more diffuse. It said, Love was Love. It said, What happened to all men being equal, then? Hadn't we just fought a war against Fascism? It said, She *is* a perfectly nice girl, leave her alone.

Both camps understood though that while the stain of bastardy was easy enough to hide - a Christmas cracker wedding ring would do at a pinch – mothering a brown baby would for the rest of your life tell the world who you had slept with, and those who hated that sort of thing would hate you. Hate your child. A lifetime of those looks. Those looks, and maybe actions. Imagine!

Bronia Salway, who had spent the last two years pretending not to be Jewish, said nothing at all. She knew there was danger everywhere. She pretended to be asleep again.

"There's talk of special homes, apparently," says Lockheart, sipping a consolatory cup of tea in the kitchen.

"What you mean?" asks Mrs Hawes. She's enjoying the scandal tremendously, though she thinks she is disgusted by it.

"For all the brown babies," says Lockheart. "Nobody wants them."

"Maybe it won't matter, in America," says Mrs Hawes.

Lockheart scoffs. "They won't let her go to America!"

"Ain't she a GI bride, then?"

"You can't be a GI bride for a black man," says Lockheart, scornfully. "It's not allowed."

"Oh," says Mrs Hawes.

On the top floor attic rooms this Friday evening there is a certain amount of dilatory packing going on. The three landgirls' time is up; they are officially standing down, as of the following month. Two of them are engaged to married. They chat about wedding plans as they sort out what items might be worth taking home again, which are best left for the rag-and-bone man. The old maidservants' rooms are alive with happiness and anticipation; perhaps they have never before held such fervour. Peace is nearly arrived, and it will last forever.

All three young women think of it as something they have helped to win themselves.

"Looked at me bold as brass," Lockheart tells Amy the nursery nurse. "I said to her, I said, You got no idea what you're up against, my girl. I'm sorry for you, I said. And I am. I am sorry for her." Lockheart's tone is far from sorry, but like most unconfident people Amy fails to trust her own senses; is ready to believe the words, and discount the tone.

"He's a lovely little thing," she says mildly, placating the tone all the same.

Lockheart sniffs: "They all look nice to start with," she says.

A small troupe of new mothers hesitantly approach the bed. There is a certain anxiety in the air, a social embarrassment; for all of them this is an unprecedented situation, slightly unnerving for everyone, whether they belong to Camp Disapproval or Camp Laissez-faire.

"Sally?"

"What?" Defensive.

"We just – well, we all just wanted to see how you are. And the baby. I mean, congratulations."

A flutter of mingled collective agreement.

Sally still on guard, non-commital. "You've heard then, have you?"

"We don't care. We're on your side," says someone from Laissez-faire.

"Can we see him?"

Eyes are soft, voices gentle.

A pause.

"Oh, isn't he lovely!"

"He's beautiful."

"Has he got a name yet?"

"Aren't you gorgeous, hallo, little man!"

Someone from Camp Disapproval waits until this sort of thing has died down before getting on with the question she knows everyone else is too soppy to ask: "So...are you keeping him, then?"

Packing nearly organised, the land girls toast one another with a little end-of-an-epoch Friday evening gin. The work has been so hard. They have carried out farm-labouring tasks that in less than a decade will be done by heavy machinery, they have climbed up high ladders lashed to lower ladders, they have driven tractors at night wearing torches, they have hammered in fence posts, built hay ricks and tied them down beneath massive tarpaulins, they have exhaustingly dug and weeded and hoed and harvested in good weather, in chill, in rain. None of them ever wants to see the rough end of a spade again.

"I suppose I might consider a very small window-box," says Julia. "Eventually."

"Perhaps a pot plant?" Tillie asks. "Just the one aspidistra?"

The youngest one, Phyllis, is pretending she's sorry it's all stopping before she fairly got going. But really she can't wait to get back home. None of them can wait, not really.

Which is a shame. For all of them, even Phyllis, the time they spent working all hours will one day come to seem the most important, the most fruitful, perhaps the richest period of their lives. They were young then, and full of laughter and friendship. They earned as much as the men for the same labour. They thought their lives would always be this free.

Right now, as their toothglasses clink together, each containing an inch of lightly-sugared gin, "Cheers!" - they imagine that they have other such comradely adventures still to come, that this was merely the first of many.

In fact responsibility of a private more isolated kind awaits them, wifedom, motherhood, housewifery. No one then will acknowledge their splendid strength, or tell them that they are feeding the nation. Advertising agents will tell them how to get their whites whiter than those of other women, their linoleum floors shinier, and for some of the time this will feel as if it is worth doing, and enough.

Friday nights

Egg's bed was still very damp when she got into it at bedtime, a nasty surprise as she had forgotten all about last night's misfortune.

For a while, that morning, she had wondered about the heavy rubber liner Aunt Norah used to put on her bed when she was little, but she had no idea where it was kept now, or whether if she found it she would be able to put it on the bed all by herself anyway. She had often helped make the beds, Aunt Norah on one side of the bed, herself on the other, in a practised ritual of spreading and tucking, the blankets pulled smooth and folded over one by one. But she'd never tried it on her own. Then the strange man had come, and she had forgotten all about the wet, until it was too late.

The outside edge wasn't too bad, she thought, but it was too narrow to lie in completely and the damp bit in the middle was very cold. It took her a long time to get to sleep, especially as the man had gone away again and she wasn't sure whether she wanted him to come back or not, either way was worrying.

After a time she woke up in the dark, sopping wet this time, and colder and colder while she lay there trying not to wake up fully, trying to hold off remembering that Aunt Norah wasn't there, and maybe never would be again, until trying got too much for her and there was nothing to do but risk Etta.

She opens Etta's door, and there is Etta sitting up in bed with the light on, doing one of her pictures.

"Bloody hell," says Etta in disgust. Egg is too lost to answer, just stands there in the doorway taking wobbling breaths while Etta jumps out of bed, yanks open a drawer and takes out her own other nightie, roughly pulls Egg's cold clinging wet one over her head and drops it with a slap onto the lino.

"Put that one on, alright?"

Egg is still not able to say anything. She does as she is told. The nightdress is far too long for her. She has to hold it up in her fingers to go over to the bed. With her eyes she says, I get in?

Etta tuts. "Go on then," she says grudgingly.

Egg folds herself up as small as she can against Etta's warm side. The pencil goes on making soft noises on the page. Time passes. Her feet grow warm again. Her breathing slows. Presently she can speak again.

"That man come back?"

"What, Barty Gilder? Yeah."

The pencil softly scribbles, these are pleasant noises for Egg, reassuring.

"Is he Auntie Norah's son?"

"Sort of," says Etta. "He's RAF. Like Tom and Percy."

"Are *they* coming back?"

"No. Don't think so."

"But Auntie Norah is, isn't she?"

"'Course she is. Go to sleep, alright?"

Etta's stopped trying to sleep herself. It's not worth bothering. Now that the sexual act has stopped being impossible to imagine, it's become impossible to stop imagining it. Ever since this afternoon she has been entirely at the mercy of sudden great sweeps of reminiscent sensation, and of detailed longing.

Jem is longing. He's in her mind all the time, barely moving into the background even when she and Egg had come home to find the front door already unlocked, a fat alien kitbag dumped at the foot of the stairs, and a half-drunk cup of tea sitting still warm on the kitchen table.

"Pretty funny sneak thief!" she had whispered to Egg, almost ready to laugh. *Jem Jem* on her mind even while she was creeping up the stairs with the poker. Not that she had felt afraid. She had felt invulnerable. Capable of anything.

She finishes the drawing, another portrait of him, regards it, turns the page, starts another, but this time something happens to the pencil, something she's met with before, and instead of Jem she begins to draw someone she has hardly thought of for years, it's long-lost Marjorie, real-Aunt Marjorie, in her good hat and her fox fur, she has raced up the turning stairs and flung herself breathlessly into the best seat on the bus, top deck above the driver.

The picture is a memory, perhaps of more than one day. She is smiling as she holds Egg, very small on her lap, they are off to Old Market for a bit of shopping. It takes Etta a little while to trace the origin of this sudden incursion.

Oh my head, says Aunt Marjorie. Bit of a party last night. Got any aspirin?

Etta cross-hatches Aunt Marjorie's hat and remembers with pleasant nostalgia the noise Barty Gilder had made, falling up the stairs when he came back from the pub.

Beside her Egg snuffles in her sleep. Etta turns the page, and has another go at capturing Jem's smile.

Norah on her narrow bunk in the dim detention cell lies awake a long time. She is barely aware of the noises above her, the shouting and arguing and singing, she's too busy wondering at herself, and at her own propensity for getting things completely wrong. Especially about herself.

"How are you all getting on these days?" Agnes Henty had asked her only the other week, at the WI, and Norah had shrugged a little and smiled and said lightly Oh too not bad, thanks.

She had thought that was true, at the time. That she had grown used to the burden of looking after the girls, got quite good at it too, at the overall arc as well as the details. That she had grown used to fitting everything else around them, accepted Egg's nightmares, Etta's sour moods, the frequent low-level antagonism between them, the occasional ferocious arguments. Used also to sitting with them both in the evening sometimes, all three of them listening to the play on the radio, Egg doing a jigsaw, Etta scribbling in her drawing book, herself knitting.

I have been such a fool, Norah told herself. How can I have reached this great age and still understand myself so little? I was actually proud of myself for making such a decent job of looking after someone else's children.

"How are you all getting on these days?"

"Oh, not too bad, thanks." Her tone amused. Detached.

But I am not making a decent job of looking after someone else's children, thought Norah now. They are not someone else's children; they are mine. And I love them with all my heart.

If I go to prison, what will happen to them? They will be alone in the world.

I'm not sure either of those kiddies can left in your care, under the circumstances.

Is it a bluff? All Thouless has to do is let the relevant authorities know. There are Children's Homes everywhere, for orphans, for the unwanted, the abandoned, the lost, thousands of them. It seems to Norah that taken to such a place Egg would collapse in on herself, perhaps forever. Etta too. In their different ways her girls are both so fragile.

If you take them away from me, Mr Thouless, my heart will break, yes, but that's not the important thing. I can hardly blame you for not understanding this, when I didn't understand it myself, but the punishment would be theirs, as well as mine. I'm not just me anymore. I am my children.

Saturday mornings

She knocks, and enters. "Sir?"

"What? You heard back from Dr Pascoe?" He's still hanging his coat up.

"Yes, sir. There's no record of a Miss Quick ever being attached to the practice."

"Well, that doesn't make sense. Unless Mrs Heyward got the name wrong. Or the job wrong."

"Yes, sir, so I thought – well, you have to be registered to work as a midwife. So I phoned the Central Midwives Board, see if they could trace her."

"I see. And could they?"

"Yes, sir. She's dead."

Dammit. "They sure?"

"Violet Quick, they had all her record. Three years ago, sir."

"Alright. Well done, Hendricks. Good work."

"Thank you, sir. There – there was something else, sir. About the case."

"What?" warily.

"I was looking at the photos again last night, sir. And it come to me that they've all got the same sort of - funny look. They're all making the same sort of face."

Thouless hesitates. Of course the poor kid's a virgin, he tells himself. This is exactly the sort of nonsense you get into when you let females into the force. Obviously the women in the dirty pictures are meant to be indicating sexual pleasure, even imminent climax. But poor stolid little Hendricks knows nothing about any of that, and most probably never will. He should at least try to be kind, he tells himself.

"I think the idea is meant to be – that they're happy," he says at last. "About what they're doing. See?"

"Yes, sir. But I thought – suppose that wasn't just something he was *telling* them to do. Suppose there was more to it."

"Like what?"

She plumps herself down in the chair opposite him and leans forward. "Dolly Wainwright had taken veronal some time before she died. Enough to make her drowsy at some point, the inquest said. And I thought – well, she looks a bit funny in the picture. As if she'd taken something then too."

"You mean veronal?"

"Well, as if she'd taken *something*, sir. Drowsy-like."

"You got it there?"

"Yes, sir. I got all of 'em. Here. This is Miss Wainwright. Her eyes. See, I thought – maybe she's not just pretending to be all swoony. Maybe she really *was*."

He looks at the soft yielding face in its frame of paper. Could it be true?

"May Tranter," says Hendricks. "The prostitute. Here she is."

He takes the photograph from her, sees more faked abandonment.

"She was found dead in bed, sir. Unexpected. October, '31."

"I know. It wasn't that unexpected," he says. "She had heart-trouble."

"Yes, sir."

"She died of a heart attack." Rheumatic fever in childhood, he remembered; he had seen the coroner's report himself.

"Yes, sir. But I wondered. If anyone would have looked very hard for veronal, sir. Or anything else. When they already knew she had heart disease."

And was a known whore besides, he thought. Good point, Hendricks. "Common enough drug," he said aloud.

"Yes, sir. I know."

"You reckon it might be part of his MO, do you?"

"Sir?"

"*Modus Operandi*, WPC Hendricks. His way of doing things. Dr Heyward's MO."

"Well – maybe, sir. I mean, I know it don't make much sense."

But perhaps it made sense, thinks Thouless, to whoever it was who had sent the photographs in the first place. Why else include May Tranter, if not to prompt exactly this sort of speculation? Though as it turned out only Hendricks had done any speculating.

He stands up. "Come on then. Get your coat," he says. "We got another visit to pay. Who we going to see, WPC Hendricks?"

She was straight off the bat: "Mrs Heyward, sir?"

It's odd, being impressed with Hendricks. Uncomfortable. "Not as green as you're cabbage-looking, are you?"

"I hope not, sir," says Hendricks.

Etta had slept a little towards morning, and woke feeling tremendous, alight with life and excitement. *Jem Jem* was her first thought. Jem.

Staying in bed any longer was out of the question. She got up slowly, so as not to wake Egg, still out for the count, and would be for hours, knowing her. Lightly Etta dressed, picked up everything she needed, and made her way out into the back garden, greeted the hens and let them out into their run, then quietly opened the garden gate and stepped out into the back lane.

She had had a thought about where to go on this particular golden morning. He would not of course be there, not on a Saturday morning, but she could still stand near the flat white rock where she had first met *Jem, Jem,* and try once more to catch the light on the next rising flank of the cliff, its changing colours, greens and purples and yellow gorse flowers, the flank's long lightly curving promontory, the sea turquoise below it, and edged with creamy foam. She could almost see the picture as she hurried as fast as she could along the familiar field paths, over the stiles, and on towards the sea.

On the way back to the station this time he was silent, until they were passing the Little Owl Tearooms, and a strong smell of toast.

"Don't know about you, but I need a cup of tea," he said.

Hendricks glowed within at this unbending.

Stupid, stupid women, he was thinking, as they sat down at a table in the corner. Why say yes to that? Why say yes to being drugged up to the eyeballs, so that someone could take photographs of you all naked and twisted about? Why choose to believe that someone, when he said it was out of kindness?

"It made it easier for me, Mr Thouless," Mrs Heyward had said. Looked him in the eye, and come out with that, in front of Hendricks! It was enough to make you sick. "I had to stay very still for a long time, in a rather – awkward position. For the camera. It was sometimes rather a lengthy exposure, you see. That's why."

Oh, Mrs Heyward, educated woman – aren't you? Why take that on trust, from the man who had promised to cherish you?

"Did you use any other drugs on you? Making it easier for you?"

"Well – of course, as a doctor he had access to several methods of sedation."

"You mean anaesthesia? He put you to sleep?" Dear God!

"No, not really. Well, almost. Once or twice. Yes."

Taking whatever he gave you, no doubt telling yourself it was still somehow love. When really it had all been about power, and making someone else powerless. The photographs weren't the point, weren't the main point at all, thought Thouless. They were just a record, of the times when Heyward had been in complete control. It had been power he wanted.

Putting himself in Heyward's shoes made him feel queasy. "I hate this case," he said aloud, rather surprising himself. The waitress brought their tea, and he told himself to get a grip. "So, WPC Hendricks. What's our next move?"

"I don't know, sir."

"Miss Wainwright's inquest. You read it?"

"Yes, sir."

"So. What am I thinking about? Right now."

"Her chemise?"

"Good girl; yes. Her chemise, noted to be on inside out. Sunday best, but her underwear inside out. What are we thinking about that?"

"The inquest said she got dressed in a hurry. Or she was a bit woozy, from the veronal."

"And what do we think now?"

"Someone else dressed her, sir. Well: he dressed her."

"Yes. I think so."

"She was unconscious."

"Already dead, probably. Gave her something that stopped her breathing. Maybe not on purpose. It was just one of the risks he ran. She ran, I should say."

"So - maybe May Tranter as well. With his – what you said."

"MO. Yes."

"Maybe even others, sir. That we don't know about."

"Let's work with what we've got, shall we? We think he brought about the death of Dorothy Wainwright, and got away with it, by making it look like suicide."

Hendricks stared, put her stubby hand to her mouth, whispered: "Oh my Lord - he threw her body off the cliff!"

"I think so. Look, you know this area. Could he have driven it? Those cliffs?"

"There's field tracks," she said, after some thought. "Risky, though."

"He was a war hero, I'm told. In the last lot. Parachuted behind enemy lines. I think he maybe went in for risk."

"Yes, sir."

"And it's his death we're looking into. No one else's, not right now. And we know that just before he disappeared – died - his wife – who should have known, she had plenty of practice - she thought he was seeing someone else. We know it couldn't be Miss Wainwright, she was dead already. So who was it?"

"Maybe Miss Quick."

"That's what his wife thought. The mysterious Miss Quick, deceased. A trained midwife, who never worked for Dr Heyward or Dr Pascoe. So who did she work for, what was she doing?"

"People might remember, sir: locals. And that other midwife, the one at the inquest, who lived with Miss Wainwright. She might know. "

"Sister Nesbit. Yes, very good, WPC Hendricks. I think she might."

Nesbit was already having a difficult morning. Almost all the current post-natal patients were due to leave that day, the bus to the station booked for the early afternoon, and as usual nearly everyone seemed to have some different individual problem to add to the general anxieties of packing for two for the first time, and for managing onward travel with a suitcase in one hand and a baby in the other: they had mislaid vital documents, forgotten their mother's telephone number, lost their left shoe, their door keys, their hairbrush.

It was as if for an hour or so they were all girls again, giddy schoolgirls at the end of term, laughing and singing little snatches of song, signing one another's autograph books with mildly risque verses and grave quotations, swopping addresses and sometimes tearful vows of lifelong friendship to come. Essentially they all needed attention; some of them needed actual nursing care, a wound re-dressed, another post-natal check, a baby with a sticky eye or a sudden outbreak of spots; yet it was on this morning, of all mornings, that Edina had for no discernible reason (thought Nesbit furiously) decided to visit the kitchen without warning just after breakfast had been cleared away, in perfect time to catch Mrs Hawes in the very act of sliding an enormous tin of pork luncheon meat into what was unquestionably her own private shopping bag.

Which was all very well and good, of course, but instead of giving the wretched woman a fierce ticking-off or a final warning Edina had sacked her on the spot.

Hearing of this disaster Nesbit had raced to Edina's office. "Who is Matron here, me or you?" she had demanded. "This sort of thing is *entirely* up to me. The wretched woman was just starting lunch for all of us - more than twenty people!"

Edina looked away mulishly.

"Are you going to do it?" shouted Nesbit, quickly calming down, however, as the idea of Eddie in an apron busily setting-to in a kitchen was so entertaining. "Heaven knows I don't like her either, but I don't know how we can replace her."

"We don't need to," said Edina.

"What? What d'you mean?"

"We don't need a cook any more. We may not need anyone anymore."

"Eddie – what are you talking about?"

"We're being closed down," said Edina.

"I don't understand. You mean, we're closing as a Lying-In hospital? Well, that makes sense, people won't need to leave the cities the way they..."

"No. Not just that. Here. Read this. This morning's post."

Nesbit scanned the several closely-typed pages. It was from the Ministry of Health, yet another lengthy screed about the coming post-war Health Service, and Rosevear Hospital's possible future within it.

"Keep going," said Edina, watching her. "It's in the last paragraph."

"Ah," said Nesbit, after a pause. She looked up. "I'm not sure I understand."

"Well, it's written in purest civil servant," Edina agreed. "But essentially it means they are not going to take us on at all. Rosevear, I mean. The new Health Service."

"You mean, close us down completely?"

"Looks that way."

"It's a mistake, it must be."

"Well, they can't accept every cottage hospital."

"But we're always so busy - where are people supposed to go, then?"

Edina shrugged. "Elsewhere. You seen the bit where I'm invited to apply for the Interim Management Panel?"

"What does - "

"Not *re-apply*, you notice. *Apply*. The last five years counting for nothing, it seems."

Nesbit looked at her. "I can't believe it. I'm so sorry - you *built* this place!"

Edina gave her a sad smile. "Not on my own."

"No, it was you, it was all you!" said Nesbit.

"Well, thank you kindly," said Edina, "but we both know none of that counts when the chaps are coming home."

"Oh, no, surely - "

"I was just good in a crisis, you see. I was wartime exigency. Time to sweep all that away now. Time for me to curtsey and withdraw." Sighing Edina sat down, pushed her chair back, and put her feet up on her desk. "You ever wonder why I keep this picture on my desk?" With the toe of her shoe she nudged the Nativity scene in its golden frame. "When I have not the slightest jot of religious feeling?"

"I thought you just liked it," said Nesbit.

"I do like it. Take a closer look. It's Late Medieval."

"I - "

"Please."

Nesbit picked up the picture. It was every Christmas carol, the angels singing overhead where the guiding star glowed in the dark blue sky, the shepherds with their crooks, the oxen and asses, three tiny wise men on camels toiling up a hill in the starlit distance, and enclosed in the glowing centre Joseph, neatly bearded, the blonde young Virgin all elongated ovals in her blue and white robes, and in her arms the golden child. She was lifting Him out of the manger, which was lined with white cloth, the barest hint of clean flowery straw showing at the edges.

"It's very nice," said Nesbit, at a loss.

"Who are the two at the bottom?" said Edina.

"You mean the little ones?"

Two small figures knelt curled in one corner, one robed in red, the other in green, each wearing a white hat like a beret. The one in red was holding another tiny version of the glowing Baby, while the other poured water into a shallow basin on the ground.

"Shepherds?" said Nesbit.

Edina shook her head. "No, not shepherds."

"Angels, then."

"Where are their halos? No, they're not angels."

"Well, they're not the Wise Men," said Nesbit. Thinking: lunch for thirty, and no cook!

"No. They're not. And that's everybody accounted for, isn't it? Jesus, Mary, Joseph, shepherds, angels, kings, the lot. So who are they?"

"I give up," said Nesbit.

"I'll tell you then. Those two are the Virgin Mary's midwives."

"What?" Nesbit looked again at the two small figures at the bottom, kneeling or perhaps sitting very curled up. They certainly *could* be women, she thought. But -

"The Virgin Mary didn't have any midwives," she said.

"Oh yes she did," said Edina. "She used to, anyway. Their names were Salome and Zelomi. Or they were one person with two different spellings, and sort of turned into two people, because that's the way these things happen in oral history - spelling can make all the difference. Either way, Joseph puts his missis in the stable and rushes out for help, meets Salome or Zelomi or both of them, they hurry back to Mary but it's too late, the poor girl's delivered all by herself."

"Well – that happens a lot," said Nesbit.

"True. There's still a lot to do, of course. Midwifery – well, it really is the oldest profession. Not whoring. That old smear, typical bloody men, always thinking everything's to do with them and their unutterably boring sex-drive. No. Helping another woman with her baby, before and during and after, that is the first work that ever there was."

"But what about - "

"Sorry, sorry. Got distracted. No, my *point* is, that Zelomi and Salome - they or she - used to be part of every Nativity scene, picture, play, what have you, everyone knew about them, knew the stories about them - a touch bawdy, some of them; one of them won't believe in the Virginity – that's after the birth as well as before, you understand, Mary is a post-natal Virgin too - and does a quick vaginal to make sure, and her hand bursts into flames, or turns black and drops off, or something. Doubt punished, you see. Though the Baby Jesus kindly puts it right again, it's all a bit panto, I suppose. Anyway, some time in the fourteenth century or thereabouts some synod or Pope or something decided that on the whole it would be better if neither of these ghastly women messed up the sacred scenery at all, so they banished Salome and Zelomi altogether, banished them and vanished them, made them literally Apochryphal! So they weren't in the Nativity at all, not in the Bible, not Holy, and what's more, what's really important, my dearest, is this: what's really important is that for centuries now *they never have been*. Have you heard of them?"

"No."

Nesbit shook her head.

"You see? No one ever has. Once the Virgin's midwives were as familiar as the shepherds, but no one knows them now. That's why I keep the picture, Marion my love. We must all of us bear in mind, d'you see, how easy it is to pretend women play no part in anything important, to take us out of the story altogether."

"You don't think..." Nesbit hesitated. She had no real doubt that Edina was being by-passed because she was a woman; but she was also aware that over the last few years Eddie's gender had become harder to overlook, because she was also odd - brusque, overbearing, assertive; in a word, mannish. She was not just female, she was unfeminine. Not a man, but still too manly; the sort of person no decent Committee would choose. Especially if any member were to suspect her of sexual deviance.

Edina has not been discreet enough, thought Nesbit, anxiously. She has been too open. But there was no time to think about any of that really, there was far too much to do. There was still lunch, for a start.

"We must talk about this later, Eddie," she said, and then she hurried off to the kitchen, to see if there was enough bread and margarine for lots of small thin sandwiches. At least they would be able to put that beastly pork luncheon meat to good use, she told herself.

Falling asleep in a German prison camp, he woke in another country, that was clear, but which one? He had dreamt of a woman in a headscarf passing him a bag of bread rolls, which had surely happened somewhere, was a real memory from some half-ruined border town. He opened his eyes and her entreating gaze faded. There was a completely unfamiliar ceiling overhead. He studied it for a while. A crack from the window right over to that corner. Wallpaper peeling there, pinkish-beige with age. The sound of someone else sighing.

His heart gave a great heave of fright, and he sat up fast, making the little girl sitting on the other bed flinch and gasp.

"Oh!"

"Sorry," he said.

"Brung you a cup a tea." Eyes huge behind the glasses. Hair in very messy plaits.

He glanced sideways, and saw the cup and saucer beside him on the bedside table. "What time is it?"

She shook her head. "Dunno."

After a while he felt calm enough to consider the tea. His hand shook as he picked up the cup. He watched the quiver with a sort of interest, as if this were someone else's problem. The tea was still hot, and tasted odd but delicious.

"Got honey in it," said the girl, and he remembered her ridiculous name.

"Egg. Thankyou."

She swung her little legs, she had fawn ankle socks on, and shoes with buckles. She seemed entirely alien, from a different species, *child*. Already complete as she was.

"You going to get Auntie Norah now?"

He finished the tea. All the better for it, what they said about hot sweet tea was all true, part of his mind was cosily nattering, even as it occurred to him that the woman in his dream, the gazing intent headscarved woman who had given him a bag of bread rolls, had not been entirely a memory at all, because she had been his step-mother, Norah.

"I can't just - " he said, then stopped. Because it seemed to him suddenly that he knew exactly what to do, that in fact he had woken up knowing it. There were perhaps a few details that needed a little active thought. But on the whole the idea seemed watertight, and what had he got to lose? What had anyone else got to lose?

"Yes," he said. "I'm certainly going to try."

"Miss Nesbit, is it, I don't think we've met before, have we? My name's Thouless; this is Sergeant Davey. May we sit down, please?"

"Do. I hope this won't take long, Inspector. Most of our in-patients are leaving today - there are a thousand and one things to do."

"I'll try to be brief. Does the name Violet Quick mean anything to you?"

"Certainly. I used to know someone of that name, a midwife in Silkhampton. She's dead, I'm afraid. Died in a car crash. One those blackout things."

"She worked with you?"

"Yes, years ago. Before the war."

"D'you know exactly when?"

"'31, I think. I can look it up for you, if you like."

"What was she doing? She wasn't working as a midwife, was she?"

"No, she was mainly here to set up what we called a Mother's Clinic. That is, family planning: contraception, for women."

"Oh," said Thouless, disconcerted by this bluntness. He could not stop himself exchanging a quick embarrassed glance with Davey.

"That was what Miss Quick did," said Miss Nesbit. "She went from place to place, setting up clinics to help often very poor women who had otherwise no control whatsoever over their own fertility. Or their own lives, as a result. It was a political act. She was a feminist."

Davey blew his lips out in a startled little snigger. Privately Thouless was also surprised; to him feminism meant corsetted Edwardian suffragettes breaking windows to get the vote. Wasn't that battle long over?

"I see," he said. "How long was Miss Quick in Silkhampton, d'you think?"

"Six months or so. Something like that. She was training me to take over – I volunteered. Then she went elsewhere, that was how she operated."

"How much did she work with Dr Heyward?"

"Not much, as far as I know. Not once she was here. He was largely instrumental in her coming to Silkhampton in the first place, petitioned the council, arranged funding, that sort of thing. He was quite forward-looking in some ways."

"They get on well? As far as you know?"

"As far as I know, yes."

"You weren't particularly friendly, then, you and Miss Quick?"

"We got on well enough. We were allies."

"Against whom, Miss Nesbit?"

"The world in general." Something about the way she said this made it clear there might be more, if he waited. So he did, a long quiet beat or two, letting her decide. He heard her breathing change.

"And Dr Heyward, in particular," she said at last.

Ah. "In what way?" he asked gently.

"He was not a competent practitioner. Particularly with regard to childbirth."

Like many people Thouless wants to believe that doctors, all of them clever men subject to the same extensive training and discipline, are therefore more or less the same in practice, all as good as each other. "How d'you mean?" he asks, after a pause.

"In my opinion Dr Heyward was responsible for several avoidable maternal deaths."

"You mean – on purpose?"

"No, no. Not on purpose. By accident. Because he wasn't any good. Careless, impatient, rough. In childbirth all those things can be disastrous."

Again it takes Thouless a while to recover. "I see," he says at last. "You reported him, then?"

He notes that for the first time she appears a little discomposed as she shakes her head. "It's next to impossible to prove that sort of thing," she says, hiding something, he's sure of it. "He was popular with patients, and good-looking, he had charming manners when he chose. And he didn't just work in Silkhampton, he had private patients across half the county, and no one was keeping proper track, d'you see?"

Again he was silent, as if considering. Then he said: "Did you ever discuss him with Joe Gilder? You know who I mean?"

"Yes, but no, I hardly knew Mr Gilder. He came to see me once, shortly after I came to Silkhampton, that was in 1921, and told me that two other women had died in childbirth in the year or so since his own wife's death. He asked me if that was normal."

"Did he name Dr Heyward?"

"No. I said it was. Normal, I mean. That the deaths were bad luck, a coincidence."

"But later you changed your mind."

"Yes."

"Miss Quick agreed with you about Heyward, did she? Is that what you meant, when you said you were allies?"

"Yes. I suppose it is. We had got as far as discussing ways to proceed – legal ways, I mean, nothing remotely criminal - when he disappeared. It was jolly good riddance, as far as I was concerned."

"Do you know if Miss Quick ever came here?"

"What, to Rosevear? No idea. Sorry."

"One more thing. Is there anyone here now who was here in '31? When the old housekeeper was alive, Mrs Givens?"

Nesbit looked doubtful. "Mrs Givens is long dead," she said. "There's sometimes a very old man hanging about the place, used to be one of the gardeners. Sam Keverne - I think that's his name, I've never actually spoken to him. He was probably here."

"Old Sam?" This from Davey, again on the edge of laughter. "You won't get much out of him, sir. He ain't said a word all his life, he's a dummy, sir. Deaf mute."

"Well, that - makes sense," said Nesbit, apparently taken aback. "But there's Minnie too, of course. The maid-of-all-work. She's lived here more or less all her life – grew up here; I gather she was one of the children here, when it was an orphanage. I'm not sure she'll be able to tell you very much either, though."

"Oh? Why not?"

"Thruppence short of a shilling, sir," said Davey, grinning. "Sixpence, more like."

Outside the door, where she has been uncomfortably crouching for some time, Minnie slowly straightens up. She didn't like them talking about herself. Nor about Sam Keverne: he was her secret.

She'd known what he was up to in the airing cupboard all along, shifting things about bit by bit. It had been funny, suddenly opening the cupboard door on him the first time, finding him lying there tucked up all snug in bed with his Bible. But she had brought him a bit of hot dinner too, so he had not looked sad for long. It had become a good game, smuggling out enough to keep him happy right under Mrs Hawes' ever-twitching nose, not that old Sam ate much. But she could tell that he was always pleased to see her. It was a lot like having a dog, Minnie thought, only better.

It occurs to her that in fact there is a great deal she could tell the two policemen, if she wanted to. She could tell them not just about Sam living in the airing cupboard but all about the strangeness of her Ma, who was sometimes Bea and sometimes Violet, though she was always kind. She could tell them about the Beautiful Lady, who had once come to stay at Rosevear, and have her little baby there in secret, so that she could pretend later on to adopt him, a puzzle her Ma had told her she need not worry about, and so she hadn't.

She could tell them about the fruit cake they always had when Mr Pender came visiting, and about little Barty on his bicycle bringing the bread, and Miss Thornby and her friend Miss Quick, who had sometimes pretended to be called something else, though Minnie could not now remember what that had been.

She could tell them about that sunny morning when arriving early as usual, for in those days she had lived down in the village, she had seen Miss Thornby and Miss Quick at the front of the house, running along together in the staggery way you run when you can't hardly run no more, as if, she had thought straight away, they had both of them been down to the lake, and caught sight of the ghostly girl as drowned herself there in her nightie, a-standing in the reeds with her ankles in the water!

She could tell them all these things if she wanted to. But she she doesn't want to. I may be slow, thinks Minnie, but I know you don't tell the police nothing. Even if they think you are thruppence or sixpence short of a shilling. Especially if.

So when Matron and the two policemen come and find her in the kitchen she makes the face that best puts them off. It's a slack blank face, the one she often pulls to punish Mrs Hawes when she's in a bate. The tall one asks her about Miss Thornby coming, or Mr Pender, or Miss Quick, and she says nothing at all, just keeps the face going until the third or fourth time he says it, when she lets the tears slip out of her eyes. They are never far away. It's easy enough to let them fall.

"For heaven's sake," says Matron crossly, "that's enough!" And when the man tries to give her a little bit of white card with his name on it Matron takes it instead, but she doesn't tell them that Minnie cannot read, though of course that is true.

"Of course if Minnie does remember anything, she can let me know – can't you, Minnie - and I'll pass it directly on to you. Alright, Inspector?"

Then she looks down at the little white card in her hand and Minnie sees something at once happen to her face. Matron looked at the card and it said something to her that makes her sad, or frightened, and when she speaks her voice is different, hard and higher.

"Inspector Thouless, is it? That's how you spell it?"

Then there is one of those silences that often arrive when Minnie is talking to someone, or being talked at. But this silence is not hers. It is theirs, the tall thin policeman and Matron's.

Matron gives a pretend laugh, and she says, "Oh, I thought you spelt it - "and then she says some letters that Minnie cannot follow.

"No," says the tall policeman, "Not like that. Thouless, that's me."

"Spelling. Can make all the difference," says Matron, and her voice is like a stranger's.

Minnie doesn't like the choking way the air feels. "I go now?"

Matron nods, and Minnie sees with interest that her face is full of pain, stiff with it. She herself says nothing more, just gets herself to the door, opens it and escapes as fast as she can down the corridor.

"Bit peculiar," says Davey, as they make their way back to the car. "What was all that about spelling?"

"No idea," says Thouless. The whole place gives him the creeps, he thinks. And everyone in it.

As Davey unlocks the car there is a sudden crunching of gravel behind them, and the Matron appears again, breathing fast, as if she's run after them all the way from her office. She has his card still in her hand, he notices.

"Inspector - I ask you something?"

"What?"

"Just this: you've been investigating Dr Heyward's death for some time now. Haven't you?"

"Yes."

"What d'you think of him? I mean, have you formed any opinion about him? As a man?"

"Why?"

"Please. Tell me."

Wouldn't piss on that bastard if he was on fire, he thinks immediately, but that's none of her business. He is none of her business. "You said it yourself: I'm looking into his death," he says. "Not his life."

She stares at him for a moment longer, then nods. "Of course. Thank you, Inspector." And she turns, and crunches swiftly away again over the gravel.

Etta was sitting cross-legged on the wiry clifftop grass, intent on the board leaning at just the right angle against a tuft of heather.

Bees buzzed in the clover on the other side of the hedge, and once a small pale blue butterfly alighted first on top of the board and then, as if deciding on a closer look, on the hand that held the paintbrush. She raised her hand to her lips and gently blew it away.

Not bad, she thought, some time afterwards, and then was abruptly herself again, Etta full of new knowledge, more specific hopes, *Jem, Jem.*

With an effort she gave the painting a more considered look. In fact it was her best yet, she decided. She had almost caught the morning light on the flowery rise of the cliff, the narrow path cutting diagonally across it, the dark rocks at its edge, the cream and turquoise of the sea below, though it was nothing like as good as the picture she had thought of when she first woke up.

The narrow pointing headland was the place Jem loved best of all, he had once told her. This was where he went as often as he could, which was never often enough, to make his way right out along the rocky path there to the very tip, to gaze out at the clean sparkling expanse of the sea all around him, to breathe it in.

Remembering this Etta took up her finest brush, and after some thought, to get the scale just right, she painted him in, a delicate stroke or two, a tiny grey-blue figure in the misty distance, Jem walking along the headland towards his favourite place in all the world.

She sat back, looked again at her picture. Yes. It was almost worth keeping, she thought.

If I were a bird I would soar across, over the fall and rise, to feel the air change. The valley would be cooler.

Suddenly she was aware that she was very hungry, and wondered what time it was, and eventually whether she would be in any sort of trouble; she often was, when she did anything unplanned, and to please herself. But then she remembered with an odd lurch at her heart that there couldn't be any nagging, not without Mrs G.

She poured away her jar of dirty water, decided the picture was just about dry enough, and closed her book. As she rose to her feet she remembered the small blue butterfly that had alighted on her hand, the feel of its delicate feet, with a pang of regret, that she had not taken proper notice. It's not every day a butterfly mistakes you for a flower, she thought.

As soon as he was back in the office he broke the rules and called home then and there, but there was no reply. Out shopping, he told himself. With her mum. She's fine. All the same he let the ringing go on and on, picturing the empty rooms full of unanswered sound, until the desk sergeant came knocking, and he hung up fast.

"What is it?"

"Sorry to disturb you, sir, but there's someone here waiting to see you, says it's important. About the Heyward case."

"Oh yes, who?"

" Barty Gilder, sir. Joe's son. The fighter pilot. Shall I show him in?"

"Where's Hendricks, WPC Hendricks?"

"She's gone off duty, sir, I could - "

"Never mind. Just - show him in, will you?"

"Sir."

Thouless heard uneven footsteps approaching down the corridor, and sat down, straightening his tie.

"So, what can I do for you, Flight Lieutenant, is it, what do I call you, anyway?"

"Mr Gilder's fine," said Barty.

"Mr Gilder it is, then, take a seat," said Thouless. He was a nervy type, Barty thought. Prone to sudden outbursts, that was the feeling he had, seeing Thouless's worn stiff face and very neatly combed hair. You'd be wary of him sharing your hut.

"I'm here to give you some information. About the disappearance of Dr Philip Heyward," said Barty, his heartbeat quickening. It felt familiar, that sudden access of speed within. It felt enticing.

"Oh yes?" The pale face perked up straight away.

"The long and the short of it is, I know what happened. And I'm hoping that when I've told you, you'll let my step-mother go. She's totally innocent. Of anything, really."

Thouless sat very still. "And why would you know what happened?"

"I was there," said Barty.

Thouless looked at him.

"I was twelve," said Barty, answering the unasked question. "If you want to know who pushed the car into the water, it was me and my dad. We did it."

"You're confessing?"

"Only to that. We didn't kill him."

Thouless stood up abruptly, went to the door. Barty heard him: "Get Davey in here. Pronto."

"Would you be willing to make a statement to that effect, Mr Gilder?"

As he spoke the door opened, and it was Andy Davey, of all people.

"Barty, mate, long time no see!" said Davey, instantly red in the face. "How are you, heard you was back! What a time you've had, and no mistake! Sir," he said, turning to Thouless, "this here's one a the Few! Barty Gilder! Put it there, mate!" and he held out his hand, only noticing the atmosphere several seconds too late; he never had been that quick on the uptake, Barty thought.

"Nice to see you too, Andy. How's Janet?" he said, as they shook hands.

"Fine thanks," said Davy, sheepishly. He glanced at Thouless: "Erm, perhaps I shouldn't be - "

"Just sit down," said Thouless wearily. "And take notes, will you."

Under-manned, thought Barty. Of course they were.

"So then, Mr Gilder. You were saying. You were at Rosevear House on the night in question, that is, March 19th 1932. is that correct?"

Out of the corner of his eye Barty saw poor old Andy Davey look up, startled. Sorry, Andy: yes, I'm here about the murder of Dr Heyward.

"No," he said. "I wasn't there that night. I came the following morning. Very early."

"What were you doing there, Mr Gilder?"

"Delivering bread, to my grandmother Bea Givens, the housekeeper there."

"What time was this?"

"I'm not sure. It was light."

"Ok. Go on."

"I cycled. I saw the car, parked in front of the house. I knew it was the doctor's car."

"How?"

"There weren't many cars in town then. I was a kid, I liked them. I knew whose it was. I went on to the house. And there was a light on at the front."

"Was that unusual?"

"Yes. It had never been on before. The front of the house – by the main staircase – d'you know it?"

"Go on."

"So I looked in the window. And I saw Dr Heyward. There was a woman standing on the landing halfway up the stairs, and he was walking up towards her, and it looked as if they were having some kind of argument."

"You know who this woman was?"

"No."

"Could you describe her?"

"Not really. She was quite small. Dark hair, I think."

"Age, roughly?"

"Sorry."

"Ok. Go on."

"They argued, he went up the stairs, and when he got to the landing he hit her, really hard. He punched her in the stomach. She fell over, he got down and started strangling her."

"Oh? Strangling her how?"

"With his hands."

"You saw this?"

"Yes, yes, and then my grandmother - "

Strange how painful it was to think of all this. I have seen more terrible things since, Barty reminded himself. Done more terrible things.

"That's Beatrice Givens, is it? The housekeeper?"

"Yes. She came running out, he turned his head, he saw her, and she just – pushed him. As he was getting up. She pushed him as hard as she could. He was right at the edge of the stairs, and he fell. Stone steps. Marble floor."

"You saw him fall?"

"Yes. I couldn't get in, the front door was locked. So I ran to the side, got in at the kitchen door."

"And?"

"I ran back along the corridor. When I got to the stairs he was lying at the bottom. He was dead."

The thick dark blood beneath his head, in a slow spreading pool. His first body. How many since? There was no counting them, thought Barty.

"How did you know?"

"I was in the Scouts. I tried to take his pulse, at his wrist. But I couldn't feel anything. Then I - I put my ear to his chest. I knew he was dead. Then my grandmother came down. She was happy. She was glad he was dead. She'd always hated him, you see."

"Why was that, Mr Gilder?"

"Because of my mother, Violet's adopted daughter."

"Grace Dimond?"

"Yes. That was her." Grace Dimond, the Silkhampton darkie. "She died when I was born. Violet was sure she would have lived, if it had been the old doctor looking after her, not Dr Heyward. Violet was - not a midwife, but a *handywoman*. That's what she called herself. You know that term?"

"No."

"Her own mother trained her, she looked after women in childbirth all her life, before there were professionals, but she was good, you know, she was an expert. Violet thought Dr Heyward did something wrong. And – well. All I'm saying is, she knew what she was talking about."

"She thought Dr Heyward was a bad doctor?"

"She was certain of it, for women, anyway, for childbirth. Don't know about anything else.

Thouless was silent for a while. Barty could hear him breathing. "Did you see anyone else at Rosevear that morning?" he said at last.

Barty shook his head. "There was no one else."

"Why didn't you call the police?"

"Didn't think of it. Just went home, fast as I could."

"And how fast was that?"

Barty half-smiled. "I used to race myself, most days. I was probably back before eight in the morning."

"So who did you talk to?"

"My dad, of course. I told him - " Barty broke off suddenly.

"Told him what?"

For the first time Davey put down his pen, leaned forward, and spoke. "I heard you got to see him," he said, "just before he died, I mean."

Barty nodded.

"I went to the funeral," said Davy. "Folk round here had a lot a time for your dad."

"Thanks, Andy," Barty said, uncomfortably. Wasn't Joe supposed to be a cold-blooded murderer, and Norah his accomplice?

"Sergeant," said Thouless, and Davey looked away, and picked up his pen again. Barty glanced over at the shorthand.

"I told my father what had happened," he said, "and he left the shop to the woman who worked there. Mrs Bettins. He told her my grandmother had been taken ill. The two of us got in the van, and went straight back to Rosevear."

"What did you do when you got there?"

"My grandmother was in the kitchen. We all went to the entrance hall. He was still lying there, the doctor. Just as I'd left him. My grandmother said her sister, Violet - who'd been dead for years - she said Violet had come out of the mirror, and helped her. That they'd both pushed him down the stairs. And my dad just says, right, ok, and then something like, Come on, Bea, it was an accident really, though, wasn't it? And she says No. She says: her and Violet, they'd done it together, on purpose, and good riddance. And then. Then we all went back to the kitchen."

"Who else was there?"

"Nobody."

"What about the woman you say you saw Dr Heyward attacking? Had you told your father about her?"

"Of course I had. But she'd gone by the time we got there."

"You mean, she'd left the house?"

"There was no sign of her."

"Did you ask your grandmother about her?"

"My dad did the talking," said Barty.

"So?"

"Nanna was cooking us breakfast. Frying bacon. She said it was just her and and her sister, together again."

"Let me get this straight. She actively denied there was anyone else in the house at all, did she?"

"Yes. She didn't seem to know what Dad was talking about, when he asked her. I mean, I knew what I'd seen. I went upstairs, had a good look round. I didn't see anyone, the place was empty. I had no idea who that woman was or where she'd gone. So. You can see how bad it was going to look. If we called the police. I didn't want my grandmother hung for murder, or locked up at Sedan Cross. And everyone knew my dad had hated the doctor. We thought people'd say it wasn't my crazy old Nanna who'd really done it anyway, they'd say it was Dad. Either way, I'd be the boy with a murderer in the family. My father didn't want that."

"So, you decided to dump him in the lake."

"Yes," said Barty, after a pause. "Dad took the keys out Dr Heyward's pocket. He didn't want me to touch the body, but he couldn't manage it himself. He had his old war wound, couldn't walk far without his stick."

"He used to joke about it, sir," Davey told his boss. "That he'd given his arse for his country - "

" - an honour granted to few," Barty finished.

"He was a character," said Davey, almost smiling.

Thouless briefly looked at him, a certain level stare, then turned to Barty. "Carry on, please, Mr Gilder. I believe you were helping your father to hide the body of a murdered man."

"Yes," said Barty. "I took his feet. I can see his shoes now. Very good brogues. Brown. We put him in the passenger's seat. It wasn't that difficult. Then my dad drove the car to the lake. I ran behind. At the edge we dragged the body across into the driver's side. And then we pushed it in. And that was it. He was gone."

Barty realised that he was trembling, breathing fast, as if he had just helped his father haul the deadweight, push the loaded car over the edge. "Can we stop for a minute?" he said.

"Get us some tea," Thouless ordered Davey, who got up and went out.

"He had a wife and three kiddies," said Thouless. "Dr Heyward, that is. You ever think about them?"

"When I do, I remember him punching that woman. I'd never seen a man hit a woman before. It seemed to come easy enough to him. What d'you think he did to his wife, in private?"

Thouless shifted in his chair, looked away.

"And another thing," said Barty, after a pause. "I'm told there's a witness, someone who says my step-mother Norah was at Rosevear, or was seen in my dad's van that morning, when we got back to Silkhampton."

"Who told you that?"

"This isn't a big place. Word gets about. But it was just me and dad in the van. And if the person telling you otherwise is the woman who worked in the shop for us, if it was Mrs Bettins, well. She had her eye on my dad, at the time. I could see it. She had ideas about him. Wasn't pleased when he took up with Norah, if you know what I mean. That's all I'm saying."

When Davey came back in with the tea he went out to the public kiosk to call home again, but there was still no answer. The morning's words swirled in his head, *incompetent, rough, impatient, disastrous, bad doctor for women* making his heart pound in his chest, making him sweatily breathless, almost like the bad days in the hospital. He promised himself that he would try again in an hour, and hurried back to the station to find Hendricks waiting for him at the front desk.

"Aren't you off duty?"

"Yes sir, but can I talk to you, anyway, sir?"

"What about?"

"Miss Quick, sir. What she was doing here."

"I know what she was doing. Nesbit told me."

"You know it was *family planning*, then?" Hendricks lowered her voice and blushed as she spoke and he felt a little surge of approval of her, for this proper feminine delicacy.

"That's right. Who told you?"

"A local person, sir," said Hendricks.

Thouless gave her a keen glance, as if he knew the local person in question had been her own mother.

(Who hadn't known where to look either. It had been awful for both of them.

"Mum! You mean – you went to see her? As a *patient?*"

A quick shamed nod. Already wishing she'd kept quiet, but too late!

"When *was* this?"

"Just after Harry was born. We couldn't afford any more, Sally, that's all it was. She had this place above the chemist's. Told you what to do, that's all. So you didn't get no more babies."

"You mean - " You mean you and dad were still -

No. Some thoughts had to be firmly squashed flat before they went any further).

"Get a description?" Thouless asked now.

"Not really," said Hendricks. "Just that she was small and thin."

"Hair colour?"

"Dark."

"Ah," said Thouless.

("Funny eyes, she had. Not good-looking. Not what I'd call good-looking, anyway. Scrawny, you know.")

"Well done, Hendricks. Confirms what Miss Nesbit said, too. Good work."

Oh dear, thought Hendricks. She was entirely unfamiliar with the phrase *don't shoot the messenger*, but something like it crossed her mind as she spoke: "There's something else, sir."

"Oh?"

It was the best bit, she thought. Yet still she dreaded telling him. "It's about where she lived, sir. Miss Quick. While she was in Silkhampton."

"Yes?"

("Ooh that were a turn up for the books," Mrs Hendricks had said, all too glad to get off the subject of Miss Quick and what she was providing in her little place above the chemist shop. "Miss Thornby, of the Square, taking in lodgers! Before the war, see, you only done that if you were skint.

And they'd been rolling in it, the Thornby's, right toffee-nosed too, what a come-down *that* was!")

"She lodged with Mrs Gilder, sir," said Hendricks. "Before she was married to Joe Gilder. When she was Norah Thornby, Miss Quick was her lodger."

He gets it straight away. "You're sure?"

"My informant was, sir. So – well, Miss Quick could have taken that brooch any time, pinched it, or borrowed it. The one in the car. And if she was having a, a love affair with Dr Heyward – "

"She would have got in the car with him."

"Yes, sir. Sorry, sir."

"What you sorry about?" He looks at his watch, then back at her. "Right, I've got a train to catch. I'll be back some time next week, do the report. Ok?"

"What? But – where are you going, sir?"

"Home. I'm going home. Everyone's dead, Hendricks. Not just the victim but everyone else. Case is closed. Tell Davey to let Mrs Gilder go, will you? And you. You go home as well, alright?"

He makes as if to leave, then stops, turns, holds out a hand: "Nice working with you."

Raptly she takes it, touches him for the first and last time. "Thank you, sir."

Barty sits on a chair in a dim sour-smelling corridor.

"Don't go anywhere," Davey had told him, then disappeared for what felt like a very long time. He tried to make his mind go blank, in the way someone in camp had told him about, some Indian method of calming yourself down, but thoughts kept intruding. One of them was, *sorry, dad.*

How morally bad was it to finger your own father for a fairly major crime? It was pretty bad, Barty thought, even if your dad was guilty. Which was likely, he reminded himself. Most of the story he had told Thouless had been true, though in fact Joe had driven off alone to Rosevear, leaving Barty behind to man the shop. He had never talked about it afterwards, but surely he really had helped with the disposal of the body, Barty told himself.   After all, someone had done it, someone had hauled the deadweight from the bottom of the staircase out into the car, and run it into the water. Who else could it have been, apart from Joe and the dark-haired woman Heyward had tried to strangle? Though Barty's grandmother had boasted true enough of pushing her enemy down the stairs to his death, it was hard to picture her being much use afterwards, not when she was eighty-two.

Sorry, dad.

Did it help at all, Barty wondered, that he had also up to a point incriminated himself? The child he had been, anyway. What would the police do about that? At the thought of finding himself a solicitor Barty felt so tired that his eyes closed all by themselves.

Though it had also occurred to him that they might not be too keen to arrest him, as a returned POW who'd spent years behind bars already, and who of course was one of their precious sodding Few. Please God, thought Barty, could that tripe come in really handy, just this once, not just in free beer?

Then the door opened and Davey finally appeared again, followed by a tall thin old lady encumbered with various bags. Despite her shabby coat and wild grey hair the old lady was rather imposing, almost grand in the half-light of the grimy corridor, and she had swept past before he understood who it was. Barty stood up, and hurried forward to catch up with her.

"Norah," he said.

She stopped dead. Instantly he could make the worn thin face, the hooded eyes, into his step-mother's. He saw too her ungloved hands clutching the bags she held, tremendously familiar hands, blue veins showing through the thin skin, knobbly fingers work-hardened, very like those of his beloved twin grandmothers, long-dead Bea and Violet. The sight of Norah's aged hands made his eyes fill with tears.

She whispered: "Barty?"

"Yes. It's me," he said.

The bags fell at her feet. Her smile was Norah's, and yet an old lady's.

"Hallo!" he said, half-laughing.

Slowly she put up a hand, and touched his face. "Hallo, my dear," she said.

On Saturday evening Norah, Barty, Etta and Egg went to the Gideon Dining Rooms, once Silkhampton's finest restaurant. It was Norah's idea, as decades earlier her father had more than once treated her there, and on the whole she was not disappointed. Much of the old Edwardian splendour remained, the heavy velvet curtains, the immaculate tablecloths; if the chandeliers remained in storage there were still sparkling crystal glasses, and a candle on each table.

You could almost forget the war, until you looked at the menu. But the potatoes had been oven baked in some delicious French way and the rissoles came with a jug of something described as sauce agnes sorel, which Etta refused to try, Egg said was bitter and Barty finished using his dessert spoon.

Watching him felt like being in an actual sweet dream, for Norah. He had been an absence for so long. Now she wanted just to sit and watch him talk to Egg and Etta, she was happy just to watch all of them chatting to each other, she almost marvelled that they could, it seemed extraordinary somehow that they even spoke the same language. Let alone had memories in common. But they all had been to the same school – Egg of course still in attendance – they had played in the same playground, shared some of the same teachers, old Mr Vowles, Miss Wordsworth, Mr Fulljames, they had sat cross-legged on the same school assembly hall singing the same hymns to the same battered piano, still played staccato by Miss Hampton, who still of course had just the one eye.

How lovely they all looked, too! Egg so pretty, proud in her new birthday frock – how long ago that seemed, yet it was only a few days! Etta glowing with happiness – who would have imagined that her own release would make such a difference, but - so touchingly! the child was simply radiant. And even Barty, poor soul, surely looked a little less seedy already.

What exactly was it that he had told Thouless? When she had asked him he had only shrugged, and said, Just a version that held water, can we leave it at that?

Absolutely not, she had thought. Well. Maybe we can, just for now.

The restaurant idea had been okay until the wine waiter scurried over and ceremonially gave him the wine list. Then he was straight away sitting with Jess in some classy West End place she knew, and she had laughed at him for being baffled, she had raised one eyebrow and said in a low voice, Goodness, you really are a peasant, aren't you!

They had spent the afternoon in bed, and her tone had been pleasantly lascivious. But he really hadn't known what to say to the sommelier, and if it hadn't mattered then perhaps it would have mattered later. After a while she might have started saying that sort of thing in a completely different voice. So maybe it was all for the best, he told himself, that she'd fucked off with the decent chap who worked in the Foreign Office. Who'd doubtless known since birth how to work his way through a wine list. Out in the wilds of Hampstead.

Now he looked up at the wine waiter, gave him back the list. "Got any beer?" he said.

Etta is still in heaven. There is not a single moment of the whole day when the thought of Jem has not sounded in her head like music. The world is so beautiful that she can hardly sit still. Everything is easier. When Mrs G told her to iron her blouse before they came out it had been annoying – it didn't need ironing, it was fine – but somehow it hadn't seemed worth arguing. It had seemed simpler, somehow, to just get out the iron board and make the old girl happy.

And she has never been in a restaurant before. It's weirdly gloomy and more like church than she would have expected had she ever even bothered to wonder what the place was like inside, which she hadn't. It was for old folk, obviously.

"Would madam care to see the dessert menu?"

"Yes. Please," said Etta.

Egg could not bring herself to decide. Though the waiter made things easier when he came round by pointing out that nearly everything on it was off.

"Sorry. Though actually we have some very nice ice cream tonight, made the real old-fashioned way. With a little strawberry sauce." He turned to Norah: "What do you say, mother?"

There was a short silence, while Norah waited for Etta to point out, in one of her many dismissive tones, that Norah was not Egg's mother at all, nor her own. But tonight, for a wonder, Etta kept her head in her menu, as if she hadn't heard at all.

"I say yes," said Norah at last. "If that's what you'd like, Egg? Is it?"

And when Egg, after a quick cautious glance at her sister, looked back, and nodded, Norah turned as if calmly to Etta herself. "Would you like ice cream too, dear?"she asked.

Etta's shoulders were stiff, she could not quite meet Norah's eyes, her voice was gruff. But: "Yeah, alright," she said.

Norah turned to Barty, but suddenly her throat seemed to have closed up, and wouldn't let her say anything at all.

Barty turned to the waiter, and spoke for her:

"Four ice creams it is then, please."

When they came out of the Gideon Dining Rooms the streets were full of soldiers, cheery young Americans spilling out of the pubs and walking arm in arm four abreast on the pavements.

Despite her long nap that afternoon Norah suddenly felt almost too tired to stand. She took Barty's arm as they threaded their way through the bustle, the girls diving along ahead of them.

"D'you know what's going on? It's not usually like this," she told Barty, as they crossed the market square.

"It's because they're off soon. Tomorrow, I think. The whole camp's leaving. That's what I heard anyway."

Etta turned round, her face sharp in the twilight.

"What did you say?" she asked.

Agnes Henty came round at ten the next day, which was a very odd time to call, Norah thought.

"Hallo, Agnes, come in, is everything alright?"

Agnes Henty has had a bad weekend. Shame and regret have kept her awake more or less ever since Friday. She has found herself shedding tears. All these years she has fought hard to expand her business, to do her duty by her country, to keep going in the face of sharp enduring fear for her children. She has never spared herself. But in the early hours of Saturday morning, wide awake in her bed, she remembered that once she had been fourteen years old herself.

She remembered, not that she had ever really forgotten him, that once she had loved Richard Sawby, who had been no more than sixteen at the time, a child himself, far younger than both her boys were now. They had walked out together in complete innocence, she told herself that Saturday morning, and yet of course when she thought about it clearly, when she thought herself back to that time, it had not been innocent at all. It had been courtship, full of sex-feeling, full of desire. They had merely not acted on the desires, because there were rules about these things, and on the whole those rules were good.

It occurred to her then that Etta and her boy had almost certainly behaved in the same way. Etta simply was not one of those girls who flaunted and flirted. She had a reticence about her, she had character, thought Agnes Henty cloudily, as she got up to make herself a cup of tea at four-thirty in the morning.

I shouted at her boy. I called him names. Would I have been so quick to assume the worst if he had been white?

Here is another source of shame, for it seems clear to Agnes Henty that she has unbeknownst - but that's no excuse – allowed herself to be infected with vulgar prejudice. She has acted with vulgar prejudice against an Allied soldier. A boy like one of her own, adrift in a foreign country. She has insulted Etta. And she has insulted Etta's lad, Etta's own Richard Sawby.

Thoughts like this have made Agnes Henty ache with misery until this morning, this bright Sunday morning, when going in as usual to check stock levels for the early Monday shift she realised what was happening at the station, and saw her chance.

"I see Etta?" she asks Norah Gilder.

Norah looks surprised, as who could blame her.

"Um – well, sorry, but I don't think so, no. I'm afraid she's not at all well this morning."

"Oh? What's wrong with her?"

Pause. "She's just a little overtired," says Norah, who in fact has no idea why Etta has so far refused to get out of bed, or answer any questions as to what might be wrong with her.

"Let me see her, please. It's important. Or I wouldn't have come."

"Agnes, it's not about work, is it? I mean, if Etta's been remiss – you do understand things have been very difficult for her here, with me being ah away - "

"It's not work."

"What, then?"

"She's not in any trouble. Let me be a friend to her, Norah. That's all I want. Alright?"

"I'm afraid she may not want to see you."

"Ask her. Tell her this: that he came to see me on Friday."

"Who came to see you?"

"Just tell her, will you? Please."

If Agnes had her usual bristling manner Norah might have stood firm and gone on refusing. But this droopy dispirited version was harder to say no to. It was vexing; but after a little more thought Norah went upstairs and knocked once more on Etta's closed bedroom door.

There was no reply, so she opened it and spoke through the gap: "Etta? Mrs Henty is downstairs. She wants to see you. She seems quite determined about it. She says you're not in any trouble. Can she come up?"

There was a sound from the bed, as of Etta turning her face to the wall.

"She said to tell you: that he came to see her on Friday. No idea what that means. Have you? Anyway that's what she says. That he came to see her on Friday. Etta?"

The sound of breathing. Then a shape stirring, rising in the darkness. "Tell her to come up," said Etta.

By the time Agnes Henty had climbed up the stairs Etta had taken down the blackouts and put on her dressing gown. She was sitting on the bed, and she did not stir as Agnes closed the door behind her.

"You saw Jem?"

Etta looked up as she spoke the name, and this pierced Agnes Henty again, for she remembered the secret luxury of naming Richard Sawby, of having some reason or excuse to say *Richard* out loud.

"I don't know his name," said Agnes Henty.

"Why'd he come to see you?"

Admit it, Agnes Henty told herself. There's no getting away from it now. Tell her the truth. "He come to give me a letter, so's I could give it to you. To say goodbye."

"A letter? He wrote me a letter? Where is it? You got it?"

Agnes shook her head. "No. Sorry. I saw red, see. I thought you were too young. Well – you are too young. Dunno how old he is."

"Eighteen," said Etta. "I told him I was sixteen. It was my fault."

"What was?" Agnes frightened. "You don't mean you - you didn't - "

"No," says Etta. I wanted to. But he wouldn't. He wouldn't, thinks Etta, and begins to cry again.

"Well, he's a good boy then, and no mistake," said Agnes firmly. "He respected you. That's important, Etta."

"Is it?"

"I'm sorry about the letter," says Agnes sincerely.

Etta has a long time ahead of her, to think about what might have been in the letter, whether Jem would have put his own address on it, and what she would have done if he had. The diagnosis of dyslexia is decades away, she only knows now, instantly, that writing back would have been beyond her. Would have betrayed her as some sort of idiot, he would have read her laborious childish hand full of spelling mistakes and realised that she was far more stupid than she looked, that she was simply too stupid to love or be loved by.

Agnes Henty interrupts the beginning of what will become a lengthy much-repeated train of thought: "I didn't come about that, not really. I come to tell you that they're at the station. Or they were, twenty minutes ago. Your boy's lot this is, the coloured troops. They're all there waiting on the platform."

There had been a crowd too, and the Silkhampton Colliery Band oom-pahing, and a little platform had been put up in the forecourt with various toffs prating about England's everlasting thanks and the special relationship, there were stars and stripes and union jacks flying, it was enough to make you sick, thought Agnes Henty.

"Go there now you might catch him," she said. "Say goodbye anyway."

"What – at the station?"

Agnes Henty hesitated, decided. "There were girls doing that. I saw 'em. You can get in through the Goods Yard. Round the back."

She herself had stood upon Platform One and openly held Richard Sawby's hand while the band played and the troop train slowly came steaming alongside. She had never for a moment suspected that she would never see him again.

Etta looks wildly about her. "I can't go like this."

Agnes understands. She means her hair, her clothes, her everything.

"Get yourself ready then," she says. "Come on, quick about it. I'll go with you as far as the station. Alright?"

Five minutes. She gets into her good skirt and the blouse still tired from the night before but there isn't another one, brushes her hair, she goes straight into Norah's bedroom and helps herself to her best lipstick, she goes back to her own room and takes a certain roll of paper from her desk, and puts her good shoes under her arm.

"Ready."

Norah is down in the kitchen, they can hear her doing something with pans, and Egg's voice raised. Neither hear Etta and Agnes Henty quietly letting themselves out of the house though Barty, leaning out of the attic window to flick cigarette ash out onto the parapet, sees them hurry cross the square and disappear into the narrow streets on the far side.

The reason you could get into the Goods Yard, it transpired, was that someone had earlier come along with a bolt-cutter and broken through the padlock that held the big gates shut.

Inside the shifting crowd is enormous, a party noisy with talk and cigarette smoke and laughter and song.

"How will I find him?" Etta almost whimpers. "I don't even know if he's here."

"You'll just have to look," says Agnes. But she is certain that over the babble of voices she can hear a train approaching. "Go on, quick! At least try, go on!"

Etta shakes out her hair, puts on her heels, squashes the plimsolls into her bag, turns, and plunges into the crowd.

She doesn't see him straight away. For several minutes she pushes through and between the people, fighting her way towards the high railings that separate the platform from the goods yard. Everywhere there are chatting groups and at the railings the crowd is particularly dense. Hands are being held, through the railings. Lit cigarettes are being shared, gifts passed, kisses given. This is goodbye, crowd-level. There have been parties, and dances, and talk, and jokes, and stories, and jealousy, and arguments, and hurt feelings, and misunderstandings, and malice: human interaction, unforgettable, for some.

Jem is standing at the far end of the railings nearest the platform edge, pressed against them, looking at her.

What does he see?

Like Agnes Henty, Jem has spent the weekend changing his mind. In fact he will change his mind about Etta over and over again in the coming years. Particularly when his own daughter turns fourteen. For now, it took him barely an hour on Friday to regret that he had failed to deliver his letter. A little longer to stop feeling that he had had a narrow escape. He was melancholy company in the George and Dragon, got half-cut thinking about her, missing her. All yesterday he suffered. This morning at the station he is ashamed of himself for feeling so soft about someone who has lied to him. He should be angry with her, he thinks, but somehow the anger keeps draining away.

When he sees her in the crowd at the station it's as if he has conjured her up from his own confusion. He sees that she is hardly more than a child, that she would have been four whole years below him at school, that she's younger than his own little sister. But she is still his sweetheart. She comes closer, stands on the other side of the railings, and his face smiles all by itself, he has no control over it at all, his face is so delighted, thrilled to see her.

"Etta! Oh Etta, hi!"

"Hallo," she says.

Now he notices that she has makeup on and her hair done like a woman's, and is relieved. He may know the truth, but he is sure the other guys behind him won't suspect: all they will see is a pretty English girl, come to see him off. His bunkhouse credit will soar. He is cravenly glad, as well as ashamed of himself, in a different way.

"I'm real sorry," he says.

"What you sorry about?"

He knows the other guys behind him are grinning and elbowing one another, and ready to josh him, So this here is one of the *Wildflowers of Western Europe*, right? He wills them to stay back, not crowd him.

"I wanted to let you know," he says, feeling the eyes on his back, trying as hard as he can to to ignore them, and be himself for her. "Just let you know that we were going."

"Never mind. I wish you weren't, though." Her eyes fill. His will not, he tells himself. He is a man. He will not make a fool of himself. Bunkhouse credit isn't fireproof. Tear-proof.

"What did you say, in the letter?" she asks.

"Just goodbye. That it had been nice knowing you. And it has been," he says.

Behind him a sudden blare of clarion noise. The train, his train, is arriving. Someone is yelling horribly, bellowing incomprehensibly, instructions, commands. Etta ignores them. She goes on looking into his face.

"Jem. Jem, I got you this."

She opens up her handbag and pulls out the roll of paper sticking out of it. "It's a picture I did. It's a portrait of you. My best one. Keep it. Alright?"

He takes it, reaching through the bars. "Thankyou."

"Goodbye, Jem."

"Goodbye, Etta."

Neither of them talk of love. Both of them think that's being grownup about it.

Jem does not look at the picture until the train is well under way. He has a seat by the window and for a little while sits looking out at the passing greenery. He remembers one of the guys in his tent telling him that back home the train he took to his initial camp had had its windows heavily curtained off so that no one in the towns they went through could be offended by the sight of black men sitting comfortably in a decent train. He will hold that story in his heart for the rest of his life, along with others that scorched him.

He thinks briefly of it now as he unties the roll of paper Etta gave him and unfurls it, and holds it to the light. It's not a portrait, he thinks at once. It's not a portrait at all, why did she say that it was? It's a landscape, a clifftop scene on a sunny day, and soon he recognises where she must have stood when she painted it. It's his place. It's his favourite place in all England and for now the world. It's the headland where you can walk right out above the sea, and look out at the horizon and know that this splendour has been here always, and is as good as anyone ever said it was, or even better. That there are true splendours in the world waiting for you, if you can find them and make sure you see them when you may.

It's a beautiful picture. Thank you, Etta.

Then he looks closer and sees the tiny bluish figure, like an elongated comma on the headland, less than a matchstick man but you can still tell somehow that its hands are in its pockets, that it's sauntering out in contentment towards the sea.

It is himself, he understands. This is a portrait after all. And a picture, too, of their love. His and Etta's. It is himself at a distance, unknowable; understood, but completely out of reach. Seeing this is a bit too much for him. He gets up and goes to the lavatory, to be private while he can.

The following week Alice Pyncheon, Norah's last remaining relative, was found dead at Sedan Cross hospital. Her funeral was a dispiriting affair, though several of the nurses kindly swelled the numbers.

"She was one of my favourite ladies," one of them told Norah over tea afterwards. "So gentle. Wouldn't hurt a fly. Of course sometimes we had to laugh."

Did you? thought Norah, smiling politely. Couldn't you have held it in, if you'd tried a little harder?

"You could never talk her out of it. Didn't matter what you said."

Alice had been found in one of her usual hiding places, beneath a particular stone seat at the back of the house overlooking the pleasantly sloping lawns. Though safely in bed at bedtime she had somehow managed to climb through an open first-floor window and make her way down through the adjacent lilac tree to the frosty ground below. No one had missed her until morning, when it was far too late.

"Convinced she was invisible!"

Though in fact, thought Norah, who had been fond of her cousin, clearly poor Alice had sometimes been perfectly correct. When it really mattered, none of you saw her. None of you noticed that she had vanished. Laugh at that, if you will.

"More tea?" she had said.

At the time Norah was back at work at Rosevear. The first time she cycled back through the gates and saw the edge of the lake behind the house her heart had thudded, she found that she could hardly bear to look at the water, as if she had committed her crime of concealment there the day before, instead of years ago. But then of course it had been only recently discovered; and blamed on someone else. On Joe.

They had been doing the washing-up, Norah washing, Barty drying, and between one sideplate and another he had told her what he had done.

"Oh, Barty!" Standing still, her hands in the hot water. "But why?"

"Is it so bad? It just seemed the simplest way to get you out."

"But he had nothing to do with it!"

"You sure about that?"

She had hesitated; decided. "I know Joe had nothing to do with the disposal of the body. Because it was me." She looked down at her hands in the sink, took up a dinner plate, and swiped at it with her dishcloth.

"What? What do you mean?"

She gave him the plate. "I was there. I did it."

"You can't have been!"

"I was there. All the time."

"I didn't see you!"

"It's a big place, Barty. I didn't see you either, but I promise you, I was there that night. I was helping Lettie. Lettie Quick."

"The woman I saw? On the stairs with Heyward?"

"Yes, that was her. She had been having an affair with him. And he was very angry when she stopped it."

"And tried to kill her."

"Oh. I'm – I don't actually know what you saw."

Barty put the plate down, laid the teacloth on top of it. "I'd just come, with the bread. I saw him knock her down, and throttle her. But he was dead when I got there. What happened to her? Who was she, anyway?"

Norah sighed. "She's dead now, you know. Lettie. She was my friend as well as my lodger. I liked her very much. But - how can I put this? She was a woman of principle. One of them was that the cards are always stacked against women, and she was prepared to even them up a little. It was a sort of sideline."

"Sideline?"

"No one got hurt! Or robbed, or anything. It was just false documents, really. Birth certificates. Several other people were involved. But essentially - we were at Rosevear that night to help someone conceal a birth. You know - the ruinous sort. Illegitimate. We were helping her."

"Okay," said Barty slowly. "So - what happened?"

"I was with the - the person having the baby. She was a very nice woman, really all of this is absolutely nothing to do with her, she never knew anything about any of it! But I came out of her room to call Lettie. And there was Heyward. Attacking Lettie, horrible man, I still don't know how he knew where we were! But he had his back to me, crouching over her. I grabbed him by his collar, just grabbed at him and hauled. And he did let go of her, but he hit me, terribly hard, he punched me! So I'm not exactly sure what happened next, though I've thought of it and thought of it so often ever since. But Bea came. And pushed him. He was right at the edge of the stairs. But to be honest - I think he tripped over Lettie, she was lying there on the floor, and I caught at his coat, and pulled on it, and well. I think we did it between us. Made him fall. We all killed him, Barty. We all did it."

"And you couldn't call the police."

"No, of course not. Lettie wasn't keen on police."

"Because of her sideline."

"Amongst other things. And the - person. The woman having the baby: we had promised her secrecy."

"So you made Dr Heyward vanish," said Barty.

She looked at him. "Yes. It was my idea, actually. The lake. We did it between us, Lettie and me. I drove the car."

"You ever talk to dad about this?"

"No. But he knew. He saw the tyre-tracks in the grass that morning, I saw him notice them. He knew everything. He just didn't actually *do* any of it."

"Well, he has now," said Barty.

Rosevear felt very different without the babies, by contrast even more hopeless and empty now than the days of its pre-war dereliction, thought Norah, especially as it turned out that on leaving under her cloud Mrs Hawes had taken the radio with her.

"I suppose I can see the sense of it," said Nesbit to Norah one afternoon over tea. Full closure was two weeks away now. "People are just going home."

For while she had spent much of the afternoon assisting Dr Broughton with an emergency appendicectomy on an eight-year-old girl, the child had been an evacuee, about to go home for good with her mother, who had until the week before been working in the big machine shed above the harbour in Porthkerris, making army shirts. With the peace the factory had abruptly shut, no notice, and at the same time the RAF had officially withdrawn from Silkhampton airfield.

"I'm afraid Edina is taking all this very badly," said Nesbit. "I'm rather worried about her."

A pause, while Norah recalibrated several ideas. She had assumed that Dr Broughton was senior partner in her private friendship with Nesbit, as she was in their professional lives. But this sounded like maternal concern.

"She does seem...not quite herself, "she agreed cautiously.

"It's been such a kick in the teeth," Nesbit went on. "Coming on top of – well, you know. The parachute. It upset her so much."

It was true, thought Norah, that Dr Broughton seemed diminished of late; thinner, as if she had been ill, and quietly moody rather than vituperative. I haven't heard her shout once since I got back, she realised: though of course there is hardly anyone left to shout at.

"She used to love swimming in the lake. It used to cheer her up somehow, no matter how cold it was. But now. She can't bear to go anywhere near it, poor darling."

There was a pause.

Norah was very vague on the subject of Lesbianism, which was itself a word she had never actually heard spoken aloud; she had never come across any of the cruder terms at all. Once she had overheard Edina and Nesbit arguing, and thought with mild amusement how like a couple they sounded, but without any vocabulary to help it along, the thought had found nowhere else to go. What good friends they are, she had concluded, with a little pang for herself, and the loss of her own best friend Lettie Quick. What loving friends they are, she thought now, this time firmly closing the thought off on purpose, before it could clarify into something that might be worrying.

"She will soon find work elsewhere, surely," said Norah at last.

Nesbit shook her head. "It's the tone as much as anything," she said. "So dismissive. As if nothing she has done really *counts*. They would never treat a man like that. But I suppose now the war's over we must all be squashed back into our places."

"I'm sure things aren't as bad as all that," said Norah.

"Oh yes? That council nursery you used to take your youngest to. Eglantine, Egg. When you started here she was too small to go to school. Could you have done the job without the nursery?"

"Well, no - "

"So. War's been over less than a fortnight. Answer me this: when will they close the council nursery, d'you think?"

"Well, I have no idea. Why should they close it at all?"

"Good question," said Nesbit. "But it's already closed."

And Barty was still talking about studying something, without doing anything about it, spending his days on building sites and his evenings in the pub; Etta had just got the sack again from her most recent little job. Agnes Henty's factory had closed the month before, and since then all Etta's jobs had been little ones, part-time, barely-paid at all, since the labour market was flooding with employable males. And she was being so extraordinarily difficult, so short-tempered; who would want to take on a sullen almost illiterate girl, when there were ordinarily educated men back coming from the fighting, and needing the work, any work, to support their wives and children?

And Egg had fallen out with her best friend at school, and felt very sorry for herself, there was never enough hot water because the boiler wasn't working properly, the various lodgers complained and wanted seconds and better puddings, and a fox had not two nights ago broken into the henhouse and murdered every occupant, even fierce old Mrs Simpson.

All these smaller things on top of the several revelations of 1945. Smaller things, against the background of enormities that kept you awake at night.

And now here was Norah, required by the Board of Trustees to inventory every last cracked sideplate and roll of bandage before the final closure, stuck for days on end at Rosevear, hardly her favourite place what with one thing and another, and depressing enough without having more or less constant run-ins with Minnie, who had never been troublesome before.

"Why can't I? I knows the place. No one knows it like what I do."

"Of course that's true, Minnie, but I'm afraid there isn't any need for a housekeeper, even if there was money to pay for one. Which there isn't."

"Can't leave the place empty. Folk need homes."

"I agree, of course it shouldn't be left empty. But it costs too much to run and it's so hard to get to and it's not divided into flats or anything – and there's no work anywhere near by, d'you see? People need to live where they work. Not miles away."

"I live here," said Minnie. "I ent going."

It must be so lonely for her, poor thing, thought Norah. Especially after all the warmth and companionship of those wartime years in the kitchen. Aloud she said: "Shall we have a quick break for tea, now, Minnie?"

It was while she was in the kitchen poking about in the bowels of the range, which had never worked properly since the sudden departure of Mrs Hawes, whose scones Norah still particularly missed, that Minnie lumbered in again, looking agitated.

"Please, ma'am."

"What is it, Minnie? Are you alright?"

For Minnie's moon face had paled. "'Tis the queen, ma'am," she said.

Norah laughed. "What?"

"Her's outside. In her car. A-waiting," said Minnie.

"The queen," said Norah. Minnie looked so serious that she knew a moment's doubt. After all, she thought: Her Majesty had to be somewhere. "I'll go and see," she said.

Outside on the weedy gravel there was indeed a most magnificent car. It was dark green, with a long bonnet, and was very clean and shining. As Norah stood hesitating at the side of the house the driver's door opened, and Queen Elizabeth herself elegantly emerged: small, erect, buxom, dark-haired, and beautifully turned out in a closely fitting suit of blue wool, delicate kid boots, and a discreet little hat with a dark lace veil. Norah swallowed, then took a few steps closer, and Her Majesty turned round, and with one gloved hand lifted the veil. The face beneath was anxious, even entreating, but devastatingly familiar. No smile. No queen.

"Hallo, Norah," said Lettie Quick.

"'Course not," she said in the kitchen much later. She had brought a large fruit cake from Fortnum and Masons, packed in a basket with other lovely and generally unobtainable things, lapsang suchong tea, and quails' eggs, pate de fois gras, and a bottle of Moet and Chandon champagne, which she stood in the sink, in cold water. "I planned it all along. Things were getting a bit hot for me, as you might say."

Now Norah was over at least some of the shock she was constantly swept with alternating waves of joy and rage, it was very hard to keep track. She could not stop staring into her old friend's face, so altered; putting on weight suited Lettie in a way; she looked softer and sweeter-natured, as well as much older. The likeness to Her Majesty Queen Elizabeth was really rather striking, Norah thought, and had to smother another laugh.

"So the police were after you?" she asked, still smiling.

"No. Not the police," said Lettie soberly. "The opposite of police, if you get me."

"I must say you look very prosperous, for a corpse. Or is it all borrowed pomp?"

"No it bloody isn't. Flaming cheek," said Lettie, without heat. "I made sensible investments. In a former life." She opened her handbag, a soft dark blue leather affair, lined in pale blue silk, delicious, Norah saw, and took out a silver card case.

"Here," she said, holding out a calling-card, a plain white rectangle, very correct. "This is me now."

"You mean you have a new name?" said Norah, taking it.

"New identity," said Lettie.

"Mildred Bright," Norah read aloud, laughed again: "Mildred?"

"Ring any bells?"

"Not really – oh. D'you mean – but that's one of the Rosevear Trustees! Miss M Bright. Was that you, all the time?" Miss M Bright, among the grand uppercrust ladies who had so patriotically come together to fund Rosevear as a lying-in hospital back in 1940; she had tried to crush Thouless with them, she remembered.

Lettie was grinning.

"That was ages ago!" said Norah. "How long had you been planning it – to disappear, I mean?"

"Years. Since Thirty-six, or thereabouts. Just a back-up plan at first. Then I sort of – saw the benefits."

"But – what have you been doing all this time? You can't work, can you – not as Mildred Bright anyway. Or can you?"

"I can pull strings," said Lettie.

"But is it safe for you now? I mean, if you had to disappear just a few years ago, why is it alright now?"

"I am dead, remember."

"Surely someone might recognise you," said Norah. "I mean, look at you, Miss Bright, or may I call you Mildred? Swanking about shopping in the West End - you're hardly unnoticeable, are you? Not in that car, for a start."

"Oh, that doesn't matter," said Lettie. "It's the car they look at, not me. And besides, I'm forty-five, Norah! I'm invisible anyway. I don't mind, I've got used to it. In fact: I like it."

"Do you?" Norah thought of poor Alice, and her sad conviction that no one could see her at all. Perhaps she had not been as crazy as all that; merely an extreme case.

"Anyway, to business," said Lettie now.

"Business? What do you mean?"

She meant Rosevear, it soon turned out.

"Is that why you're here?"

"I am the largest backer."

"And I thought you'd come to see me - that's a bit rich, Lettie! All these years I've been - well - mourning you. Missing you."

"Hold on," said Lettie. "I saved your bacon, didn't I?"

"What?"

"It was me got you out of the nick!"

"What do you mean, it was you who put me *in* there! You and my mother's brooch - they found it in the car, Lettie!"

"What brooch, what are you - oh. Little thing, garnets?"

"Yes, the one you - you pinched! And I wouldn't mind. I *don't* mind. But you dropped it in his car, that was how they got to me the first place!"

"Oh," said Lettie. "I see. Well. I did wonder what had happened to it. I only meant to borrow it. Sorry. But I did get you out again, you know."

"No, you didn't, it was Barty who got me out. Joe's son, remember? He explained everything. He went to them and told them Bea Givens pushed Dr Heyward down the stairs."

"What about the car, then?"

"He said Joe did that. Got rid of the body, I mean. For Bea's sake."

"And the cops were happy with that, were they?"

"Convinced enough, anyway. Why did you think it was something to do with you?"

"Maybe it wasn't, then. Maybe everything would have worked out fine without me."

"What did you do?"

Lettie shrugged.

"You've got to tell me now, please!"

"Oh, alright then. I just happened to have a set of his personal keys at one time. Heyward's, I mean. So I knew more about him than most. And I took one or two of his belongings, held on to them. Insurance. Kept 'em safe. Until I sent them to the police. Gave 'em something else to think about. We leave it at that? Because this hospital of yours. I want it kept open. I want it kept useful."

"So do we all, but the council won't budge. Dr Broughton's tried everything. She's written dozens of letters."

"Council," said Lettie scornfully.

"And she tried several contacts in London."

"I got contacts in London," said Lettie. "Important contacts. People who wouldn't want to upset me, if you know what I mean. This place is staying open."

"But people are going home. Evacuees and so on. The war's over, we don't need safe places in the middle of nowhere anymore."

"I think we do. Women do. I want this place for a mother and baby home. Full time. Residential. Subsidized. But mainly, and this is the real point: no shame. None of that. They're having a baby and good for them, see! If people want to be secret, they can be, because they're in the middle of nowhere, if they want to pretend it never happened and have the baby adopted, they can. But if they want to keep the baby, we help them, because it's not easy, doing it on your own. Especially if you're being shunned. Or moralised at. And this place: all set up here. Ready to go. It's perfect."

"What about the cottage hospital?"

"It can stay open. For the time being anyway. Place is still big enough to stay private. Secret. We proved that a long time ago, didn't we? You and me both."

"You have dropped the sideline, Lettie, haven't you?"

"You bet. That was the last one. Good money, but Christ, never again! Think Edina'll go for it? The mother and baby idea? It was me recommended her in the first place. Knew her in London before the war."

"D'you mean you got her the job here?"

"I told you. I've been pulling strings."

"Oh, Lettie! How hard?"

"Don't look at me like that," said Lettie. "It's not blackmail. I don't do blackmail. Not any more, anyway. Don't need to: Mildred Bright's been chucking money about for years. Funding this and that. Good causes all. Well - arguably. See what I mean? That's what gets you influential. You got any glasses, for that champagne?"

"No."

"Shame. I'd've brought them, if I'd known. Never mind. We'll have to make do with teacups."

Nesbit is writing up notes late one morning the following week, when there is a knock on the door, and someone comes straight in.

Nesbit looks up in surprise, then puts down her pen, stands.

"Ah," she says. "Hallo. I thought you would come. Eventually."

Detective Inspector Thouless takes off his hat. A moment passes. "Please," she says. "Sit down." She notes his pallor, his breathlessness, and pours him a glass of water from the jug on her desk, puts it in front of him, waits while he struggles for control, takes a sip of water. Then: "May I ask – how is your wife?"

Now he can speak. "Well, thanks. She's very well."

"And - the baby?"

His smile is unexpectedly sweet. "Lovely little boy," he says. His breathing does not seem to be getting any easier. But no point beating about the bush, she thinks.

"You've come to make sure," she says.

"Yes. Please."

"Alright, then. Was your mother's name Rosina May Thouless?"

He closes his eyes, and nods.

"Rosina May Thouless, born March 1892," Nesbit recites from memory. "Died April 21 1920. She lived at Lowerberry Farm, on the coast road outside Wooton."

He nods again, clears his throat. "Were you there?"

"One of my earliest cases. One of the first disasters."

"So. You called Heyward?"

"No. You have to understand, everyone thought he was the best, in those days. Your father thought he was doing his best for his wife."

"Booked him."

"Yes. I'm sorry."

Head bowed, he takes out a clean folded white handkerchief, and wipes his eyes.

"When did you start to suspect?" she asks softly. "Was it when I told you he worked all over the county?"

He shakes his head. "No. Earlier. I kept thinking about her. My mother. All that talk about – other women who'd died. All the time I was trying to remember. I didn't know any names."

"I would have worked it out straight away, I think, if I'd known how you spell yours. I thought Thewlis. You know, with a W. Until I saw your card, I just didn't make the connection - there was talk at the time you were local."

"My dad sold up after mum died. That's when we moved. Everyone said, it was just one of those things. Sad but, inevitable. All this time I've thought that. Except that it wasn't. Tell me straight, will you: would she have lived, if it hadn't been for him, Heyward?"

"That's what I thought at the time. Yes. I felt he had shown neither judgement nor skill." And I didn't stop him, Nesbit reminds herself. I let shock rule me, I just stood there and meekly played the woman's role, bystander, subordinate.

A long silence. Finally he looks up, directly at her. "D'you remember her, my mother? That's what I really came to ask. Not just as a case, I mean. Can you remember *her*?"

"Yes. I remember everything. She talked about you. Her boys. You were staying with your grandparents."

He covers his eyes with one hand.

"Are you – are you Harry?" she asks.

He nods.

"You were...eight?"

It takes him a while to reply. "Seven."

"She was very proud of you," says Nesbit after a pause. "She said, You were a really kind older brother."

He looks at her. "Did she? Did she say that?"

"Yes, honestly: she did."

"I can remember her, a bit. Not much. Pete can't remember her at all. I've thought about her a lot though. When I did badly, or did something good, when I joined the force. Got married. Got ill. When they carved me up in the hospital their wonders to perform, I thought of her then. When I went back to work. When Jen told me about the baby. Then."

She waits, until he has control of himself again.

"But your own little boy was born safely," says Nesbit firmly. "And your wife is well."

He wipes his face with both hands.

"And you know the truth," says Nesbit, "which is very hard. But still the best thing."

"You sure about that?"

"No. All those years, though," says Nesbit, who has given this matter some thought, "all those years down in that haunted water. Sitting there in the dark. I think: it was no more than he deserved. I'm only sorry they found him."

There is a silence. "I should be getting off now," he says. "Thanks for talking to me."

She holds out her hand, and he takes it. "Well. Goodbye then, Harry. Good luck."

"Thanks," says Thouless.

After a stint in a government Civil Resettlement Unit for ex-POW's in Devon, Barty was finally demobbed and went to live in the cottage set against the harbour wall in Porthkerris, once his mother's. Soon he began helping with the rebuilding there, hands-on work shifting rocks and mixing concrete.

One mild Sunday afternoon in November Norah walked down from Rosevear to meet him and his recently-acquired dog Bill, a small light-brown whippety mongrel. There was something he wanted her to see, he had said on the telephone.

"What?"

"Show you when you get there."

"Think I might do some engineering," he told now, Norah as they reached the clifftop path.

"You mean, at university?"

"Maybe," said Barty vaguely.

Norah was on the whole worried about him. He still seemed so lost, though whatever it was he'd been doing in Devon had clearly calmed him a little. ("What sort of things did you do?" she had asked him, but he had only shrugged, and said, Talked to the other blokes.)

And was the dog a good thing, or not, she wondered? Barty had come home from work one rainy evening, he said, to find it stretched out asleep, or unconscious, on the rug in front of the empty grate. It was starving and sick-looking and very timid; when, he'd poured it a little milk in a saucer it had wagged the tip of its ratty tail, but not dared to drink until he had retreated back to the kitchen doorway well out of reach.

Like Barty himself, thought Norah now, the dog was at least looking better for a few square meals.

They reached the top of the hill, and stopped for a moment, both of them winded. "It's just along a bit from here," said Barty.

"What is, exactly?"

"Not completely sure, to be honest," said Barty. "Though I've got some ideas." They walked on, Bill picking his way along quietly to heel. After a while she said:

"We're not going far, are we?"

"No, this is it, actually. What I wanted to show you. Look. Over there. See what I mean?"

They were standing now at the edge of one of the long flat fields, bordered with low stone walls, that stretched all the way along the coast from Porthkerris to Rosevear and beyond.

"Come up this rise," said Barty. "It's easier to see from a height."

Both of them puffing again, the dog lagging behind now, lying down at once on the scrubby grass when they stopped.

"Now then," said Barty. "Look down there. What d'you think that is?"

Norah looked. She saw rust and decay, ancient-looking machinery half hidden in bramble, coils of chain, bits of wood, things that looked like broken baskets. There was a surprisingly large amount of it. There. Another set over there, in the far corner of the field.

"Farm machinery?"

"That's what I thought, at first," said Barty. "But there's too much of it. Anyway. Who'd abandon tractors and whatnot in the middle of a war? No. It's nothing to do with farming."

"That looks like a pylon. That bit over there," said Norah, pointing to another collapsing stretch of wooden struts and rusted metal. And was that the remains of a hut, over there? "How old is it, d'you think?"

"No idea. Maybe five years? So what is it - any guesses?"

Norah shook her head.

"'Course I'm not sure," said Barty. "But I think this was a fake airfield."

She stared at him. "A what?"

He was pleased at her incomprehension. "You never heard about them? That's good. They were a supposed to be a secret. Secret from us too sometimes, at first anyway. See that there – that bit?"

"Yes."

"It's a stand. It was high up, you could tilt it over. So it would pour what was in it onto the brazier below. See where the brazier was?"

"I think so."

"It's a fake airfield. This whole couple of fields. Trying to steer the Jerries away from RAF Silkhampton, I reckon. There were lots of them one time. All over the place."

"But how? What do you mean?"

"You light it up at night. You make it look like a real airfield, from the air. Or a shunting yard. Or even docks. Whatever you want, you fake the lighting. You fake trains, doors left open, windows lit up. They had people in from the films doing it, cinema people."

"You mean, like film sets? Oh my goodness!"

"Yeah. People whose job it is to do pretend stuff, make it look real. From a distance anyway. Especially at night."

"So - using lights?"

"Yeah. And fire. Nice big bangs - you get a fire going *boom*, cinema-stuff, keep topping it up so it looks good and big.   So Jerry's night-flying, looks down, doubts his own charts, nothing on the ground makes sense. He feels lost, drops on the wrong place, but he thinks he's done for RAF Silkhampton, 'cos he sees it all lit up burning. Goes home happy. Clever, eh?"

"I didn't know we did things like that," said Norah.

"We didn't. Not officially."

Norah was silent for a moment, thinking. "So - wouldn't a site like this mean – well, it would actually attract bombers, wouldn't it?"

"That was the idea. So they didn't go for the real thing."

"So who manned them? Were they manned? Who put the lights on, knowing that they were there to bring the bombers in on top of them?"

"Yeah, well, it's not a job I'd fancy," said Barty. "Though I think you could do some of it from a distance. Hope so anyway," he added.

Another pause. "So," said Norah after it, "If it looked like an airfield from the air, and you were in trouble – say your aeroplane was damaged, and you were lost – did people ever try to *land* on these pretend places?"

"Happened twice, I heard," said Barty soberly. "Our chaps, this was. Early on. Bought it, thinking it was real."

"Oh no!" Norah could hardly bear to think of it; some young man like Barty himself, thinking he had found a desperate last chance, coming in, flying low, trying to land a damaged plane on rough ordinary hopeless ground.

With stone walls, she thought. And oak trees.

"Then they changed the lighting so we'd know," said Barty. "Not to land. Because it was a trap."

Norah was remembering how quickly she and the German pilot she had pulled from his wrecked aeroplane had been surrounded by RAF men. She had wondered even in the daze of the moment where they had sprung from.

Keep me and the lads out of it. She could still see the mysterious young officer's charming lively face, and the way he had tapped the side of his freckled nose.

The German pilot – my pilot - must have been trying to land on this very fake airfield. The others were there because they were operating it. Holding the trap open. They brought him down. He was a *win*. And I -

I told them about Rosevear, she thought. The map spread out in the waiting room, herself tracing out her way along the lanes, her bicycle ride from the newly opened hospital barely a mile away. "What, women there now?" the freckled RAF man had asked. "Having babies and so on?" No wonder he had looked nonplussed.

Was that why they had abandoned this place, just walked away and left it? Because of course they wouldn't want to up the chances of a lying-in hospital full of mothers and babies getting a direct hit. And maybe, thought Norah, that's why those baffling raids on Silkhampton itself, on Porthkerris, in the grounds of Rosevear, on poor Alice's house, all stopped; the timing was certainly right. Maybe some of those early bombs really had been strays, leftovers off-loaded on the way home, as the ARP had insisted. But some of them, surely, had been a side-effect of this strange feat of open-air theatre, this film set of covert fakery now rusting in the weeds.

I could tell him, she thought. I could tell Barty now all about the German pilot and why he was almost killed and how he was saved. Should I?

"There's something I've often thought of telling you," she starts, and straight away her voice trembles with emotion.

"What is it – you alright, Norah?"

"Yes, yes," says Norah impatiently, and then says something completely unplanned, it just falls out her mouth: "It's about Joe. Your father. When he was dying. I felt you should know. Something important." Her voice breaks, but before he can say anything she takes a quick breath and continues: "On his deathbed. He called me by her name, he called me

Grace. I wanted you to know. That at the very end, he never forgot her. He thought of your mother. Very lovingly."

She weeps. It's as if she has never cried before, she can hardly breathe for crying, though at the same time she is desperately embarrassed, how awful for him, she's making such an exhibition of herself!

"Sorry, sorry," she says, through her sobs, aware of him patting her shoulder, and saying the usual things people say, Oh don't please, don't apologise, it's alright...

She pulls away from his awkward hand, blows her nose, a fierce trumpet.

"Come back to the cottage," says Barty. "I'll make you some tea."

"No, no. Thank you. So kind." She tries to smile. "But I'd better be getting back to Rosevear."

"Yeah, I think Bill's had enough," says Barty. "Ran completely out of steam yesterday, I had to carry him home, he's heavier than he looks." He turns, moves off a step, turns back again:

"I'm not sure he was – thinking about Grace. My mother, I mean."

She can't speak, can't yet trust herself not to make a fool of herself again.

He goes on: "I mean – I'm not sure what I'm saying here, I'm trying to work it out – I don't think it was Grace he was talking to, it was: his loving wife. I think he meant you, no matter what name he used."

This gives her pause. It is a thought she will come back to later, and consider, and, eventually, be able to hold on to. Sometimes.

She can't grasp it right now though. She remembers also that Joe had asked her to sing to him. *One a the old songs.* But this she will never tell to another living soul.

"It must have hurt, though," says Barty soberly. There is a silence, while they negotiate a narrowing in the path. "I'm sorry about the baby," he adds. "I never said, did I."

"I – didn't know you knew."

"Dad told me. Wanted me to lay off a bit."

Oh, Joe!

"I'm sorry I was such a git."

She has to smile. "You weren't, honestly. You were just – well, very polite."

"Yeah. A git. You know when I got my glider's licence, when I was sixteen? You and dad came to watch my first solo flight, d'you remember?"

"Yes, of course I do."

"When you turned up, before I took off."

"What about it?"

"You looked sick. And I thought, What's she looking like that for, what's it got to do with her if I mess it up? And I was angry, I thought, why does she think I can't do it, why does she think I'm such an idiot anyway? I was furious."

"I was terrified," says Norah. "We both were – you could have been killed."

"Dad was better at hiding it. When I got back. You looked so different. So happy. For me. And it was my best day ever, then, qualifying, it was great. And I just stopped being angry with you. Didn't quite know it at the time, I thought I still resented you. But I didn't really. Not from that day."

They reach the place where the path divides, steeply downward to Porthkerris, straight ahead for Rosevear House.

"Will you still be at Rosevear next week?" he asks her. "Come for tea, if you like, bring the girls."

Egg will want to make a special complicated cake, she thinks, and a tremendous fuss about getting it to the cottage unscathed, with floods of tears if anything goes wrong. Etta will refuse to come at all, change her mind at the last minute so that we all nearly miss the train, and then spend the afternoon sulking and staring out of the window or drawing pictures of Bill. While I chatter brightly, and try to keep the peace.

"Say about four?" says Barty.

Something in his voice gives Norah pause. An astounding new thought occurs to her: that maybe when the waiter at the Gideon Dining Rooms had mistaken her for everyone's mother, Barty too had been content, even pleased for a moment, to pretend he had a family, that he was out celebrating his homecoming with his mother and his two little sisters. Not one of them, in fact, had tried to correct the waiter's mistake. Was that the same as embracing it?

Not really, she thinks. But still - close enough.

Norah smiles. "Four then," she says. "That will be lovely. Thank you, Barty."

Acknowledgements

My affectionate thanks, as ever, to my first reader and brilliant editor Sheila McIlwraith.

I took information and atmosphere from First Light, by Geoffrey Wellum (Penguin 2018) Cornwall at War, by Peter Hancock, (Halsgrove 2002) Forgotten, the Untold Story of D-Days' Black Heroes, by Linda Hervieux (Harper Collins, 2015) and A Crowd Is Not Company, by Robert Kee (Eyre and Spottiswode, 1947).

I first heard of the faked wartime runways and shunting yards at the ex-MOD observation post at Nare Point, Cornwall, now manned by Coastwatch volunteers.

Apart from Cornwall itself, all places and people are fictitious. The wartime jokes were my mother's; mistakes and inaccuracies are all my own.